# DROPPED DEAD

# ALSO BY S.L. MENEAR

## The Jettine Jorgensen Mystery Series

Dead Silent

Dropped Dead

Dead Ends

## The Samantha Starr Thriller Series

Flight to Redemption

Flight to Destiny

Triple Threat

Stranded

Vanished

Life, Love, & Laughter: 50 Short Stories

# DROPPED DEAD

## A JETTINE JORGENSEN MYSTERY
### BOOK 2

## S. L. MENEAR

Book and cover design by eBook Prep
www.ebookprep.com

September 2022
ISBN: 978-1-64457-270-2 (Paperback)
ISBN: 978-1-64457-323-5 (Paperback Large Print)

*ePublishing Works!*
644 Shrewsbury Commons Ave
Ste 249
Shrewsbury PA 17361
United States of America

www.epublishingworks.com
Phone: 866-846-5123

*Dedicated to Chief Pilot Kelly Mahon
and the unique Mid America Flight Museum
in Mount Pleasant, Texas, where vintage
aircraft are maintained in flying condition
and come alive for the visiting public.*

# ONE

*The banyan tree strains,*
*bearing a tragic burden*
*caught in leafy limbs.*

Just when I thought my life had returned to normal, the strangest thing happened.

Sophia DeLuca, my trusted friend, and dog nanny, strolled beside me as we followed my four-month-old Timber-shepherd puppies across the broad back lawn. A cool breeze blew in from the Atlantic Ocean on my six-acre estate on Banyan Isle, a residential barrier island off the eastern mainland of South Florida between Singer Island and Juno Beach.

She pointed at the dogs and laughed. "I love to watch them wrestle and play."

"They're smart too. I think it's the timber wolf in them." I watched as they paused under a tree and stared up at something.

"That's odd. Look how still they're sitting with their noses in the air."

I glanced up. "Buzzards are circling."

"Something stinks." She wrinkled her nose. "Maybe a hawk left his kill in the tree."

I called, "Here, Pratt! Here, Whitney!"

The puppies, named after my favorite aircraft engine manufacturer, looked back at us, hesitated, and ran to me.

Pratt, a honey-colored male, and Whitney, a black and tan female, seemed agitated about something. Each dog gave a sharp bark then bounded back to the tree.

Sophia frowned. "Might be an intruder hiding. Where's the armed guard?"

"I think he just started his check of the front yard, and I didn't bring a weapon." I pulled out my cell phone in case I had to call for help. "I wasn't expecting trouble, especially this early in the morning." The ground was still moist with dew.

"No worries." She pulled a Glock from under her shirt at the small of her back. "I've got us covered."

At five-nine, I towered over her four-ten, slender, hour-glass frame. Now sixty, she looked too tiny for the weapon in her hand, but she wasn't afraid to use it. The Italian beauty and feisty daughter of a late New York Mafia kingpin feared nothing.

A massive banyan tree, its canopy spreading over multiple trunks, looked like a small forest. We eased under it to where the puppies sat, their noses skyward.

I brushed aside my waist-length black hair and gasped. "Holy cow, I wasn't expecting this!"

Glassy blue eyes, wide open in a macabre look of terror, stared down at me. His clothes ragged and torn, a man in his late twenties, tangled in stout branches, had his arms bent at odd angles. A thin line of dried blood ringed his neck. But it wasn't until my gaze traveled to his lower legs that murder was evident. His feet formed the most bizarre pieces of the puzzle, mired in concrete-filled buckets wedged between branches.

Sophia, accustomed to seeing corpses because of her Mafia family, commented, "Looks like somebody meant to fly over and drop him in the ocean but hit fifty yards short." She shook her head. "Reminds me of my relatives. I don't approve of what they do, but they're pros. They wouldn't have missed the water."

My stomach churned. "This is terrible. His family will be devastated, and what will the police think when I call in another dead body?"

"Who cares what the cops think? You don't know the guy in the tree, right?"

I studied his face. "Oh geez, I didn't recognize him at first." Memories of awkward teenage kisses and fun dates to the movies flooded my brain. We had been classmates at Banyan Isle Prep School all four years and briefly dated in our junior year.

"Who is he?"

"Chad Townsend. His parents live five houses down." My voice caught. "Haven't seen him in years."

"A sad waste of a handsome young man, and his parents will be crushed." Sophia put an arm around me. "I'd be devastated if anything bad happened to one of my boys."

I bit my lip and hit the number for Mike Miller, my old boyfriend from college days, now a detective with the Banyan Isle Police. Six years ago, he broke my heart when he stopped speaking to me because I joined the Navy. Recent events had forced him to talk to me again, and his cold attitude toward me had thawed now that my stint in the Navy had ended.

"Mike, it's Jett."

His deep voice held a neutral tone as he answered, "You sound upset. What's wrong?"

I hesitated, not sure how he'd react, considering the murders here last month. "Sorry about this, but I found a dead guy in one of my trees."

Silence for a few beats. "Are you sure he's dead?"

"Positive."

"I hope he isn't hanging from a noose."

"No, I think he fell from the sky."

"His parachute caught in the tree?"

"No parachute."

He groaned. "How high up is he?"

"About fifteen feet, and you'll probably need Fire Rescue and a CSU."

"What makes you think he was murdered?"

"His concrete overshoes were my first clue, and the bloody ring around his neck looks like a garrote injury."

A sharp intake of breath on his end was followed by, "Do you recognize him?"

I choked out the words, "It's Chad Townsend—we were friends in prep school."

Another groan. "Did you touch anything?"

"No way. He's fifteen feet above me."

"Okay. Which tree?"

"The one with the buzzards circling it." I pocketed the phone, nausea gripping my stomach.

Sophia glanced at her watch. "I'll take the puppies back to the house before all the cops and emergency vehicles roll in."

"Thanks. I'll wait here, not that poor Chad's going anywhere." I looked down at the dogs and pointed at the house. "Pratt, Whitney, go with Sophia."

"Come along, my angels." She turned and trotted toward the house, which was actually a four-story, Nordic-themed, stone castle. It was built over a hundred years ago by my great-great-grandfather from Denmark as a tribute to his Viking heritage. An only child, I inherited the estate after my parents were murdered in a plane crash two years ago.

The puppies followed Sophia onto the back terrace where she sat with them.

Before long, Mike jogged around the house and headed toward me. Thirty, fit, and six-two with movie-star good looks and sexy brown eyes, he looked boyish with his black hair tousled in the ocean breeze. A blue polo shirt and tight jeans hugged his muscular body in a way that sent my heart rate into the danger zone, despite my sadness over finding Chad's mangled body. Emotions are such complicated things.

I had been home from the Navy almost three months, and Mike and I were still in the not-trusting-each-other phase. Our mutual attraction was obvious, but neither of us wanted to risk getting hurt again.

He stopped beside me and looked up. "You're right, it's Chad Townsend." He sighed, clenching his fists. "The garrote injury reminds me of my brother's murder years ago." He sighed. "He was only sixteen."

"I remember." I clutched his arm. "Matt and I were classmates, and everyone was traumatized after that." I hugged him. "Sorry to stir up painful memories."

"His unsolved murder is what drove me to become a police officer." Mike's voice caught. "This is going to devastate Chad's parents."

# TWO

After I gave Mike my official statement, I joined Sophia and the puppies on the terrace. We watched the CSU techs and the Fire Rescue crew work on extricating Chad.

Sophia pocketed her cell phone. "While you were gone, I called one of my sons in Brooklyn and asked if he knew anything about a Mob hit on the guy in the tree. He said it wasn't anyone connected to the family, and it sounded like an amateur trying to make it look like a professional hit."

"Well, thanks for asking, but I'm leaving this one to the cops. The murder can't have anything to do with me because I haven't seen Chad in about ten years. We went to different colleges after prep school, and then I joined the Navy." I checked the time. "Karin Kekoa will be here soon to interview for the part-time position as my special-events chef. Think I should reschedule?" My stomach was still churning.

"Not if you're planning to use her for your charity ball next month. Time is short."

"You're right. Even though it's the end of the social season, I'm hoping to have at least a hundred guests, and I need to make a great impression with my first ball."

"And you'll bring in plenty of money for the women's shelter."

"That reminds me, I met a woman at the shelter who's an expert hacker. She's the perfect cyber person for my new Valkyrie Private Detective Agency."

Sophia's jaw dropped. "You met her at the shelter for battered women? I hope you did a thorough background check."

"Of course. She's twenty-five and deserves a chance at a good life."

"Good. Your apprenticeship starts soon, and she can help you with cases."

"She'll be living here, but I'm not sure how to handle her dating and possibly having men spend the night. I mean, she must not be good at choosing quality men or she wouldn't have ended up in a women's shelter. Any suggestions?"

"I've been out of the game ever since my Vinnie took a permanent dive into Long Island Sound twenty years ago." Sophia paused a moment. "If she meets someone she likes, maybe suggest inviting her date here for a meal so we can get a read on him."

"Good idea." I checked my cell phone for messages.

"I can only imagine how she'll react to your Uncle Hottie when he visits. She'll probably swoon over him." She smoothed her shoulder-length auburn hair. "Just a glimpse of him makes my day."

"Hunter already has more women than he can handle, so there's no danger of him getting too friendly with a new resident."

"The danger is her going crazy over him, but no worries." Her hazel eyes twinkled as she drew her Glock. "I'll protect him."

I did an eyeroll. "I'd rather you find a way to maintain order without gunplay." I reached down and ruffled the fur on Pratt and Whitney. "The puppies have already seen two people shot in this house. I'd hate for them to think that's normal behavior."

"Hey, I only shot one dirtbag here. You and Mike shot the other guy." Sophia holstered her pistol.

"That's the thing. You and I are raising the puppies, which makes us their role models."

"Look at the bright side. Gunfire doesn't scare them because they became accustomed to it in their first weeks here. Could be an advantage when they're older."

I looked at my adorable fur babies. "I guess you're right."

My cell rang. Hugo, Gwen's French chef from next door, was calling. "Jett, what is happening?"

I explained what we'd found. "The police are handling it. Must've happened overnight." I hesitated. "Are you sure about the chef candidate you recommended?"

"*Oui*, Karin Kekoa, originally from Hawaii, graduated from *Le Cordon Bleu* in Paris." He paused. "She'll be there in ten minutes. I hope the police won't be a problem."

"I guess it's better if she knows what she's in for right from the start. Would you like to be here for the interview?"

"*Mais non*, I'm making hors d'oeuvres for today's Art Appreciation Hour. *Au revoir*."

Hugo Fournier's fiancé, Leonardo Pérez, owned the Gourmet Art Gallery on Main Street in Banyan Isle. Art Appreciation Hour was a lot like Happy Hour at a bar, except the food and one glass of wine per customer were free. Select art was offered at a discount from five to seven every evening.

Hugo and Leo lived next door with my best friend, Gwen Stuart Pendragon, and Leo managed her household. Gwen recently earned her detective shield with the Palm Beach Police. That was also the month her last name changed from Stuart to Pendragon. Not by marriage. Her uncle, Lord Clive Pendragon, Duke of Colchester, England, having no children, legally adopted his niece so she could inherit his ancestral estate and titled land, including Colchester Castle.

My thoughts returned to the present when I glanced at Sophia, who watched the firemen hand down the body, bucketed feet first. My stomach twinged.

She commented, "Guess they'll have to jackhammer his feet out of the concrete so he'll fit in a casket for the funeral."

I shook my head. "That's not the sort of problem grieving families usually encounter."

"Speak for yourself. My late husband is still wearing concrete overshoes."

"Your family is hardly the norm." I glanced at my watch. "The chef candidate will be here any minute. Feel free to participate in her interview."

The dogs bared their teeth when a security guard rounded the corner. He pointed at the police and emergency vehicles. "What's happening back there?"

"Somebody dropped a murder victim into my tree last night. Didn't the night guard report it?"

"No, ma'am, nothing unusual was noted."

"Then he must've been sleeping on the job." Sophia shook her head. "We need better guards."

"I'll ask Hunter to help me find a new security company."

The dogs' ears perked up an instant before the doorbell blasted Wagner's "Ride of the Valkyries" throughout the house. I hurried inside and jogged between ten-foot winged Valkyrie statues in the spacious foyer.

A curvaceous, exotic-looking woman smiled when I opened the door. She had bronze skin, long brown hair, and a round face with expressive blue eyes and full lips. At thirty-four, she stood five-six in flat sandals and wore a pink cotton sundress.

"Welcome to Valhalla, Karin." I offered my hand. "I'm Jett Jorgensen. Thank you for coming."

She shook my hand and glanced around. "Thanks for granting me an interview." Her eyes paused on a life-size portrait of my late mother. The painting hung on the foyer wall partway up the south staircase and depicted her with long black hair, high cheekbones, and golden skin wearing buckskin. Flanked by wolves, Mother's golden eyes seemed to look directly at us.

Karin looked at me. "You look like the woman in the painting, except for your electric-blue eyes."

"My mother was a Cherokee shaman, but I have my late father's eyes—his family was from Denmark." I took her arm. "Come out to the terrace and meet Sophia. We'll have iced tea and a nice chat." I led

15

her through the spacious great hall, which had a magnificent thirty-foot vaulted ceiling and oak-paneled walls adorned with ancient Viking weapons. Tall windows and French doors on the east side showcased the ocean view.

Outside, I waved in Sophia's direction. "Karin Kekoa, meet Sophia Calabrese DeLuca, house manager and pet nanny to my puppies, Pratt and Whitney."

Sophia stood and shook Karin's hand. "I hope you like Italian food."

"I love Italian." She leaned down, petted the puppies, and noticed the police activity. "What's going on back there?"

"I guess it's only fair to warn you." I paused. "Unusual stuff tends to happen here."

"What sort of stuff?" She glanced from me to Sophia.

Sophia told her about the guy in the tree and finished with, "And he was wearing concrete overshoes." She waited for her reaction.

Karin's eyes widened. "No kidding? Is there more?"

I deferred to Sophia, who said, "In January, Jett found the mayor dead under a guest bed upstairs." With a smug grin, she added, "And my first night here, I shot an armed intruder."

"That's a lot for such a short time." Karin glanced at me.

"There's more. Sophia helped me solve my parents' murders, and the guy who sabotaged their airplane was shot and killed in my bedroom."

Karin grinned. "This is my kind of place."

I wasn't expecting that response. "Really? Why?"

"I miss the excitement of being in the military, but I like being free to do what I want."

Sophia leaned forward. "Tell us more about your background."

"I was an only child from a mixed marriage. Dad was Hawaiian, and Mom was British—"

I interrupted, "Like my parents—Mom from the Aniwaya (Wolf) Clan and Dad second-generation Danish with strong ties to his Viking ancestors."

"Ah, your unusual doorbell and the circular fountain with the huge Viking statue and four snarling wolves make sense now." She smiled.

"Please, tell us more about yourself," I encouraged.

"After graduating from the University of Hawaii, I served eight years on Navy destroyers. Then my parents were killed in a car crash, and I was devastated. Everything felt wrong—"

I couldn't help interrupting again. "I served in Navy Intelligence six years and resigned recently." I bit my lip. "And, like I said, I lost my parents suddenly too."

Karin's jaw dropped. "I didn't know we had *that* much in common. After my parents' accident, I quit the Navy and attended *Le Cordon Bleu* in Paris, thinking a drastic career change would fix things. I also wanted to prove wrong all the people who said I'd never learn to cook."

"Chef Hugo told me you attended his alma mater."

Karin grinned. "I graduated at the top of my class. After working in fine restaurants in San Francisco, Chicago, and New York, I realized I missed living in a tropical climate." She reached down and petted the puppies again. "I'm renting a room in a furnished condo on Miami Beach, but I'd rather live in Palm Beach County where it's not so crowded."

I glanced at Sophia, and she smiled and nodded her approval.

"We have a lot in common," I said. "We're the adult equivalents of orphans, and so is my best friend, Gwen, next door. And Sophia is a Mafia widow."

Karin smiled. "I feel like I'll fit right in."

Sophia pointed at the cops under the tree. "Any safety concerns?"

"Nah, I have a black belt in Tae Kwon Do, and I'm an expert marksman." She glanced around. "This mansion is as big as a hotel. How many would I be cooking for at your special events?"

"The charity ball next month will have one hundred to three hundred guests. I also plan to have some large dinner parties, and of course, I'll hire temporary staff to help you with the events."

Karin glanced from Sophia to me. "How would you feel about me living here rent-free in exchange for cooking your meals? I'd still work at some outside events."

"That would take the burden off Sophia, who has graciously prepared most of our meals since she moved in. I'm starting a private detective agency, and one of my employees will be living here, so we'll have four residents, counting you."

Karin's eyes lit up. "Any chance I could help with the investigations too?"

"After I get my license, I'd welcome your help. But that's down the road. First, I'll have to work as an apprentice for a licensed P.I." I stood. "Would you like to see the kitchen?" The distraction of talking with her had settled my stomach.

"Yes. Show me everything, please." Karin followed us into the house.

Sophia pointed out all the modern appliances in the twenty-by-thirty-foot kitchen and showed her the spacious pantry.

"This is a chef's dream come true." Karin glanced around, smiling. "I love it."

"And we've got a dining table that seats forty people, more if we put in the leaves." Sophia waved. "Come on. We'll show you. And then we'll take you to the ballroom. It's bigger than a basketball court."

I walked beside Karin, and the pitter-patter of puppy feet trailed behind us. "You already passed a background check. When would you like to move in?"

"Would tomorrow be too soon?"

"Tomorrow is perfect. Do you have a lot of stuff?"

"No furniture. I have clothes, shoes, a few personal items, my set of chef knives, and a Glock 19." She hesitated. "Is it okay to keep the weapon?"

"Yes, if you have a license to carry. Would you like an ocean-view suite or an island-view? You'll have a private bath and plenty of closet space."

"An ocean view would be wonderful." She stepped into the huge dining room where teal, silk-covered, twenty-foot-high walls matched the upholstered chairs that accompanied an enormous mahogany table. "You can throw some fabulous dinner parties here."

Sophia grinned. "If you like the dining room, you're gonna love the ballroom."

The ballroom stretched across the north end of the first floor. Fifteen-foot-high windows and French doors covered three sides opening to a wraparound terrace.

"I feel like a princess in a castle." Karin gazed up at magnificent crystal chandeliers.

"Since you're moving in tomorrow, let's go pick out your bedroom." I led her to the twin staircases. "We also have an elevator." I pointed at it. "Would you like a suite on the second, third, or fourth floor?"

"Fourth floor. Nothing like a view from the top." Karin bubbled with enthusiasm.

Sophia stayed downstairs with the puppies, and Karin chose a three-room suite in the northeast corner with a view of the ocean and the north inlet to the Intracoastal Waterway. A king-size bed with an elaborately carved oak frame dominated the bedroom, and a spiral staircase led up to a turret room in the northeast corner of the castle.

The decor was heavily antique. Karin tested the bed, sitting first, then lying on it.

"I love this. It's so comfortable." She grinned. "I can't wait to move in."

I glanced out over her east balcony and spotted a woman standing on the beach, staring at my home. She was too far away to see her face. Probably just a curious tourist.

The doorbell blasted Wagner throughout the house.

"The contractors must be here for the final inspection. They converted the bowling alley on the first floor into a two-lane shooting range so we can practice our marksmanship at home." I explained, "After last month, I want to stay prepared for whatever craziness might come."

# THREE

W e trotted downstairs and found Sophia standing beside two handsome men, one in his late twenties wearing a snug T-shirt, jeans that hugged his fit physique, work boots, and a toolbelt. He had short brown hair, long lashes over dreamy brown eyes, a warm smile, and a body that oozed testosterone from every well-formed muscle. He looked like a clone of the silver-haired man beside him. Both six feet, they towered over tiny Sophia.

She beamed. "Jett, Karin, I'd like you to meet these nice Italian men, John and Joe Caldarelli of Caldarelli and Sons Construction. Joe is John's grandson. They're here to approve the shooting range."

Karin seemed a bit flustered and blurted, "I just love men with toolbelts."

I offered my hand. "Hi, I'm Jett Jorgensen. Thanks for coming."

To my surprise, they kissed Karin's hand and mine in turn, and said, "It's a pleasure to meet you both."

Sophia grinned. "Such gentlemen."

I took John's arm because he was the senior partner, and Joe's testosterone would've spiked my blood pressure. "Let me show you the indoor pistol-shooting range. Your crew did a great job."

We strolled north toward the ballroom. Joe, Sophia, Karin, and the dogs followed us.

A heavy oak door led to our destination. "Here it is. I did a few test shots yesterday in each lane, and the target controls and video scoring screens worked perfectly."

John and Joe stood, hands on hips, gazing at the long room with a twenty-foot ceiling.

John smiled. "The shooting booths look comfortable."

"And I'm sure the four feet of sandbags behind the back wall are sufficient to stop all the bullets. No ricochets, am I right?" Joe glanced at me.

I stared down a sixty-foot shooting lane. "No problems, and the soundproofing stops all the firing noise from penetrating the rest of my house. It's perfect."

While Karin stared at Joe with a silly grin, Sophia smiled at John.

Not as affected by handsome men because I used to work with hot Navy SEALs, I nudged Sophia. When she snapped out of her trance, I said, "They should sit outside with us and enjoy some cannoli and coffee."

"Good idea." She turned and grabbed Karin's arm. "Come and help me set up something on the terrace for our guests."

As we walked out, I snuck a look at Joe's well-formed bottom when he sauntered ahead of John and me. It had been three months since my heart-wrenching breakup with a Navy officer in Afghanistan, and men were starting to look good to me again. Especially men like Joe and Mike. But Mike and I had baggage from our past breakup. It was obvious Karin and Sophia thought Joe and John were hot. Maybe romance would flourish for at least one of us here at Valhalla.

In minutes, we were enjoying coffee and cannoli on the terrace.

Joe and John pulled out chairs for us before they were seated— definitely raised right by their mothers. The men noticed the activity under one of my banyan trees.

John asked, "What's going on in your backyard?"

"Somebody killed my neighbors' son and dropped him into the tree

—another reason for my shooting range." I handed him a cup of coffee.

"Jett left out the most interesting part." Sophia paused for emphasis, then mentioned the feet encased in concrete-filled buckets.

Joe and John exchanged surprised glances.

Joe accepted cannoli from the platter. "Sounds like a Mob hit."

"Is your family connected?" Karin asked.

"No, but we have relatives who are. We steer clear of Mafia business." Joe took a bite. "This is the best cannoli I've ever tasted, but don't tell my mother I said that."

Sophia served John and then set the platter on the table. "I'm from Brooklyn, and my family is as connected as you can get. I don't approve of their business, so I moved to Florida after my boys were raised."

"Your husband didn't mind moving away from the family?" John asked.

"My cheating husband is wearing concrete overshoes on the bottom of Long Island Sound." She held up a hand. "Long story. My father was Don Calabrese."

"*The* Don Calabrese of New York Mafia fame?" Joe asked.

"That's him, may he rest in peace." She crossed herself.

Joe's jaw dropped.

John looked at Sophia with obvious interest. "So, I guess you're a widower like me."

"For the past twenty years."

My cell rang. "Hi, Gwen."

The puppies jumped up, ears perked and tails wagging.

"Hi, I'm letting myself in. I was getting ready for work when I heard sirens, and Hugo and Leo told me about all the cops in your backyard."

"Yeah, here we go again. Come out back."

———

Gwen had a key and Jett's security codes. Her long red hair glistened in the morning sun as she strode onto the terrace. She wore a light-blue blouse with navy slacks and her Glock 40 and badge clipped to her belt. She stopped in her tracks when she spotted the handsome men sitting with the women.

Jett stood, and so did the men. "Gwen, I'd like you to meet John and Joe Caldarelli. They just inspected my new shooting range." Jett glanced at the men. "Gentlemen, this is my best friend and next-door neighbor, Palm Beach Police Detective Gwen Pendragon."

Gwen grinned as the men took turns kissing her hand. "Such rare gentlemen."

Jett added, "And, Gwen, this is my new chef, Karin Kekoa. She arrived just in time for all the excitement."

The women exchanged greetings, then Gwen turned to Jett. "Who died?"

"Chad Townsend." She explained what she and Sophia had found in the tree.

Gwen shook her head and sat beside Jett. "Just when I thought the murders here had ended. Poor Chad. I dated him in prep school a few times our senior year."

Sophia joined in, "Oh, Gwen, I forgot to ask if you caught whoever killed those horrible Palm Beach men back in January. How's that case going?"

Gwen's face blanched. *Can't let anything slip about Guinevere's Lance, but I hate keeping secrets from friends.* She quickly recovered. "Um, no luck there. The killer must've been a pro. I wish I hadn't failed on my first murder case, but life goes on."

Jett asked, "Do you think the killer will return when the social season ramps up again this winter?"

"I hope not. Palm Beachers aren't patient people, especially when it comes to three unsolved murders." Gwen glanced at her watch. "I have to run. Nice meeting everyone."

———

I watched Gwen leave. *That triple-murder case must be a sore spot with her. I've never seen her look so flustered.*

Mike jogged across my back lawn, and Karin leaned in and whispered, "Are all the men on Banyan Isle this hot?"

"Sometimes it seems that way. Excuse me." I trotted down to meet him.

He took in the group on the terrace. "Odd time for a party."

I explained who was there and why. "Anything new about Chad?"

"You know as much as I do." He hesitated. "Any chance the murderer used Chad to send you a message?"

I stepped back. "You're kidding, right? I've been gone for most of the past six years, and Chad was just a neighbor and my classmate at prep school. It must be a coincidence that he landed in one of my trees. I mean, considering the concrete boots, the killer must've meant to drop him in the ocean."

"I hope you're right. Does your new chef know about the murder?"

I glanced back at the house. "Yep. She's moving in tomorrow. I'm looking forward to her cooking."

# FOUR

The following morning, Sophia and I had just come inside from walking the grounds with the dogs when Uncle Hunter called my cell.

"Good morning, Jett. I'm parked out front. Is it okay if I let myself in?"

"Of course. We just walked in from the backyard. Join us for breakfast." I pocketed my phone and met him as he sauntered into the great hall.

"Oh, joy. My favorite man is here." Sophia ran over for a hug.

A full-blood Cherokee, six-foot-three, and muscular with thick black hair, golden skin, and golden eyes like my mother, Hunter looked like a god. No wonder women swooned over him. He scooped up Sophia, planted a kiss on her lips, and gently set her down. Then he pulled me in for a hug. Afterward, he leaned down, and the puppies made a fuss over him, wagging their tails and covering him with doggie kisses while he ruffled their fur.

"I just returned from an airline flight and heard about the body in your tree. It was all over the news." He stood and glanced from me to Sophia. "Are my favorite girls okay?"

"Have breakfast with us on the terrace and we'll tell you all about it." I led him to the kitchen to help us carry everything outside.

The timer dinged, and Sophia pulled a large pan of ham and Gruyère quiche out of the oven. Bowls of cut fruit complemented the meal.

We gathered at a round glass-top table on the terrace under the overhang roof and passed around the food and coffee.

After we explained the guy in the tree, Hunter said, "I hope this was just a weird coincidence and has no connection to either of you."

I frowned. "Mike was concerned about that too."

Sophia's eyes widened. "*Me*? My husband was killed years ago, and no one came after me. Of course, my father was still alive and a powerful Mob boss back then."

He arched an eyebrow. "The murder looked like a Mafia hit."

"But dropping him in the tree had to be a mistake," Sophia said. "Otherwise, why bother with the concrete overshoes?"

I turned to my uncle. "I forgot to tell you I hired a live-in chef. She's moving in this morning, so you'll get to meet her."

As if on cue, the doorbell blasted the famous Viking tune, and Hunter and I rushed to the foyer. He opened the door to Karin, and her jaw dropped the instant she saw him.

I jumped in, "Karin, I'd like you to meet my uncle, Hunter Vann. Hunter, this is Karin Kekoa, my new chef. She's from Hawaii."

He took her hand and kissed it as he gazed into her blue eyes. "A pleasure to meet you, Karin. May I help with your luggage?"

She just stood there with a silly grin on her face, so I answered for her. "Yes, please. We'd better take the elevator. Her suite is on the northeast end of the fourth floor." I shoved a suitcase toward her and broke the spell.

Flustered, she said, "So nice to meet you, Hunter. Thanks for helping."

We grabbed everything and crowded into the elevator. Karin didn't seem to mind pressing against Hunter. It was obvious he found her attractive too. Oh boy. Sophia would not be pleased.

A long walk to the north end of the top floor brought us to Karin's three-room suite. We deposited her things in the sitting room and invited her to join us down on the back terrace for coffee.

Sophia and the dogs greeted Karin. "Do you need help bringing in your bags?"

"No, Jett and Hunter helped me take them up to my suite." She smiled at Hunter.

He changed the subject. "Sophia, any news from your family?"

"My sons aren't happy about me living here. They think this place is a murder magnet."

Karin poured a cup of coffee. "The killer could be a weirdo looking for the thrill of publicity."

I glanced at my watch. "My new cyber tech will be here any minute. She's quite a character, and I doubt the dead-guy-in-a-tree incident will bother her."

The dogs' ears perked up, and they looked at me and gave soft woofs a moment before the doorbell rang.

"I'll bring her out here." I jumped up and jogged to the front door with the pups tagging along.

Hunter followed me. "She might need help with her stuff."

I opened the door to Mona Wang, dressed in black leather, five-six and slender, and originally from L.A. She looked like a night creature with her pale skin, short, spiked black hair, and Asian/American features enhanced by violet eyes, smoky eye shadow, and blood-red lips. Three identical small diamond studs trailed up each ear lobe.

A large, black leather bag was strapped to the back of her black Ducati motorcycle parked behind Hunter's McLaren sportscar. I focused on the bike. "Whoa, Mona, is that a Streetfighter V4S?"

"Yeah, it's scary fast. Do you ride?" She unstrapped the bag and set it on a step.

"Sorry, I should've made introductions first. This is my uncle, Hunter Vann." I thumbed at him.

Hunter smiled and kissed her hand. "A pleasure to meet you, Mona, and your bike's a beauty. I've got a restored pan-head Harley."

"Ah, an old-school gentleman." Mona grinned at Hunter. "I like it."

I checked out her bike. "Hunter turned me into a motorhead, and yes, I love to ride."

She handed me her steampunk helmet. "Go for it."

"Now? Are you sure?" I pulled on the helmet.

She gave my uncle a side glance and grinned. "No time like the present."

He arched his eyebrows. "Which room?"

"Any empty bedroom she wants except my parents' room and the murder room. I'll only be a few minutes." I climbed aboard the sleek bike, known as the Ferrari of motorcycles for its beauty and handling.

Mona's eyebrows shot up. "Murder room?"

"Hunter will tell you all about it. Be right back." I started the quiet engine.

The soft purr transformed into a high-pitched whine when I raced around Odin's fountain and out to Ocean Drive. What a rush! Super smooth. What felt like 45 mph was actually 130. That's why I didn't buy one of these Italian speedsters. I knew I'd ride it way too fast. Better to stick with my aesthetic cruiser, a teal Harley-Davidson Softail Classic with white sidewalls. I was never tempted to go over 60 mph on my bike and usually kept it under 40 on the two-lane island roads.

———

When I returned, I put Mona's Ducati in the garage beside my Harley. I found her on the terrace, laughing and joking with Hunter and the women.

"Your bike is awesome—fast and smooth. It's in the garage." I handed her the ignition key and a remote for the gate and garage door.

Mona glanced at the banyan tree surrounded by crime-scene tape. "Sophia told me you've had a lot happening here."

My dogs jumped up and smothered me with kisses. "Yeah, hopefully the future will be calmer." I leaned down and petted each pup. "Did you find a room you like?"

"There were so many beautiful rooms, it was hard to choose. I took a suite on the third floor halfway down the east side." She grinned, her triple earring studs sparkling in the sunlight. "The ocean view is fantastic."

Hunter leaned back. "Excuse me for asking, Mona, but why do you need free housing if you can afford a new Ducati?"

She blushed. "Oh, that. I didn't buy it. A rich boyfriend in the middle of a divorce put it in my name so his wife wouldn't snatch it." She shrugged. "His wife ended up in prison after stabbing him to death."

Karin patted Mona's hand. "Sorry for your loss."

She checked her black nail polish. "We weren't that close. He just used me to stick it to his wife, but hey, I ended up with a free Ducati."

We shared a collective jaw-drop.

# FIVE

I glanced out toward the ocean and spotted a woman looking at my house from the beach. Was she the same woman I'd seen yesterday? Hard to tell from fifty yards away. Probably just another tourist roaming the beach.

Hunter asked, "Mona, what was your college major?"

"Computer Science." She looked sheepish. "Full disclosure: I'm an expert hacker, but I want a legit career in computers, focusing on Internet searches and computer security."

"I have friends at the NSA from my Navy Intelligence past," I offered. "They'd probably be interested, but I'd like you to give my new P.I. agency a fair shot before I recommend you."

"That won't be a problem. I'd rather work for you than the government."

I explained to Mona and Karin, "Sophia's our house manager. She'll help you get settled. The rules are simple. While you're living here at Valhalla, no foul language, smoking, or illicit drugs. Any questions?"

Mona and Karin looked at my uncle, and Mona asked, "Does Hunter live here?"

He smiled. "No, I live about a half-hour drive west in a pilot community called Aerodrome Estates."

Karin's eyebrows shot up. "You're a pilot?"

"I'm a captain with Luxury International Airlines, and I also do some flight instructing in small airplanes." He glanced at me. "I taught Jett to fly. She's licensed as a commercial pilot and flight instructor."

They looked at me and responded in unison, "Awesome."

"I'm not an airline pilot like Hunter. I mainly fly vintage airplanes for fun and fill in for him occasionally teaching flying lessons."

Sophia grinned. "Well, I love that we have a professional chef and a computer expert in our household now."

"I also *parle français*." Karin shrugged. "I learned French while I was in Paris."

Mona added, "I don't know any French, but I speak Korean."

"That's four languages covered: English, French, Korean, and Italian," Sophia said.

"Five," Hunter asserted. "You're forgetting Jett and I speak Cherokee."

Mona's eyes widened. "Cherokee? That's so cool."

"And I speak enough Spanish to get by," I said. "You never know when one of these languages might come in handy on a case."

Hunter stood. "Well, ladies, it was a pleasure meeting you, but I must go. I have flight students this afternoon." He smiled at everyone, hugged me, and gave Sophia a little kiss on the lips before departing.

After my uncle left, Karin asked, "Sophia, is Hunter your boyfriend?"

"In my dreams." She sighed. "He's forty and a god. I'm short and sixty, old enough to be his mother. But I do enjoy his hugs and kisses. What a man!"

"I wouldn't get too excited, ladies. Flight attendants are constantly knocking on his door," I explained. "The man is never without a date."

"I think John Caldarelli is interested in Sophia." Karin grinned at me. "Remember how he focused his attention on her yesterday?"

"And his grandson, Joe, is quite the hottie too," I said.

"Don't forget that handsome police detective—what was his name?" Karin asked.

"Mike Miller." I paused. "I may as well tell you; he was my boyfriend before I joined the Navy. Then he ghosted me for six years. We're on speaking terms now, but we don't trust each other with our hearts."

"Think you'll ever get back together?" Mona asked.

I frowned. "My heart was stomped on by a Navy lieutenant four months ago. Men are just starting to interest me again. The last thing I need is another heartache."

The women nodded.

I continued, "Now that Hunter is gone, ladies, time for a tour."

I started at the north end of the first floor in the ballroom with the same initial tour Karin had received. We continued through the great hall where Mona paused and admired the life-size painting of my parents above the hearth.

"Looks like you have your dad's blue eyes and your mom's raven hair," Mona commented.

We continued into the south wing to the music room, a TV and movie room with stadium seating, an exercise room, and a study lined with floor-to-ceiling oak bookcases.

———

That night, we gathered at one end of the formal dining table for dinner. I started the conversation, "The theme for the charity ball will be Renaissance gowns for the women, and I'll pay for yours. We'll keep it simple for the men—they'll wear tuxedoes. Designer Cameron Altman will be here tomorrow morning to fit us for our gowns."

Sophia's cell phone rang. She glanced at it and smiled. "It's Snake. I'll put it on speaker." She hit the button. "Hi, Snake, how're you doing?"

"Not so good, darlin'. I have bullet wounds in my right leg, and I need a place to recuperate. I'd love to stay with y'all unless Jett's involved with someone. Wouldn't want to interfere with her love life."

Sophia looked at me and raised her eyebrows.

"Hand me the phone." I grabbed it and left it on speaker. "Snake, it's Jett. Sorry you're wounded. Of course, you can recover at my place. Where are you? I'll pick you up in a Jorgensen Industries' corporate jet."

"I'm at the SEAL base near Virginia Beach. Fly into Norfolk." He hesitated. "Can I ask one more favor?"

"Anything. You've always been there for me when I needed you."

"It sure would be fun to make my teammates jealous. Any chance you and Gwen could show up in sexy nurse outfits?"

"It will be our pleasure, and maybe I'll bring an extra nurse and lay it on thick. We'll pick you up tomorrow at 3:00 p.m. and have you back here in time for dinner. And expect Sophia to spoil you rotten."

"Thanks, Jett. I'll look forward to seeing everyone tomorrow."

I slid the phone back to Sophia and explained to Karin and Mona, "Snake is a handsome Navy SEAL who helped me investigate my parents' murders. Would anyone like to volunteer to play nurse when we pick him up?"

Everyone raised their hands.

"Mona is in, but I'll need Karin here to prepare a delicious meal for him." I glanced at her. "He's easy to please, and his favorite meal is a juicy steak, medium rare." I turned to Sophia. "And I need you to look after the puppies and make Snake's favorite cannoli."

"I'll arrange a room for him close to the elevator on the second floor," Sophia said. "Do you have a wheelchair?"

"Yes." My mind raced. "I need to call Cam about the nurse outfits."

He answered on the first ring. "Jett, darling, I'm looking forward to seeing you."

"Hi, Cam. I have an emergency rush job for you." I explained about needing three sexy nurse uniforms before lunchtime tomorrow, and he said he'd get right on it.

I called Gwen and explained the plan. She happily agreed to go with us. Next, I arranged for a doctor friend to examine Snake at my place tomorrow after dinner.

My doorbell boomed, and I ran and opened the door to Mike. "Is everything all right?"

"I interviewed Chad's parents. Turns out he mentored a man once a week who runs a minority-operated business in Riviera Beach. Chad's car was found parked outside the man's office the night he was killed, and all four tires had been slashed. No security cameras or evidence of physical violence."

"Am I correct in assuming the guy he mentored didn't kill him?"

He nodded. "No motive and no means to drop a body on your land."

"Are you thinking someone knocked Chad out while he was bent over checking his tires and then dragged him into their car and drove to an airport?"

"That seems logical, except there wasn't a bump on his head or any evidence of chloroform. No obvious means of abducting a fit man over six feet."

I thought about that. "What about his cell calls. Maybe he knew his abductor."

"We checked. No calls an hour before or any time after he arrived." Mike stepped closer. "We're dealing with a clever killer. Stay vigilant. He might come after you next."

My jaw dropped. "What makes you think I'm a target?"

"No evidence yet. Just a gut feeling. Be careful, Jett." He turned and left.

# SIX

The next morning, Mona and I had a good workout in the pool before breakfast. We met Sophia and Karin on the terrace after we dried off and pulled on robes.

Mona poured a cup of coffee. "Ooh, scrambled eggs, bacon, and cinnamon buns."

The puppies gave a hopeful sniff at the table before Sophia gave them her get-down glare. They dropped to prone positions on either side of her. Good dog nanny.

After the meal, I said, "Time to get ready for our ballgown and nurse-outfit fittings with Cam."

After showering and dressing in white lace lingerie and robes, Mona and I met Karin and Sophia in the ballroom. Crystal chandeliers reflected off the polished oak floor.

Cam arrived at 10:15 a.m. so we'd have plenty of time to get fitted before the flight.

He kissed my cheeks and glanced around. "Are they my hot nurses?"

Mona sashayed over. "I'm one. We're waiting for Gwen. Sophia and Karin are just here for the ballgowns."

We turned as Gwen strode in.

Cam greeted everyone and hugged Gwen. "Help me pull out the nurse outfits, you naughty girls." He unzipped a big dress bag.

We sorted out the three sizes, and he turned his back while we giggled and slipped into the nurse uniforms. We wore the garter belts, stockings, dresses, and our white stilettos for the full effect.

"Okay, Cam, you can turn around." I struck a sexy pose, hands on hips, chest out.

He examined me first. "It should be tighter at the bust to accentuate your cleavage. The waist and hips fit well. I'll just take in a little up here, and you'll be good to go."

Gwen stepped forward. "What do you think about my uniform?" She twirled around. "Is it too tight?"

Cam grinned. "Not if you want to look like a slutty nurse. It's perfect." He reached over and unzipped the front two inches lower to give her ample bosom breathing room and show extra cleavage.

Mona's uniform needed tightening at the chest and hips. In thirty minutes, he had us tarted up to the maximum.

He stepped back and looked us up and down. "Perfect. Who's the lucky guy?"

"You remember Snake. He's a Navy SEAL from Texas, and he's coming here to recover from leg wounds."

Cam glanced at Gwen. "I remember you telling me about him back in January. Does Clint know about this?"

"Not yet, but he won't mind. I'm just playacting." Gwen admired her outfit in a floor-length mirror.

He arched an eyebrow. "Playacting with the same guy who gave you a steamy kiss two months ago?"

Gwen blushed. "Snake is really hot, but that was before I started dating Clint." She glanced at everyone. "And Clint doesn't ever need to know. Understood?"

We all nodded, grinning.

"Now that the naughty nurses are ready to roll, let's get cracking on the ballgowns. Ladies, think about what color you want, and I'll show you the styles for Renaissance gowns." Cam opened a binder of his designs.

When it was Mona's turn to choose a gown, Cam checked out her spiked hair, piercings, and makeup. "Are you into Goth or steampunk?"

"Both. I like variety." She paged through the photos. "Any way you can modify a gown to match my style?"

"My dear, I can make you the Renaissance Goth Queen." He pointed at one. "Imagine this in black satin with red lace and black leather accents, a blood-red tiara and matching earrings. And, of course, you'll wear red lipstick and nail polish."

Mona grinned. "I love it!"

Sophia said, "I'm too short for these full skirts. I'll look silly."

"You're taller than Queen Elizabeth." Cam gave her the once-over. "You'll look like an Italian Countess when I'm finished with you—elegant and regal with a slender skirt."

Cam had everyone fitted and their gowns picked out by lunchtime. We gathered on the back terrace for a quick meal before driving to the airport.

———

Jorgensen Industries' Chief Pilot, Captain Dan Duquesne, did a double-take when we walked into the private jet terminal.

"Hi, Dan. I'm sure you remember Gwen from our roundtrip flight to London two months ago." I nudged him out of his trance, and he took her hand.

"Good to see you again, Gwen. I, uh, didn't know you were a nurse."

She laughed. "No, silly. We're just playacting to cheer up a wounded friend and make his teammates jealous."

"Oh." He glanced at our trio and grinned. "Lucky guy."

I introduced him to Mona, and then we boarded the company Gulfstream jet.

A curvaceous blond flight attendant displaying long legs under her short uniform dress greeted us. "Welcome aboard, Miss Jorgensen. I'm

Dani, and I'll be taking care of you and your friends today. Is there anything I can do for you?"

"We need a blonde to complete our TLC Squad." I explained our mission, and she agreed to help us fawn over Snake and make his buddies jealous.

———

We arrived in Norfolk right on schedule, two hours and ten minutes after takeoff. Snake hobbled onto the ramp on crutches, his teammates carrying his bag and giving him moral support.

We looked out the windows at the men.

Mona said, "Ooh, the guy on crutches is tall, dark, and sexy."

Dani peered at the men. "You weren't kidding, Jett. SEALs are super-hot."

Everyone did a quick primp before the copilot opened the door and extended the stairs.

I addressed my nurse squad, "Remember, we'll take turns giving Snake enthusiastic kisses, and then we'll help him aboard. Gwen and I will go first because he knows us. Ready?"

Everyone stood, and I led them outside. We sashayed to where Snake and his team stood, staring.

"Snake, you poor darling." Eager to set an example for the other women, I slipped my arms around his neck and gave him a passionate kiss.

He responded with the same intensity he'd given me two months ago when he tried to seduce me. I could barely catch my breath when Gwen took my place.

Gwen's mouth devoured his with a long, steamy kiss. Then Dani plastered herself against him, slipped her fingers into his thick brown hair, and pulled his lips to hers in a smoldering embrace. Afterward, she said, "I'll go and prepare a nice comfy bed for you on the airplane." She gave his team a million-dollar smile and strolled back to the jet.

I introduced Mona. "She lives with me now, so you'll have plenty of women to take good care of you." I grinned as she kissed him like it was an Olympic sport.

"Time to go." I smiled at his team. "Good seeing you guys, and don't worry. We'll nurse Snake's wounds and bring him back good as new." I waved goodbye.

We crowded around our patient, helping him up the steps and into the jet.

Dani guided him to a central recliner and placed his bag under his right foot. "Use the bag to support your foot until after takeoff. Then you can recline your seat."

He grinned at her and the rest of us. "You ladies gave an Academy Award-worthy performance out there. I'll be a legend by the end of the day. I can't thank y'all enough."

Mona stroked his cheek. "Oh, I'm sure we'll think of something you can do."

All the women, including me, laughed.

Dani fastened his seatbelt and turned to us. "Okay, everybody buckle-up until after takeoff." She leaned down and caressed his cheek. "I'll be back soon, sugar."

I strapped in beside him, and Gwen took the seat on the other side. In minutes, we were airborne.

I squeezed his hand. "Are you in pain?"

"Not when I look at you in that hot nurse outfit. Dang, you're sexy." He glanced around. "All of you are. Any chance y'all might wear these outfits when we're at home?"

I grinned. "Turn on your Texas charm and we might be persuaded."

After the plane leveled off, Dani took charge. "Dear, are you on any meds that prohibit drinking alcohol?"

"No meds at all, darlin', and I'd love a cold beer."

Gwen knelt beside his right leg. "Would you like me to massage your leg? Where does it hurt?"

Snake wore cargo shorts and a snug T-shirt that hugged his muscles. He pointed. "I've got stitches in my thigh and calf, so no massaging the leg."

A naughty glint flashed in her eyes. "We could massage the rest of you."

He grinned. "Now, ladies, don't tease me."

Mona reached over, squeezed his biceps, and exclaimed, "Your muscles are so hard."

Snake shook his head. "That's not the only thing that'll be hard if you ladies don't simmer down."

We giggled and backed off as Dani handed him a beer.

Gwen nudged him. "It's so nice to see you again. I wish we could pick up where we left off, but I have a boyfriend now. He's the lead detective with the Palm Beach Police."

He squeezed her hand. "If you're happy, I'm happy."

"Jett has three women living with her now, and one's a gorgeous professional chef who's preparing your dinner tonight."

Snake turned to me. "And Mona lives with you too? I thought you just said that to make my team jealous."

"It's true. Sophia, Mona, and Chef Karin live with me."

He smiled. "I was goin' to ask if anything interestin' has happened since you and Mike nailed your parents' killer. Looks like you've been busy."

Gwen and I shared nervous smiles.

She said, "Actually, the murders haven't quite stopped yet."

"What the heck happened?" He glanced from Gwen to me.

I told him about the guy in the tree.

He shook his head. "I've never heard of anything like that."

"Neither have I, and the police have no leads." I sighed. "I'm hoping it's a one-time thing that has nothing to do with me."

"I may not be able to walk so good, but I can still shoot straight. Loan me a weapon, and I'll protect you and your roomies."

"I have a shooting range in my house now. It has two lanes, and maybe in a week or so you'll feel up to training Mona to shoot."

"I don't know. A house full of armed women sounds dangerous." He grinned. "Is Sophia planning on guardin' my room?"

"Well, you know she adores you. She'll spoil you rotten, and there's no telling how much weight you'll gain from her cannoli."

He glanced around at us. "I'm not sure if I'll survive stayin' with y'all, but I'll have a big smile when I die."

"I have a feeling you'll manage just fine. Isn't that what SEALs do?"

"Right. We adapt to the situation, and I'm likin' this situation."

# SEVEN

G wen gave Snake a quick kiss goodbye before we dropped her off next door. Mona and I helped him into the house, and Sophia and the puppies made a big fuss after we put him in the wheelchair. The dogs remembered him and slobbered over his arms while he ruffled their fur. Then he pulled Sophia close and hugged her.

"I can see you haven't changed a bit, you rascal." She grinned.

He caught her hand. "I've been dreamin' about your cannoli."

"Well, dream no more, sugar buns. You'll have some for dessert right after the delicious steak dinner Karin made for you." She turned. "Snake, I'd like to introduce our chef, Karin Kekoa."

Karin grinned and stepped forward. "I've heard a lot about you from Jett and Sophia."

"Don't believe everything you hear, darlin'." He took her hand and kissed it. "You can trust me."

Sophia laughed. "You can trust him with everything except your virtue."

"Hey, give me a break. I kinda behaved last time." He playfully swatted Sophia's backside.

We put Snake's wheelchair at the head of the long dining table, and we gathered near him on both sides. After we enjoyed a mixed salad,

Karin passed around platters with juicy ribeye steaks, asparagus tips, and twice-baked potatoes topped with cheddar cheese and bacon bits. There was a large decanter of red wine for the women and a frosted pitcher of beer for Snake.

I sat at Snake's right. "A doctor will be here at seven to check you over and advise us on how best to help your recovery. He deals with leg injuries every day in his Sports Medicine practice."

"Thank you, Jett. It never hurts to get a second opinion."

We filled him in on our plans for a charity ball and my new P.I. agency.

Karin added, "Snake, we have the Navy in common. I served on destroyers before I attended culinary college."

I nodded at Mona. "And Mona's an expert with computers and Internet research."

He glanced around the table. "Sounds like you have everyone you need for the private detective agency you're startin', Jett. Especially with dead-eye Sophia for backup."

I laughed. "Yeah, lucky for me, Sophia never misses, but I have to work as an apprentice under a licensed P.I. for a year before I can have my own agency. The apprenticeship is normally two years, but Florida is willing to waive a year because I served in Navy Intelligence."

"No problem," Snake said. "Your roomies will still be here in a year. Plenty of time to set up everythin'."

Sophia walked in with a platter of fresh cannoli and served Snake first. After we finished enjoying the delicious dessert, the doorbell boomed "Ride of the Valkyries."

Snake chuckled. "Can't help laughin' every time I hear that doorbell."

"That's probably the doctor, right on time." I stood. "I'll bring him in here."

The doctor was fit and forty and all business. He examined Snake's wounded leg. "The stitches are holding, but that could change if you put any strain on the leg. Stay off it for ten days, and then I'll come back and remove the stitches and set you up on a rehab program." He glanced at Mona's and my sexy nurse outfits. "If you want this man to heal properly, he needs to remain on his back during intercourse. Otherwise, he'll pop his stitches and be worse off than he was before."

Surprised and a little embarrassed by his candor, I looked away. No point in telling the doctor Snake and I were just friends. He'd never believe me in my naughty attire.

I walked the doctor outside and thanked him for coming. As he drove away, I paused and admired the black, star-filled sky. Just as I turned and headed up the entrance steps, I heard the distinctive deep drone of a Pratt & Whitney R-985 radial engine as the airplane flew overhead. The aircraft didn't have its position lights on, and I couldn't see it clearly in the dark sky—just a brief shadow covering some stars as it flew past.

Odd.

When I turned to go inside, a strange whistling sound made me pause. In a split second, something heavy crashed onto Odin's bronze statue. I turned and lurched back against the door, facing the circular fountain in the middle of my driveway. A sickening thud was followed by something hard clanking against the bronze figure hidden in dark shadows.

I froze.

Nothing moved.

The sound of the airplane faded into the distance and silence reigned once again.

With a shaky hand, I reached inside my door and switched on the outside floodlights. I gasped, and my stomach churned, as I inched closer to the grisly scene.

Odin stood with his sword held high. A body hung, impaled through its chest on the massive sword. The man's head was slumped forward, facing down. His feet were encased in concrete buckets, and those buckets had clanked against Odin's bronze back. Below, snarling wolves guarded Odin, facing the four cardinal compass points and spewing water from their fanged mouths.

I eased closer, pulled out my cell phone, and fumbled with the flashlight function, praying I wouldn't recognize the victim's face.

I did.

I looked into the glassy blue eyes of Roger Thornton, one of my former classmates from Banyan Isle Prep School. Another guy I had briefly dated in my teenage years. His neck was ringed with a thin line of dried blood, probably from a garrote.

My knees gave out, and I turned and collapsed onto the marble rim of the fountain. Leaning forward, I put my head between my legs to ward off nausea.

Recovering, I faced my open front door with my heart racing, unsure who I should notify first—my housemates or the police.

My dogs must've sensed something sinister. They bounded up to me, raised their noses, and howled. That brought Sophia running. Soon everyone was gathered around me, including the night guard who'd been checking the backyard when the body hit.

Snake wheeled down the ramp my grandfather installed years ago. He squeezed my hands. "I've got you."

Everyone stared up at the body. No one spoke.

The guard pulled out his cell. "I've gotta report this."

I snapped a picture with my cell and then called Mike.

"Hello, Jett. What's up?"

"Another body was dropped here. This one's impaled on Odin's sword."

"Get everyone inside the house. I'll be right there." He paused. "Did you recognize the body?"

"Mike, it's Roger Thornton, another classmate from Banyan Isle Prep." I glanced up at the body. "Better call Fire Rescue. The sword tip is twenty feet high."

He groaned. "I'll talk to you inside after the scene is secured."

I stood unsteadily and gripped the back of Snake's wheelchair. "The police want everyone inside." I glanced at the guard. "Except you, of course."

He stood beside the fountain. "I'll wait here."

I called Gwen so she wouldn't freak out when the police and fire trucks rolled in. She answered as we headed back into the house and closed the door.

After listening to me, she said, "Again? Who was it this time?"

"Roger Thornton."

"Roger? How awful. He was a star running back on the football team. I dated him our junior year, and I think you dated him when we were seniors. He owns a successful property management company, or he did, poor guy."

"I read about his recent engagement to that heiress, Christy Carrington." His gory image returned and made my gut churn.

"Right, the rich widow. She was seven years older than Roger." Gwen hesitated. "Want me to come over?"

"No need. I have Sophia, Snake, and the new roomies. I'll be fine."

When I slipped the phone into my pocket, Sophia hugged me. "You look pale. Sit and have some red wine."

We gathered in the great hall, and Karin carried in wine for the women and beer for Snake.

I hugged both puppies beside me on the sofa, and they licked my shaking hands.

Snake rolled up and slid onto the sofa. He picked up Pratt and put him beside him so he could pull me closer. I snuggled against his broad shoulder and sipped the wine Karin handed me.

After a few moments of silence, Snake asked, "How well did you know the victim?"

"We went to prep school together and took most of the same classes. He was very popular. I went out with him a few times." I took another sip. "Haven't seen him since before I joined the Navy."

Sophia moved closer. "One body could be accidental, Jett, but two, that's intentional."

"Hittin' the sword had to be dumb luck." Snake shook his head. "Nobody can be that precise when droppin' a body out of an airplane."

I was about to respond when the dogs' ears perked up an instant before loud sirens shrieked outside my front door and then fell silent. I sighed and took another gulp.

Snake squeezed me. "As soon as the cops leave, arm me with a Glock and extra mags."

"Of course, and just so you know, Sophia, Karin, and I are armed too."

# EIGHT

W agner's Viking tune boomed into the great hall. The doorbell reminded me of the myth about Valkyries escorting warriors to Valhalla after they died valiantly in battle. My father had loved that crazy doorbell.

Sophia answered the door and returned with my ex.

Mike stood, hands on hips, looking down at me. "Another body, Jett? What's going on?"

I bit my lower lip. "I don't *know* why bodies are dropping onto my property."

He glanced at Mona and me, then did a double-take when he noticed Snake, remembering him from two months ago. "Why is *he* here, and what's with the nurse outfits?"

I glanced at Mona. "As for Snake, he was wounded, and we wore these outfits when we picked him up in Norfolk today so his teammates would be jealous. He's staying here while he recovers."

Snake smiled. "Lucky me."

Mike ground his teeth and pulled out his electronic tablet. "Now, who saw the body fall from the sky?"

I sighed. "Just me. Everyone else was inside when it happened."

"Alone? What were you doing out front in the dark?"

I explained about walking the doctor out and pausing to admire the stars. "Then an airplane flew overhead with no lights, and the body crashed into the statue."

He made a few notes. "Were you able to recognize the aircraft type or get an "N" number?"

"No, the plane was a few thousand feet up, but I recognized the distinctive sound of a R-985 radial engine, which means the airplane is probably an antique. You can narrow it down even more by eliminating airplanes that can't be flown safely with the door open or ones that wouldn't be feasible for the pilot to shove out the body."

He rolled his eyes. "And how am I supposed to do that?"

"Hunter will know." I pulled out my cell and punched in his number.

When my uncle answered, I filled him in and said, "Mike wants to ask you a few airplane questions. I'm handing him the phone."

Mike paced and took notes as he listened to Hunter. After several questions, he said, "Thank you. I'll be in touch. Here's Jett." He handed me the phone.

I replied to my uncle's concerns, "Don't worry. Snake's here, and he'll protect us." Hunter asked me to hand the phone to Snake.

Snake listened and replied, "I agree. I'll call a retired SEAL friend who started a high-end security company down here."

I said goodbye to my uncle and pocketed the phone.

Mike had been busy tapping data into his tablet. When he finished, he glanced down at me. "What's your connection to Roger Thornton?"

"We dated a few times during prep school. That's it. I haven't seen or spoken to him in years."

Sophia broke in, "I have a theory. I suspect the first body was a mistake, meant to drop in the ocean. After the national publicity, the killer decided it would be fun to drop another body on Jett's property and get more notoriety."

"Fun? I doubt it." Mike thought it over. "The killer is targeting these men for a reason. Both were successful businessmen. Maybe it has nothing to do with Jett, but the fact they all went to the same school at the same time means Jett could be a target too." He looked at

Snake. "If you want to call in some retired SEALs to protect Jett, I'm all for it, but leave the investigation to the police."

"Understood." Snake glanced at me. "We'll keep everyone here safe."

When Mike left, Snake called his team on a conference call and got the number for a friend's security company. Within minutes, he had an appointment scheduled.

Snake squeezed me and gave me a little kiss. "Tim Goldy and three of his best men from Trident Security will be here in thirty minutes. He'll do a much better job than those wienie guards you have now."

I pulled out my cell. "I'd better tell Mike they're coming so he doesn't block them at the gate."

Thirty minutes sped by, the doorbell boomed, and Sophia escorted the men into the great hall. Dressed all in black, they wore helmets with night-vision gear, bullet-proof vests, and pistols in thigh holsters.

Snake smiled. "Hoo yah! Thanks for comin', guys. Some looney is killing men Jett knows and droppin' them on her land."

The leader said, "We saw the body impaled on the sword." He turned to me. "Miss Jorgensen? I'm Tim Goldy. Your background check revealed a lot has happened since you came home from the Navy in January. We can help."

The men glanced from Snake to Mona and me, still in naughty nurse outfits. Although they remained granite-faced, their eyes twinkled.

Tim noted Snake's bandages. "You're on injured leave from Alpha Team?"

"Yeah, I just got here a couple hours ago." He thumbed at our little nurse squad. "Jett and Mona flew into Norfolk in a private jet to pick me up and make my teammates jealous."

Tim grinned at us. "Mission accomplished, ladies."

I introduced everyone to Tim's team. "Sophia, Karin, and I are armed with Glocks and are licensed to carry. I'd like you to teach Mona to shoot in my indoor shooting range, which is alongside the ballroom at the north end on this floor."

Tim glanced from Mona to me. "First, your property must be

secured. Who's monitoring your closed-circuit camera surveillance system?"

"Elite Security in West Palm Beach. Can you handle that, or am I stuck with them?"

"We have a state-of-the-art facility that can meet all your security needs. I noted on the property description that you have six acres. Until we catch the killer, I'll post four men outside to cover the grounds in eight-hour shifts." He glanced around. "Your home is as big as a small hotel. Would you like guards patrolling the interior at night?"

I glanced at Snake, who shook his head. "No, I have an excellent security alarm and my dogs hear everything." I pointed. "Pratt and Whitney are part of my family, and I want them protected too."

"Understood." He pulled a small laptop and portable printer from a shoulder bag and plugged the printer into an outlet. "I'll prepare a contract. I need the full names of everyone living here and anyone else who has a key."

I sat beside him and gave him all the info. In minutes, I had a printed contract.

"We can start right now if you'd like, or would you rather have the other company finish out the night?" Tim put away the printer.

"I definitely want you guys right away. Can you send someone out to fetch the security guard while I call Elite Security?"

Tim nodded at two of his men. One went out the front door, and the other went through the terrace door.

I called and canceled my contract. They grumbled about not refunding the remainder of the month's charges, but I didn't care. Their guard never even noticed the first body.

Tim tapped on his laptop. "Your video feeds have been transferred to my facility, and tomorrow, we'll change your locks and codes and provide high-tech gate openers."

Something about Tim's calm competence eased my fears. He and his men definitely inspired confidence. I felt like everything would be okay.

I assumed my new roommates felt the same way.

# NINE

I gave Tim the codes, keys to the house, and door openers for the garage and front gate. He assured me they'd patrol my grounds all night and would be relieved by new guards in eight hours, so I locked the doors behind them and activated the alarm system.

The CSU and police were still at my fountain. At least the body had been removed.

I glanced at my watch. Eleven o'clock and I was ready to call it a day. "Let's tuck in Snake and get some sleep."

We wheeled him into the elevator and took him up to his room on the second floor. After we helped him into bed, I brushed his cheek with my lips. "I'm glad you're here. You've helped me already by calling Tim's security team. Sweet dreams."

He snatched my hand. "Will you be okay alone tonight?"

"I won't be alone. I have Pratt and Whitney." I smiled and waved while Sophia, Karin, and Mona fussed over him.

———

Snake was about to fall asleep when his bedroom door opened and then closed with a soft click. A slender form inched toward him. He reached for the Glock Jett had loaned him but stopped when a soft floral scent wafted over him.

Mona lifted the covers and slid in beside him. "I hope you don't mind me joining you. I'm too scared to sleep alone tonight."

He pulled her against him. "I'll protect you."

She slid her hand down his muscular chest. "I haven't been with a man in over a year. Is this a bad idea?"

He pulled her on top of him and tossed aside her nightie. "It's the best idea you've had all day."

She stripped off his boxers. "Don't forget what the doctor said about staying on your back."

"I can live with that if you can." He slid his arms around her and kissed her the same passionate way she had kissed him in front of his buddies.

Steamy kisses preceded steamier sex. Afterward, she returned to her bed so no one would know about her nocturnal escapade.

Snake fell asleep with Mona's scent lingering.

———

Snake glanced at his watch at five in the morning when he heard the door click. The space beside him was empty. Then someone slipped into his bed. He assumed Mona had returned. *Good thing she gave me several hours to recover from our first session.*

She woke him gently, snuggling her naked body against him and sliding her hand across his chest.

Half awake, he caressed her voluptuous curves and realized she wasn't Mona. Snake looked into Karin's blue eyes. "This is a welcome surprise."

"I don't normally do things like this, but I haven't been with a man in over a year, and you're super sexy." She straddled him and kissed him deeply, communicating her desire.

Without thinking, he was about to roll her under him when she pressed his shoulders down. "You have to let me stay on top. Doctor's orders, remember?"

"Whatever you say, sweetheart." Snake responded with intensified passion.

After a heart-pounding romp, they lay entwined in ecstasy.

Before she left, she whispered, "Thanks for the good loving, Snake. Sweet dreams."

"Comin' here is the best idea I've ever had," he murmured before passing out.

———

At eight in the morning, Sophia and I peeked into Snake's room. He was sound asleep.

Karin sidled up to us. "Wounded soldiers need extra sleep to heal. He'll wake when he's ready."

"He does look deep in sleep," Sophia agreed.

Karin smiled and gently closed his door, then headed downstairs with us.

At breakfast on the terrace, Mona asked, "Where's Snake?"

Sophia said, "He's still sleeping. The poor guy's really tired."

Mona snickered.

"What's so funny?" I tried to read her face. "I didn't think anybody would be laughing after last night."

"Oh, I was just thinking about how much fun we had as naughty nurses." Mona grinned.

My cell rang. It was Gwen.

"Hey, Jett, I'm heading out to your terrace. How is everyone today?"

"We're good. Snake is still asleep. What's up?"

Gwen reached us and pocketed her phone. "I'm working a missing-person case."

"Tell us about it." I waved her into a nearby chair, and the puppies showered her with kisses.

"There's an elderly couple who live in a huge, oceanfront mansion in Palm Beach. The husband went missing last evening. The weird thing is their security cameras show he never left the house."

"What does Detective Hottie think?" I asked.

"Clint thinks the old geezer found a blind spot in the system and sneaked out."

"Really?" Sophia offered Gwen a warm biscuit. "What do you think?"

"Something feels wrong. Why would an eighty-five-year-old man sneak out?"

Karin handed Gwen a cup of coffee. "How big is the house?"

"About forty thousand square feet. I thought he wandered into a hidden closet or something, but we've searched the house from top to bottom with no luck."

"I have an idea. Let's take Pratt and Whitney over there. Their half-wolf noses detect everything." I reached down and petted them.

Gwen looked down at the pups. "Good idea. My boss won't authorize a police dog because he's convinced the man isn't there. I'm worried the old guy might die if we don't find him soon." She pulled out her cell. "I'll tell Mrs. Pickering to expect us."

"Okay, give me a minute to wrestle them into their harnesses." I stood.

Sophia jumped up. "I'll help."

It only took a few minutes, then I followed Gwen's car in my mom's mid-size SUV with the dogs in the back. We drove inland over the Banyan Isle Bridge, south on US 1, and east over the northernmost Palm Beach bridge, finally turning onto South County Road. We passed Mar-A-Lago and finally pulled into an enormous estate on the ocean. The huge stone mansion looked like it was built before 1920, not long after my house.

Pratt and Whitney sensed something was up, kind of like when I took them to cure Marjorie Wentworth's migraine. The butler answered the doorbell and ushered us in. The dogs trundled into the mansion on their leashes, following Gwen and me.

The butler led us to a grand salon where we met with Edith Pickering, eighty and razor-thin but elegant with perfectly coiffed white hair and a designer frock.

She wrung her hands. "I'm so worried. Roland's been missing since last evening, and my staff and the police can't find him anywhere."

"I'm hoping my dogs can help. Do you have a piece of clothing with his scent on it?" My dogs looked alert and ready for action.

"Yes, of course, but aren't they just puppies?"

"Smart puppies." I smiled.

"Alright." She walked away. When she returned, she carried a slightly soiled polo shirt.

I kneeled and held the shirt in front of my dogs' noses. "Find the nice man who wore this shirt."

I wasn't expecting much. After all, they were only four months old. I was surprised when they pressed their noses to the floor and trotted forward.

I clutched their leashes and walked behind them. After a few turns, they entered a long corridor and stopped about halfway. The dogs sniffed along the lower part of a life-size oil painting of a man in an expensive suit. The painting was seven feet tall with the bottom edge of the frame a foot above the oak floor. They concentrated on the left bottom corner of the painting, looked up at me, and barked.

I grabbed hold of each side of the four-foot-wide frame, but it was firmly secured against the wall. When I tried to lead the dogs farther down the hall, they pulled me back to the painting.

Glancing at Gwen, I said, "Time to call in a professional. I plan to apprentice under Darcy McKay and her Sniffers Agency. She has dogs specially trained to locate lost people, and most of her work is pro bono." I punched in her number on my cell.

"Sniffers Agency—The Nose Knows, Darcy McKay speaking. How may we help you?"

"Hi, Darcy, this is Jett Jorgensen. We discussed me doing my apprenticeship with your agency."

"Oh, yes, good to hear from you. When can you start?"

"How about now? My friend, Palm Beach Police Detective Gwen Pendragon, needs your help with a missing-person case. My puppies tracked the man to a painting inside his Palm Beach mansion, and we aren't sure what to do now."

"As I recall, you said your dogs are Timber-shepherds, right?"

"Yes, half wolf and half German shepherd."

"Okay, I'll bring Max. He's a German shepherd, and he'll act like a big brother to them. Things are pretty quiet here today. Give me the address and we'll come right away."

I texted Darcy the address, and she arrived in a half hour with a beautiful honey-colored dog like Pratt. Max proudly wore his bright orange work bandana with a GPS locator beacon. He sniffed my puppies and gave them an I'm-in-charge look. My fur babies were in awe of him, so tall and confident, and they immediately deferred to him. We walked into the expansive salon beyond the foyer and met with Mrs. Pickering and Gwen.

"Let's see if Max leads us to the same spot where the puppies stopped." I handed Darcy the shirt.

She leaned down and held the shirt under his nose. "Max, take scent."

He barked once, put his nose to the floor, and trotted toward the same long hallway where Pratt and Whitney had gone earlier.

We hurried after Max on the smooth marble floor, my dogs eager to keep up.

The big dog stopped in front of the same painting, sniffed the left side of the frame, barked once, and sat.

Darcy brushed her long red hair away from her face with a quick sweep of her hand. Her intense green eyes examined the frame. Five-two, she slid her small hand down the left side and stopped near the bottom.

"I found something." She pressed it, a latch released, and the painting swung open like a door.

"What the heck?" I peeked through the doorway.

Darcy said, "Ooh, a secret passage, but to where?"

Stale, musty air filled my nostrils when I stuck my head inside. A dark, narrow walkway seemed to run in both directions.

I turned to Edith Pickering. "Did you know about this?"

Shocked, she said, "We bought the house from the original owners in 1970. No one told us this was here."

Darcy unhooked his leash. "Max, search and find."

Max leaped into the darkness, and my dogs raced after him, jerking their leashes out of my hands.

# TEN

I wedged my purse against the door and switched on my cell's flashlight. Gwen and Darcy turned on their flashlights, and we raced into the darkness after the dogs, leaving Mrs. Pickering. Max's bark echoed down the passage, guiding us. After we'd covered about sixty feet, our lights revealed stairs leading downward. We paused at the top.

A man lay at the bottom of the steps in the shadows.

Gwen eased down to him and checked his pulse. "It's Roland Pickering. He's alive, but he's unconscious with a large lump on his head."

The dogs licked his face while Gwen called for an ambulance.

I turned to Darcy. "Looks like he got trapped when the painting swung closed. He followed the passage in total darkness, didn't expect stairs, and fell." I shined my light on his head injury. "Poor guy."

Soon, Roland was on his way to Good Samaritan Hospital, which was just across the northern bridge from Palm Beach Island.

Mrs. Pickering gripped my hand. "Thank you. Is there anything I can do for you?"

"I'm throwing a charity ball next month." I reached into my purse and handed her a flyer. "Maybe you know some people who'd like to attend."

"I know loads of people, dear. Don't you worry. I'll fill up your ballroom." She left with her chauffeur to visit her husband at the hospital.

I grinned at Darcy. "I'm so proud of my dogs. If I had trusted them, maybe I would've found the picture-frame latch and not needed to call you." I hugged them and told them what smart little pups they were.

Max sat proudly as Darcy handed him his reward—a large dog biscuit. She broke another one apart and gave halves to Pratt and Whitney. "This is how I reward my dogs after they complete a job. I'd be happy to show you how to train your dogs. They're really smart."

"Sign me up. Do you have time to stop by my house on Banyan Isle?"

"I can follow you home now. I guess Gwen will be busy with paperwork."

"You've got that right," Gwen said. "Thanks for the help, Darcy. I'll call you tonight, Jett."

———

It was 11:00 a.m. when I led Darcy and Max into the great hall and introduced them to Snake and the women. We settled on a dark-brown leather sofa, and I recounted our search, ending with, "Mr. Pickering is recovering in the hospital now."

Darcy jumped in, "Pratt and Whitney are quite remarkable, only four months old and finding that man with no prior training."

Max sat calmly beside Darcy, looking ever alert, and my puppies copied him. So cute.

Sophia served Darcy an iced tea and gave Max a bowl of water.

Snake wheeled up to Max and glanced at Darcy. "Okay if I pet him?"

"Go ahead. He loves attention." She rubbed Max's ear.

He petted the big dog. "How many K-9s do y'all have in your P.I. agency?"

"Five—a Great Dane, Doberman Pinscher, Labrador retriever, dachshund, and Max. I call my company the Sniffers Agency, and our motto is, 'The nose knows.'"

Karin stood beside Snake's wheelchair and petted Max. "Do you use the dogs for all your investigations?"

"Yes, my detective agency specializes in K-9 investigations, and we often work with police departments. The dogs sniff out drugs, dead bodies, arsonists, and missing people and pets." Darcy glanced around. "It looks like your living situation is similar to mine, Jett. Did you inherit this estate?"

"Yes, it's been in the family ever since my great-great-grandfather built it over a century ago. I inherited it after my parents were murdered."

Darcy sighed. "Sorry for your loss, Jett. My home and money didn't come from family. I inherited my estate from a serial killer under unusual circumstances."

That comment piqued Sophia's interest. "Ooh, do tell."

Everyone leaned forward, eager to hear her answer.

"My dogs found all his buried bodies, and we also found where the killer and his accomplice were hiding. I had no idea his will stipulated that if anyone ever uncovered his crimes and caught him, his vast fortune and everything he owned would go to that person."

"Is he in prison now?" I asked.

"No, a cop shot him, and he died. His accomplice is serving a life sentence." She shook her head. "But now I have an animal shelter on the estate, and we do a lot of good for the community, solving crimes and helping people find missing loved ones and pets."

"Any chance your dogs might know how to catch a killer who drops bodies out of an airplane? So far, he's dropped two here."

"I saw the stories on the news. If you can find the plane, or narrow it down to a few aircraft, my dogs can probably sniff out which one was used."

"That would help a lot. Just so you know, I already passed the written test for my P.I. license."

"Consider yourself signed up. I'll help you with on-the-ground investigations using K-9s, but you'll need someone else to teach you the cyber stuff. My work rarely involves the Internet."

I smiled at Mona. "I have someone in-house who can handle that." I paused. "On another subject, we're holding a charity ball here next month, and I'd love for you to attend. Bring as many guests as you wish. The women will be wearing Renaissance gowns and the men tuxedoes. Designer Cam Altman makes fabulous ball gowns. If you'd like, I'll text you his contact info."

"Ooh, yes! And put me down for … ten tickets. My friends and I love to dance. I'll bring my dad and his new wife too." She paused. "If you want to sell more tickets, contact the Calder twins, Mary and Molly. They're widows who love to hold charity balls, and I'm sure they'll want to attend yours. I'll text you their phone number."

"The more the better." I reached into my purse. "Here's a flyer for the ball. It will benefit the women's shelter I founded."

Darcy stood. "Good meeting everyone. Call me if you find an airplane that needs to be sniffed out, Jett."

I walked her and Max out. My puppies followed him to the door and looked disappointed when he left.

I was about to close the door when my new security head, Tim Goldy, walked up.

"Good afternoon, Miss Jorgensen." He thumbed at a man behind him carrying a tool case. "My locksmith will change all your door locks today and give you keys. I brought secure high-tech gate openers that also open your garage doors." Tim looked well-rested and handsome in his sleek navy business suit.

"Why aren't you tired after being up all night?"

"Oh, a man replaced me. I always come to meet a new client and ensure all their security needs are met, but I don't do guard duty unless an attack is imminent."

"Please, come in." I led him into the great hall. "I have to ask— have you ever been in a client situation where an attack was imminent?"

He smiled. "A SEAL friend, who aptly nicknamed his sister Danger Magnet, sent me and my team to protect her at her mother's oceanfront mansion from an expected assault by Chinese Secret Service agents intending to kidnap her."

"And did they come?"

Everyone seemed eager to hear his answer. He looked around and smiled.

"Twenty commandos parachuted in on a dark, moonless night. My team consisted of six men and two dogs patrolling the grounds." He shook his head. "I felt like I was back in the SEALs. We were outnumbered, but they weren't expecting us, so we had an advantage. It was a fierce battle. We took out fourteen on the ground and three who landed on her roof. Our client and her dog nailed the three who entered through her third-floor bedroom balcony before we could get there." He grinned. "Her German shepherd's name is Romeo, but he wasn't a lover that night. He bit the crap out of those Chinese commandos."

"Was anyone on your team hurt?" I searched his eyes.

"No, my guys are former SEALs with one-shot-one-kill skills, and our dogs act like fur missiles." He smiled, remembering. "I've been in two shootouts since I started my security company, and both were with the client we call Danger Magnet. She's an airline pilot with Luxury International Airlines."

"My uncle is a captain with them. I bet he knows her."

"*Everybody* there knows her. She's a legend. The Queen of England knighted her. Clients like her keep us on our toes." He glanced at the women. "No nurse outfits today?"

Mona grinned.

Snake asked, "What does this Danger Magnet look like?"

"Ah, a man's question." Tim chuckled. "She's twenty-seven, five-nine, long blond hair, blue-green eyes, beautiful face, a curvy body with long legs, and she has a genius IQ." He paused. "Before you get too excited, her boyfriend is a badass captain with the British SAS."

Snake smiled. "There's always a downside."

Tim shook his head. "Looks to me like you already have enough beautiful women here to keep you busy."

Snake blew out a sigh. "You have no idea."

Mona and Karin grinned.

I broke in, "Tim, I want to talk to you about our charity ball, just in case the body-drop killer isn't caught before then. I'd like at least ten men protecting us that night, but I want them to wear tuxedoes so they blend in and don't frighten the guests."

"No problem. We provide security for lots of events that require formal attire, and my men are discreet. Give me the date and time, and I'll set it up." He pulled a sack out of his briefcase. "These are your new gate and garage-door openers. Are ten enough?"

"Yes, that'll be plenty. Hold on a sec while I grab you a flyer for the ball." I jogged down to the study, snatched one off my printer, and returned. "This has all the info."

Tim glanced at it and put it in his briefcase. He smiled at me and the other women. "Call me any time, day or night, if you need me." He was about to leave when the doorbell rang.

Sophia trotted out and brought in the mail. She opened an envelope addressed to her and blurted, "What a sicko!"

I hurried over to her. "What's wrong?"

She handed me the note, written with glued-on words cut out of magazines. It said: *It's your turn. Are you ready for concrete boots, Sophia?*

"Oh, no." I hugged her. "Don't worry. We'll figure this out and catch him."

"I'm not worried, I'm angry. That creepy note doesn't scare me." She pulled out her cell phone. "I'm calling my boys. Someone is going to be very sorry." Sophia stomped out to the terrace.

I waved Tim over and showed him the message.

He glanced around. "Don't touch this. The police might get prints off it." He turned to me. "Call the police."

I placed the note on a hall table and pulled out my cell phone, while everyone gathered and read the note.

"Mike, it's Jett. Better come over right away. Sophia just received a threatening letter that might be from the killer."

# ELEVEN

O ne advantage to living on a small island is the cops are never far away. Mike arrived five minutes after my call. He read the note and slipped it into an evidence bag.

He glanced around. "Where's Sophia?"

I pointed at the terrace. "She's on the phone with her sons."

"You mean her sons in the *Mafia*?"

I put a hand on his shoulder. "Now don't get all fired up. She's probably just asking them to look into whether the note has any connection to their family."

"This had better not start a Mob war on Banyan Isle." Mike glared in Sophia's direction.

Sophia pocketed her phone and strode in.

Everyone looked at her as I asked, "Any news from your sons?"

"My eldest boy, Dominic, will meet with my late husband's side of the family. He'll check if anyone is holding a grudge over the concrete boots my Vinnie earned after betraying me and the Calabrese family." Sophia looked at me and hesitated. "And my younger boy, Marco, is flying down for a visit. I'll book a suite for him at the Banyan Harbor Inn."

I shook my head. "Marco is family. He'll stay here with us. What time is his flight landing?"

"Day after tomorrow at 9:00 a.m., and he already rented a Hummer for the drive to Banyan Isle." She pulled out her phone. "I'll text him your address."

Tim stepped forward. "I'll need his full name and description and the same for anyone traveling with him so my men will know who to let in."

"Marco DeLuca. He's thirty-six, five ten, and keeps himself fit. He has dark, wavy hair, brown eyes, and a strong chin. See?" She showed him pictures from her cell phone. "He'll probably bring some muscle, two or three guys. Just let in whoever arrives in the car with him."

Tim glanced at me, and I nodded my approval.

Mike sucked in his breath. "Let's sit down and discuss this." He waved Sophia and me to a nearby sofa.

Before he had a chance to ask a question, Sophia said, "My husband took a fatal dive into the Long Island Sound twenty years ago. At the time, my father was head of the Calabrese family and Don of the New York Mafia. No one dared come against us."

"Do you think someone in a rival family is coming after you now?" Mike asked.

"After twenty years? I doubt it." She glanced from Mike to me. "I think someone from New York is messing with my head after seeing the news stories about the bodies dropped here."

Mike stood. "I hope you're right."

"I'd like to know what you plan to do about this." I glanced at my watch. "Will you join us for lunch and discuss this further, Mike?"

"Thanks, but I have to go." He squeezed my shoulder. "Don't worry. I'll contact the FBI." He paused. "Just be careful, okay?"

I watched Mike leave, and then turned to Tim. "Stay for lunch. We need to discuss the note."

When lunch was ready, I turned to help Snake with his wheelchair and noticed he'd fallen asleep. Sophia walked beside me as I wheeled him onto the terrace.

I nudged Snake. "Wake up. Lunch is ready." He snored softly. "Snake?" I checked his pulse. Normal.

Sophia poked him. "Wake up, sweet cheeks."

"Huh?" He sat up straighter. "Sorry, what did I miss?"

I put my hand on his forehead. No fever. "What's wrong with you?"

"Nothin' a good night's sleep won't fix." He covered a yawn with his hand as Mona and Karin snickered.

I turned and glared at them. "What the heck is going on with Snake?"

Mona hung her head and blushed. "Sorry, Jett, I, um, visited him last night."

Karin sighed. "I spent some time with him early this morning, but I thought it was after he'd had a good night's sleep. Sorry." Her face flushed.

Tim made a Herculean effort not to laugh and ended up covering it with a cough.

I looked at Snake, softly snoring again, and I couldn't stop myself from laughing.

Sophia stood, hands on hips. "Ladies, I'm all for giving the man good loving, but this won't do. You're killing him when we're supposed to be nursing him back to health." She glanced at Snake. "Here's what will happen. Nobody gets in his bed tonight or tomorrow morning. Let the man rest. Got it?"

The red-faced women nodded.

I glanced around the table. "Now let's discuss what we're going to do about the sicko who sent Sophia the note."

"I'll warn my men to add mobsters to their list of potential suspects. They'll nail anyone who tries to sneak in here." He glanced at his watch. "I have to go."

My cell rang right after Tim left. I checked caller ID and answered, "Hi, Darcy. What's up?"

"Garnet Police just called my Sniffers Agency to help find a kidnapped teenage girl. She was taken from the picnic area in the Florida Wildlife Refuge on the west side of Diamond Lake. You're my apprentice now, so I'd like you to join my team in the search. Bring your handgun and meet me at the lakeside picnic area."

I glanced at my watch. "I can be there in thirty minutes." I pocketed my phone. "Darcy just called me to help with a case. I have to run. I'll call when I'm on my way home."

The magazine in my Glock was full, and I had a spare in my jeans pocket when I jumped into my SUV and floored it. I'd have to hurry to arrive in thirty minutes.

When I pulled into the picnic area, squad cars and Florida Wildlife vehicles covered the parking lot. I parked beside Darcy's Chevy Suburban where all her big dogs sat lined up on the pavement, looking ready for action.

"Jett, glad you're here. The men are already searching the forest. Come and meet the boys. You already know Max." She gestured at a black and white Great Dane. "This is Tiny, the yellow Lab is Laddie, and the Doberman is Dobie."

I petted the four big dogs and noted they wore bright orange bandanas with GPS trackers attached.

Darcy gave me an orange police armband and an orange ballcap with POLICE on the bill. "Wear these so you don't get shot by mistake."

She held a pink jacket under the dogs' noses. "Take scent and find the girl."

The dogs took off with their noses to the ground, and we chased after them. Darcy had all four GPS signals on her phone's screen. The four red dots stayed within a few feet of each other.

High-pitched barks from the dogs signaled they had picked up the scent.

Darcy and I ducked under low branches as we weaved through the trees, underbrush, and jungle-like plants in the Wildlife Refuge.

She said, "The guy who took her had this planned. A game warden found his pickup truck parked on a dirt road beside the west boundary fence, and a hole had been cut in the wire."

"I guess he planned to drag her through the forest and emerge where his truck is parked." I paused a second and caught my breath.

"Why don't they stake out the truck and nail him when he gets there?"

"They're worried he might not go to his truck until after he does whatever he's going to do to the girl. We have to find her before he hurts or kills her." She pointed. "The dogs turned that way."

As we rushed after the dogs, they barked every five seconds or so. We moved so fast mosquitoes didn't have a chance to bite us.

The barking stopped.

Darcy grabbed my arm and whispered, "The dogs stopped about twenty yards ahead of us. That means they found her and are waiting for my signal to attack the kidnapper." She drew her weapon. "Don't shoot my dogs."

We sneaked forward and crouched behind a thick bush where the dogs hid, waiting for us. I peeked through the branches and spotted the man and his victim.

The girl, a pretty blonde about fourteen, was gagged with her hands bound. The burly kidnapper stood well over six feet and brandished a large hunting knife near her throat. Wild eyed, he scanned in every direction, probably wondering where the barking dogs had gone.

I drew my pistol and waited for Darcy's signal.

She whispered, "Don't shoot unless the dogs need help. They'll take him down." She spoke to her dogs, "Max, take point, Tiny, come from behind, Laddie and Dobie, come from the sides. Attack the bad man."

The dogs silently slipped through the forest, staying hidden behind the heavy foliage. Max waited until his team had time to get in position, then he bounded into view of the kidnapper and stopped in front of him, baring his fangs and snarling.

The kidnapper waved the knife at Max, yelling, "Get back, you mangy mutt!"

Two seconds after the man removed the knife from the girl's throat, Dobie sprang into view and clamped his jaws around the man's right wrist. Laddie bit into the man's other wrist that had been holding the girl, and Max moved in and nudged the girl out of the way. Tiny leaped onto the kidnapper from behind and drove him face-first into the ground. The Great Dane sat on him, pinning him down, while Dobie and Laddie kept their jaws clamped on his wrists.

Darcy and I rushed out and grabbed the girl. I removed her gag, cut the zip-tie, and hugged her. Poor thing was crying and trembling, her eyes wide with terror. I checked her for injuries. It looked like he hadn't hurt her. Probably no time.

Darcy secured the knife and blasted an airhorn. Then she called the leader of the search team on his cell and gave him our GPS location.

We ignored the kidnapper as he screamed, "Get these dogs off me! They're killing me!"

Max crouched in front of him, snarling and snapping his jaws inches from his face. The man stopped screaming and wet himself.

The police search team arrived and froze, taking in the scene.

Chief McKay, Darcy's father, said, "Good job, honey. Now call off the dogs."

She stepped forward and said, "Dobie, Tiny, Laddie, release! Max, stand down!"

The dogs instantly left the kidnapper and grouped around Darcy. She reached into her cargo pockets and handed each dog a large dog biscuit. "Good boys."

Meanwhile, one of the cops bandaged the creep's bleeding wrists and cuffed him.

A handsome police detective with dark hair and brilliant blue eyes rushed in and hugged Darcy. "Good job, sweetheart."

She turned to me. "Jett Jorgensen, meet my boyfriend, Detective Scott Logan."

I grinned and shook his hand. "That was some chase your girlfriend led me on."

He reached out and pulled her in for another hug. "Darcy and her sniffers always get their man."

"Darcy, I don't suppose you'd be willing to volunteer your handsome boyfriend for my bachelor auction at the ball, would you?"

She smiled. "Good idea. He'll bring in big bucks."

He looked at us and stepped back. "Wait a minute. I don't want to be bought by some old biddy."

"Relax, sweetie. Chances are I'll be the only billionaire there, and I guarantee no one will outbid me." Darcy chuckled. "How much should I spend on you?"

"Whatever it takes to save me from the dowagers, especially those Calder twins."

She laughed. "Consider yourself saved."

Darcy looked at her dogs. "Lead us to the car, nice and slow."

Her dogs led us back to the parking lot.

"Thanks for including me on the hunt. Your dogs are amazing. I hope my puppies will be like them when they grow up."

"You handled yourself well back there. I'll enjoy working with you during your apprenticeship. Give your puppies a hug for me." She waved and loaded her dogs into the big SUV.

I texted Sophia that I was heading home. During the drive, I imagined Pratt and Whitney as adult K-9s doing amazing things for my Valkyrie Detective Agency.

# TWELVE

At dinner, I regaled everyone with a detailed account of Darcy's dogs taking down the kidnapper. "The dogs were awesome. They seemed to understand what was happening. I want my fur babies to grow up to be just like them."

I looked over at Snake. "We have way more women than men signed up for the ball. Any chance a few of your teammates would be willing to participate in the bachelor auction? I'd supply the transportation, lodging, and tuxedoes. They'd just need to dance with single women and stay over long enough to take winning bidders to lunch or dinner at my expense."

Snake yawned. "They might be persuaded if they can get another glimpse of the naughty nurses."

I covered my own yawn. Stress can be exhausting. "I'm turning in early. Good night, everyone. See you at breakfast."

I took the dogs out for a quick run in the backyard and then headed upstairs. Moments after I slipped under the covers and my dogs snuggled beside me, I fell into a deep sleep.

Pratt and Whitney woke me at 1:00 a.m. with cold noses and firm nudges. I struggled awake and sat up as my dogs snarled toward the balcony door that I had left open, their hackles up. I grabbed my Glock from under a pillow and racked the slide, tensing when my cell rang. Caller ID displayed Tim Goldy, which couldn't mean anything good at this hour.

"Sorry for the late call—"

"Hey, Tim, I think someone might be on my east balcony."

"No one's there. I'm below you, in your backyard. Get dressed and meet me on the back terrace. And bring Mona. We've got two bodies, and she might know one of them." He ended the call before I could ask questions.

Oh boy. I dressed, grabbed my handgun and cell, and hurried down to her room. In minutes, we were headed downstairs with the puppies on our heels.

Tim, dressed in black combat gear with an MP7 submachine gun strapped across his chest, waited for us on the terrace. "Come with me. I need to see if you can identify either of the dead men." He searched Mona's anxious eyes. "Are you okay looking at the bodies?"

She bit her lip. "I don't know. Why are they dead? Did you shoot them?"

"No." He took her arm and started toward the north end of my property bordered by a wide inlet that connected the Intracoastal Waterway to the Atlantic Ocean.

I trotted after them with the dogs sticking close. "Tim, wait! What happened? Are you sure there aren't more bad guys out here?"

He said over his shoulder, "The grounds are secure. Looks like the Asian guy tried to sneak onto your property via your boat dock. He'd just secured his boat to the pier when a body wearing concrete overshoes landed on him." He shook his head. "It appears the impact killed him."

I grabbed his arm. "Another body was dropped? Did you see the airplane?"

"My men heard the engine, but the position lights weren't on, and it was too high for them to identify it in the dark. They called me right after the impact." He stopped and faced me. "The body wearing concrete boots is in better condition than the guy who broke his fall. Maybe you'll recognize him, like you did the first two, and I'm hoping

Mona might ID the Asian guy. He came here for a reason. I'd like to know who we're dealing with before I call in the police."

Dark shadows under the banyan trees reached toward me in the Stygian night as I glanced left and right, searching for movement. *Stop worrying. Tim said it's safe now.*

My puppies kept close, sensing my apprehension. They growled as we approached the boat dock and Tim's men.

I stopped and crouched by my dogs. "It's okay. They're good men. Be nice."

They stopped growling and wagged their tails.

A small speedboat I'd never seen before bobbed alongside the floating pier. My parents' yacht, which was usually tied there, was in dry dock for maintenance at a boatyard.

Tim's men stepped aside, revealing two bodies. The concrete-filled buckets that held the falling victim's feet had crashed through the wood pier, leaving him visible from the waist up. My dogs sniffed him, yowled, and pushed me backward.

I led the dogs onto the grass, held out my palm, and said, "Stay." They sat still while I walked back onto the pier.

A man dressed like a ninja had fallen face-down after one of the buckets cracked his skull open. A long thigh holster held a silenced pistol, and a scabbard strapped to his back held a curved sword. His body lay on its stomach alongside the man sticking through the pier, and blood had pooled in a dark halo around the Asian man's head.

Mona gasped and covered her mouth when she looked at the hideous bodies. She stared wide-eyed at the curved sword and froze.

The night was dead silent. Even the crickets remained still.

Anger and revulsion competed for the top spot in my emotional landscape.

I nudged Tim. "Shine your light on the face of the guy stuck in the pier."

He did, and I recognized him. Memories of my senior prom flooded my mind, and nausea twisted my gut. Like the previous two men dropped from an airplane, the former prom king had a thin ring of encrusted blood around his neck from a garrote.

"Do you know him?" Tim kept the light on the man's face.

I blinked away tears. "It's Ben Aaronson, another guy I dated in prep school." My voice broke. "Haven't seen him in eight years. He's a lawyer with a firm in West Palm Beach, or he was until tonight. His parents still live on Banyan Isle."

Tim met Mona's eyes. "Ready to look at the other guy?"

She clutched my hand. "Let's get this over with."

Mona and I edged around Ben's body. Tim turned the other guy over, and we peered down at him, his head illuminated by Tim's powerful flashlight.

Mona gasped and backed into me. "It's Jin Kang. He's an enforcer for my uncle." Trembling, she glanced around. "They're coming for me!"

Tim pulled her into his arms. "Calm down, Mona. My men won't let that happen."

I pulled out my cell. "Want me to call the cops now?"

Tim nodded and waved his men off the pier. I dialed Mike's cell.

"Jett?" His voice sounded groggy. "It's one-thirty in the morning. What—"

I interrupted, "There are two bodies on my pier. One is Ben Aaronson. I'll explain the other guy when you get here with the usual crew."

"Wait, if they're on your pier, we don't need Fire Rescue, right?"

"Wrong. Ben's body is stuck halfway through the wood slats. They'll have to cut him out."

Mike groaned. "Don't touch anything. I'll be right there."

Pocketing my phone, I walked back to my dogs and shivered, more from the shocking death scene than from the brisk sea breeze. Mona stood nearby hugging herself, her eyes wet with tears.

Tim stood between us. "Come with me, ladies. We'll wait for the police in your home where you'll be warm and safe." He walked us back across the lawn under the banyan trees' dark branches.

Sensing my emotional distress, the dogs stayed close beside me on the way back.

*Three of my classmates murdered. And why did they all land on my property?*

I felt a little unsteady as I leaned into Tim. "Should we wake everyone before the sirens do it for us?"

"Good idea. That'll give me a chance to reassure them they're safe."

Mona said nothing and kept a tight grip on Tim's arm.

"I'd better call Gwen so she won't worry." I made the call and ended with, "Tim has everything under control, and Mike will be here any minute."

Gwen yawned into the phone. "I can't believe we lost another classmate. I'll go reassure Leo and Hugo before they freak out. Stay safe, and I'll see you after breakfast."

We entered the house from the back terrace, surprised the great hall lights were on. Snake, Karin, and Sophia sat with handguns on their laps.

Tim took in the scene. "You're up. Good. Police are on the way, and my men have the property secured." He helped Mona to a chair and then explained what happened while I sat next to Sophia on the sofa. My puppies snuggled against us.

Mona still looked shellshocked when Snake asked Tim, "How's the Korean guy connected with Jett's classmate?"

Before Tim could answer, Mike knocked on the glass French door and entered.

Mike looked at me. "I checked the bodies. Who's the dead Asian, and why was he here in the middle of the night?"

Everyone turned to Mona, assuming she'd been outside with us for a reason.

She wrung her hands and stared at her feet. "My father was American, and my mother was from South Korea. We lived in L.A., and I was orphaned at twelve. My uncle, Chul Han, became my legal guardian. He's head of *Geom Do*, which means Way of the Sword. It's a violent gang in Los Angeles. All the gang members are from South Korea. They each carry a *Samjeongdo*, the traditional sword awarded to Korean military generals. It's a curved, single-edge blade they use to hack off their enemies' arms and leave them helpless as they bleed to death."

Mona looked at me, her eyes wet with tears. "So sorry, Jett. I lied about running from an abusive boyfriend. I spent the past year hiding from my uncle in women's shelters. He never lets anyone leave the gang, but I didn't want to live as a criminal."

"How did you get away?" Mike asked.

"The Ducati wasn't a gift from a rich boyfriend. My uncle gave it to me after he forced me to hack into a rival gang's business accounts. I escaped on the motorcycle late one night and stayed in women's shelters everywhere I stopped. I wanted to live in a tropical climate far from California, so I came to Florida." Her face flushed. "I never should've come here. I'm so sorry for the trouble I caused." She stood on wobbly legs. "I'll leave right away."

I pointed a finger. "You'll stay right here. I get why you lied, and I still want you to work with me like we planned. We're in this together." I walked over and hugged her.

"Thanks, Jett. I wish I knew how he found me. I thought I'd been super careful."

My mind raced, retracing everything I had done that involved Mona. The answer came to me. "Sorry, Mona. This is my fault. The background check I did on you must've triggered something on his end."

# THIRTEEN

I looked at Mike. "Tim's security team will protect her here, but we need to find a long-term solution."

Mike turned to Mona. "I can try to get you into witness protection and put you in an FBI safe house—"

I interrupted, "She's already in a safe house. This is way better than a place with just two cops guarding her."

Mike took me aside. "The problem is we can't arrest anyone unless we catch them doing something illegal. I hate to say it, but we'll have to wait for them to make a move on Mona."

Mike's cell rang. He answered, listened, said, "Thank you," and pocketed the phone. "We ran a check on that speedboat Jin Kang docked at your pier. It's stolen, but he's dead, so that's a dead end."

Trembling and hugging herself, Mona's eyes were wide with panic.

Snake wheeled over and sat beside her. "It's okay, baby, we've got you."

Mona buried her face against his shoulder as he tried to soothe her. He hugged her and glanced sideways at Sophia.

Sophia stood and patted Mona's shoulder. "We'll take turns guarding you. Snake needs sleep."

Tim kept a straight face, but his eyes twinkled. Mike was unaware of the nocturnal escapades involving Snake, and this time the women didn't snicker.

Mike settled beside me on the sofa. "Did you date Ben Aaronson in prep school?"

I held Pratt on my lap. "We went out a few times. Nothing serious, but he took me to Senior Prom because he was Prom King, and I was Queen."

Mike clenched his jaw, never a good sign. "Jett, we've got three murdered men who dated you years ago. Ben landing on the Korean couldn't have been planned, but the killer is obviously targeting you."

I bit my lip. "The concrete overshoes make no sense since he's not dropping the bodies in the water, although this last one came pretty close."

Mike's eyes bore into mine. "Can you think of anyone from your class who might do something like this?"

"Everyone I hung out with seemed pretty normal. The guys I dated were jocks from wealthy families. They were a bit full of themselves, you know, like a lot of teenaged boys."

Karin, who had been sitting on the sofa listening to everything, broke in, "Those boys were nice to you, but what if they bullied some nerdy guy who ended up holding a grudge?"

Sophia added, "And what if that nerdy guy had secretly been in love with you?"

"That would make sense if our time at prep school had ended a few days before the first body dropped, but we graduated ten years ago." I collected my thoughts. "What if the three men were involved in an illegal activity, and a fourth man killed them to keep them quiet?"

"Why are you assuming the killer is a man?" Mona asked.

Mike said, "Because a woman would have to be tall enough and strong enough to strangle men six feet or taller who were former athletes."

Sophia suggested, "Ask guys who went to school with the victims if they ganged up on a boy often enough to make him hold a ten-year grudge."

An idea flashed into my head. "We should check and see if any male students took flying lessons." I turned to Mike. "Did you find a likely airplane?"

"Turns out Florida is a haven for vintage airplanes. The state is covered with private airports and hangars full of small planes. And there are way too many with Pratt & Whitney R-985 radial engines. Hunter said all of them can be flown safely if the entry door is removed before takeoff. The plane could be anywhere. Your uncle even has one."

"Right, he has a 1944 Staggerwing Beech. Its engine sounds exactly like the one on the airplane the bodies were dropped from. I guess it's possible someone could be using it when Hunter is away on airline flights."

Mike shook his head. "He checked. Nobody flew it while he was gone."

"Then circle back to checking if any of the Banyan Isle Prep School students in my class took flying lessons."

"You took flying lessons back then, didn't you?" Mike asked.

"Yep, earned my private pilot license and instrument rating my senior year, but I don't remember encountering any flight students from my prep school."

Tim joined in, "There are lots of airports nearby. The killer could have taken lessons anywhere. I'll have my cyber guy run the student list from your class against FAA pilot records and see who pops up."

"Thanks, Tim, but this is a police matter. My investigators will look into that." Mike glanced at his watch and stood. "Jett, I need a word in private. Walk me out."

I followed him to his car. "What's up?"

"Looks like victim number two, Roger Thornton, was abducted in a way similar to the first guy. We found his car with all four tires slashed, parked at a baseball field where he coached Little League. No other signs of foul play and no security cameras."

"There must've been loads of people around. Did you find any witnesses?"

Mike shook his head. "After the game, Roger sent everyone ahead to a pizza restaurant and said he'd catch up after he called his fiancée.

When he didn't show, the others assumed he'd gone to see her instead."

"The killer must've been lurking in the baseball field's parking lot, waiting for an opportunity to grab Roger."

"Which is why I wanted to warn you once again to remain vigilant, Jett." He paused and looked into my eyes for a long moment. "Don't let this Korean thing distract you into forgetting about the body-drop killer."

A familiar warm feeling washed over me as I remembered years ago when we were lovers. "I promise I'll be careful, and it's not like he can get to me here with all the armed guards patrolling."

"I have to deal with the news vans and reporters camped outside your gate."

I waved goodbye as he drove away.

When I returned to the great hall, I sat beside Tim. "Never mind what Mike said. Have your cyber guy run that check. Normally, I'd ask Mona to do it, but she's too upset, and I want to know who's killing my schoolmates."

Snake cuddled Mona and asked Tim. "What about the Korean gang? Do you have a plan for takin' them out?"

Tim glanced sideways at me. "Yes, but Jett might not like it."

I said, "Hey, I'm all for anything that keeps us safe and eliminates the threat, assuming we stay on the right side of the law. What do you have in mind, Tim?"

"This is now what I consider an imminent attack situation. But unlike the Danger Magnet assault, I have a lot more men now." He looked at me. "You have several empty bedrooms, right?"

"Yes, they're on the second, third, and fourth floors. I'm guessing you want to station some men inside. Tell me what you need."

"I'll put a man in an east-facing bedroom on the top floor in the north wing and another in the south wing. Same thing on the west side in both wings. They're snipers so they'll want rooms with balconies. And I'll spend every night on one of these sofas here in your great hall until the Korean threat is over."

"We'll provide meals for your team. Karin will keep us stocked with plenty of food and beverages. How many men should we plan on, including the guys on the grounds?"

"Twelve men at all times, plus me at night, and two dogs patrolling the grounds. Tomorrow, I'll have perimeter alarms installed." He looked at me. "And we need to secure all the entry points up top."

"This house was designed like a castle fortress. The flat concrete roof is reinforced and bordered with stone parapets and battlements. Four turret rooms have doors that access the roof, and their spiral stairs descend into corner bedrooms."

"Then count on fifteen men. I'll reinforce the access doors and put two men on the roof to defend against an aerial attack. This property can be accessed from the air, land, and water. That's a lot to cover." Tim made a call to his headquarters.

I nudged Karin. "Counting us, that's twenty-two people. Want me to hire someone to help you?"

Tim pocketed his phone and interrupted us, "I don't want more civilians here while an attack is imminent. Ask your housemates to help."

I glanced at my watch. It was 3:00 a.m. "Tim, is it okay if we go back to bed now?"

"Of course. I've got everything handled. If anyone is sleeping in a room on the top floor, hang a piece of clothing on the doorknob so my men will know the room is occupied when they come in and choose their sniper rooms. I'll see you in the morning."

Sophia grabbed Tim's arm. "Don't forget my son is coming here the day after tomorrow."

"Call him and tell him to cancel the visit."

"There's no way he'll agree to that, especially after what happened tonight. You'll just have to make allowances for him and his goombahs."

"We'll make it work," Tim agreed.

I thought about the fifteen retired SEALs patrolling, some of them snipers, and Sophia's mobster son and his men coming. *Geez, this isn't how I imagined life would be when I decided to leave the Navy and start a P.I. agency.*

Sophia said, "I'll get Tim a pillow and blanket."

He smiled at her. "Just a pillow. Thanks."

We all piled into the elevator, too drained to take the stairs.

I looked at my sleepy roommates. "I'd wish everyone sweet dreams, but we know that isn't going to happen tonight."

# FOURTEEN

I woke at 9:00 a.m. and trotted downstairs with the doggies. Outside, the sun warmed me as a brisk breeze carried a briny scent from the sea.

Tim's men were busy installing perimeter alarms, making my property an impregnable fortress.

My cell rang. It was Hunter.

"Jett, what the heck's going on there? I heard on the morning news another body dropped in and something about a dead Asian."

I explained what happened and our security plan. "Tim thinks the Koreans may attack soon. He has fifteen men and two K-9s protecting us."

"Tell him I was a Navy fighter pilot, and I'm coming there armed. Snake is still there, right?"

"Yes, he's guarding poor Mona. The woman is terrified her uncle will chop off her arms."

"Nice relatives. Tell your guards I'll be there in ten minutes."

"Right. They'll have to let you in because I have new codes, keys, and gate openers. Your set is waiting for you. See you soon." I called Tim and then trotted inside to start breakfast in case Karin wasn't up yet.

I found her on the phone in the kitchen placing a groceries order. She said, "I'll expect the delivery in two hours," and ended the call. "Hungry? I just made a comfort breakfast of whole-grain pancakes with fresh strawberries and plenty of bacon and scrambled eggs with diced tomatoes and cheddar."

"Sounds yummy, but I'll wait until Hunter arrives. He's due any minute. Let's set the table."

She caught my arm. "Tim wants us to dine indoors until further notice."

"Okay, no point hauling plates from here. We'll use what's stored in the dining room buffet and breakfront. I'll show you, and we'll plug in the hotplates."

In ten minutes, we had everything staged with a full banquet-size coffee pot and hot food ready on the buffet. The table was set for twenty-four in case we needed a few extra.

Hunter walked in. "What smells so good?"

I hugged him and thumbed at the buffet top. "Pancakes, fresh strawberries, maple bacon, and scrambled eggs. Join us for breakfast."

We filled our plates and settled at the table. I savored the delicious pancakes and made a mental note to swim laps in the pool and burn off calories.

Hunter stared out over the back lawn toward the ocean. "Does Tim have any idea when the gang will attack?"

"No, but it could be tonight." I pointed at the men installing the perimeter alarms. "He's making this place more secure than a military base."

Snake rolled in looking rested. "Mona and I slept like logs last night."

Mona brought him a plate with everything on it and kissed his cheek. "Thanks to Snake, I felt safe and was able to sleep."

Sophia and Karin joined us a few minutes before Tim and the night shift arrived.

"Help yourselves, gentlemen." I nodded at the buffet.

Tim sat near our end, and I introduced him to Hunter. After the pleasantries, Tim said, "Worst-case scenario would be a shootout inside the house. I doubt that would happen, but I like to be prepared, so I recommend installing steel crossbars on the inside of the shooting range door. That would make that room like a panic room. It's already bulletproof."

Snake said, "I like it. The instant we come under attack, Hunter and I will hurry all the women in there and hunker down."

"Right," Hunter agreed. "If anybody makes it through that door, they'll get ventilated by at least five shooters."

Tim made a call on his cell. "I just got approval. Install the steel crossbars now."

I looked across at Mona. "Aren't you glad you warned us about your uncle?"

"I just wish he hadn't found me. It's been a year. I thought he'd given up and forgotten about me." Mona bit her lip. "Jett, I'm so sorry."

"Don't be. It's not your fault you have a dangerous relative." I tried to soothe her. "Tim's team will keep us safe, especially now that we've had time to prepare."

Gwen joined us from next door. She put her hand on my shoulder. "I saw them installing the perimeter lasers and trip alarms. Looks like they're transforming Valhalla into Fort Knox."

"Yep, got any gold bullion you want to store here?" I grinned, trying to minimize the tension.

Gwen grabbed an extra chair and squeezed in beside me. "Seriously, when do you expect an attack?"

Everyone looked at Tim.

He answered, "Tonight, maybe, but first he'll send another scout to gather intel for an all-out assault a few hours later. We're ready."

"How do you know he won't just launch the assault?" Gwen asked.

"He might, but it makes more sense to learn how many guards are on patrol rather than just burst in with no plan." Tim glanced at Mona. "He's been hunting you for a year. That tells me he's a patient man and a careful planner. Better to send in one man first."

Mona whispered something to Snake, and he said, "Tell him."

She looked at Tim. "You're wrong about Chul Han. He cares nothing about his men and won't hesitate to sacrifice a few."

Tim crinkled his brow. "What do you mean?"

"He'll send in two, maybe three scouts, each one entering from a different direction. That way, one might succeed even if the other two fail." Mona shivered and rubbed her arms, even though the room wasn't cold. "He won't care if they die as long as he gets the intel."

A guard entered silently and tapped Tim's shoulder. "UPS just delivered a package addressed to Jett Jorgensen and Mona Wang."

Tim sucked in his breath. "Explosives?"

"Our dogs checked for drugs or explosives. None there, but something feels wrong." He glanced at me.

I stood. "Where is it? I want my dogs to sniff it." My puppies looked up at me and wagged their tails. "Pratt and Whitney are half wolf, and we have a strong bond. If something bad is in that box, they'll tell me."

Gwen stood. "I'm coming with you."

Mona moved to stand, but Snake stopped her. "Stay here with me."

"The box is in the middle of the driveway, about fifty yards from the house, ma'am," Tim's teammate answered.

Hunter stood. "Let's go."

Tim and the guard led Hunter, Gwen, and me outside. My puppies stuck to my heels. When we reached the box, which was three-feet square, I pointed at it and said to my dogs, "Sniff the box."

They pressed their noses against it and sniffed it up and down like little vacuum cleaners. Then they howled and aggressively pushed me away from the package. I'd have to be a total moron not to understand they were warning me.

I glanced at the guards. "Was everyone wearing gloves when they touched the box?"

They nodded.

Tim asked, "What are the dogs telling you besides stay away from it?"

"They reacted the same way when they sniffed the man impaled on

Odin's sword and the dead men on the pier. I think they're warning me something dead is in that box."

Gwen said, "Do you want to call Mike, or should I?"

I pulled out my cell and hit his number on speed-dial. "Mike, it's Jett. Bring a Crime-Scene Unit. I think somebody just sent me a dead body in a box. No need for Fire Rescue this time."

He groaned. "I'll be right there. Don't touch the box."

It wasn't long before Mike's unmarked police car roared into my driveway. He stopped fifty feet from the box and jumped out. The CSU van pulled in behind him. Must have been a slow crime day for the CSU team to arrive so quickly.

I held up my palm. "Before you ask, Tim's bomb-sniffing dogs already verified there are no explosives."

Mike stood, hands on hips, studying the box. "It's too small to hold a human body."

Tim shook his head. "Not if the body has been cut into pieces."

That was a grim thought. I led the dogs back several feet and waited with Gwen and Hunter for the techs to open the package.

Two men in white-paper jumpsuits used box cutters to remove the lid. They reached in and pulled open the plastic wrapping. What happened next made me clutch Hunter's arm.

The CSU techs peered inside and stumbled backward. Tim and Mike looked in the box, then turned away, covering their noses.

The scent of rotting flesh drifted past us on a light breeze.

Tim hurried back to us. "Don't look inside. Once you see something like that, it can never be unseen."

I grabbed his arm. "What's in there?"

He glanced at Hunter, who said, "Tell us."

Tim hesitated. "Four severed arms. Looks like they were cut off two women. Obviously, a warning meant to scare Jett and Mona."

My gut churned, wondering who the unlucky women had been.

Tim gently turned me around. "Let's go back inside."

Gwen paused and stared at the box. "I'll send Hugo and Leo to Atlantis in the Bahamas for a few days. Count on me staying at your place every night until this mess is settled." She strode to her car and drove home.

Hunter and Tim walked on either side of me as we returned to the dining room.

Just outside the door, I stopped and whispered, "Should we tell everyone about the arms?"

"Not in the dining room," Hunter said.

I glanced at my dive watch. "Sophia's son will be here tomorrow morning. No telling what he'll do if he finds out about the severed arms."

Tim held the door open. "Let's deal with Mona and the others first."

The instant we entered, Snake asked, "What's in the box?"

Mona, Karin, and Sophia studied us. Their faces were clouded with worry.

I bit my lower lip. "Meet us in the great hall when you're finished with breakfast."

"We finished ten minutes ago." Sophia glanced at Karin and Mona, then looked at me. "Please, tell us now."

I settled across from them. "Brace yourselves. Tim will tell you what he saw. He warned me not to look."

After Tim explained the contents of the box as delicately as possible, Sophia's eyes flared, Karin clenched her fists, and Mona hugged her arms.

Tim concluded, "The police are investigating the delivery, and the FBI has been notified. Don't worry. My men will protect you, and your property is secure."

Sophia said, "My son, Marco, will be here tomorrow, and I'd appreciate it if you didn't mention the arms in the box. And Tim, please ask your men to keep quiet about it too. If Marco finds out, half the New York Mafia will descend on us. Nobody wants that, especially me."

# FIFTEEN

The rest of the day passed under a cloud of tension with everyone worried about another body drop or a deadly attack from Chul Han's gang. After dinner, unexpected drama arrived when Gwen's boyfriend, Detective Clint Reynolds rang my doorbell. My guards must've checked his police credentials and allowed him through the gate.

I opened the door. "Hi, Clint, I'm glad you're here. How's everything?"

"I'm not sure. I understand you're expecting an attack by a violent Korean gang."

"It's a possibility, but you must've noticed my beefed-up security. I'm confident they have everything handled." I did my best to appear calm.

"I wish you could get police protection, but they can only respond to actual attacks, not perceived threats." He glanced around. "Where's Gwen?"

"In the great hall. Please join us." I led him there. "Can I get you a drink?"

"Thank you." He focused on an open bottle of merlot. "The red wine looks good."

Hunter and Snake sized up Clint as I introduced him and then handed him a glass of merlot. Gwen and Mona were seated on either side of Snake, and Sophia and Karin flanked Hunter on another sofa.

Gwen stood and kissed Clint on the cheek. "What a nice surprise. Is everything all right?"

He frowned. "I stopped next door, but no one was home. Then I tried your cell and got no answer. After everything you told me about the Korean gang and your former classmates dropping from the sky, I was worried." He pulled her close. "Why didn't you answer my call?"

She patted her empty pockets. "Oh, no wonder. I must've left my cell in my purse upstairs. Sorry, honey." She pointed at an empty chair. "Relax and I'll get you a plate of Sophia's delicious cannoli."

He glanced at his watch. "No thanks, Gwen. Let's go home to my place until this thing with the gang is resolved." Clint's gaze swept over the male houseguests.

Was his real reason for coming here jealousy?

Gwen stepped back. "I told you I'm spending the nights here for as long as Jett needs me. I won't abandon my best friend."

He stiffened and shot another glance at the men. "Are you sure that's the *real* reason? Maybe I should stay here with you."

Apparently, Clint had forgotten about redheads and their tempers. Gwen's green eyes flashed as she clutched Clint's arm and dragged him to the foyer. Unintelligible yelling preceded the front door slamming with a resounding boom.

Gwen stormed back. "The nerve of that man. I apologize for my boyfriend's rude behavior. Honestly, I don't know what got into him." She gripped her wine glass and took a swig.

Sophia squeezed Gwen's shoulder. "Clint is jealous of Hunter and Snake."

Gwen arched a brow. "Really? He's jealous of my beloved 'Uncle' Hunter? And Snake is with Mona."

Hunter smiled and shot a quick glance at Karin.

Uh oh, there was already too much drama going on at Valhalla. I silently prayed that everyone would get through the next day or two unscathed.

I jumped at the sound of the doorbell. "I'll get it."

Tim strode in wearing black combat attire and carrying a big duffel bag. "Hey, Jett, I'd like to borrow three of the male mannequins from your ballroom."

"Of course, Tim, but I'm curious. Why do you need them?" I couldn't imagine why he'd want the props I'd brought in to add ambiance to the charity ball.

"Decoys. I'll dress them in combat gear and flak jackets wired to send us signals if someone shoots them. The dummies can draw fire while my men stay hidden and pinpoint the attackers' locations." He glanced at our gathering. "An attack could be imminent. Everyone should stay inside." His voice had a hard tone.

"I'll help you." As we walked to the ballroom, my gut tightened. I tried to diffuse the tension by asking, "Any progress on finding flight students from my prep-school class?"

"Yeah, do you remember a guy named George Stavros?" Tim held the ballroom door open for me.

"Yes, but we weren't friends. What about him?"

Tim surveyed the ballroom, his eyes pausing on the six glass French doors standing tall and wide, two sets on the east side, two on the north, and two on the west. "Don't you have any shades to cover those doors?"

"Sorry, just curtains for the windows."

He sighed. "Then keep this room empty when we finish here. We wouldn't want it to become a kill zone." He pulled out his tablet and showed me George's class photo from senior year. "Remember him?" A nerdy-looking guy with glasses stared into the camera like he was posing for a mugshot.

Tim pulled off a mannequin's tuxedo jacket. "Stavros earned his private pilot license during prep school, continued flight lessons in college, and earned his commercial pilot license and instrument rating. The thing is, he never finished college. Dropped out and took an executive assistant job working for Harold Bright, the CEO of Bright Investments in West Palm Beach." He shot glances at the glass doors as he worked.

"George was a shy geek who hated sports and worshipped money. He took all the business courses at prep school and was hoping to get into Harvard Business School. Is that where he dropped out?" I asked.

A bullfrog on the pool side of the ballroom croaked loud enough to make me jump.

Tim squeezed my shoulder and smiled. He checked his electronic tablet. "No, he attended Palm Beach State College and filed numerous complaints about male students bullying him. He was halfway through his second year when he dropped out and took the job with Bright."

"Bullying? That could be the link we're looking for." I folded all the formal wear we'd removed from the mannequins.

"See if you can find a former classmate who remembers if George was bullied by the men who were dropped onto your land. If so, maybe the murders have nothing to do with you." He paused before asking the next question. "Do you recall George asking you out and you turning him down?"

"No way. I have an eidetic memory, and I'm sure he never even talked to me, except as my lab partner in chemistry class." I frowned. "Why didn't he pursue a pilot career?"

Tim handed me black combat clothes for one of the dummies. "Probably because flight instruction is expensive. My helicopter lessons for the firm's Bell 429 Global Ranger cost a fortune. I'm guessing George didn't have enough flight experience to qualify for a commercial pilot job." He placed a dummy aside. "And it sounds like he wasn't the sort of guy who'd fit in with typical macho pilots anyway."

"Which means he wouldn't be offered free stick time as a copilot on freight runs. And he never earned his flight instructor certificate because he ran out of money." I zipped up the flak jacket on dummy number one.

Tim stiffened, listening to someone talking into his earpiece. "Where and how many?" He paused a beat. "Keep me informed."

My stomach did a flip-flop. "Is everything okay out there?"

"Two speed boats raced past your north boundary on the inlet, and a motorcycle gang just cruised past on Ocean Drive." Tim handed me clothes for the last dummy.

"We don't get motorcycle gangs on Banyan Isle." I dressed the decoy for combat.

"They're probably casing your property." Tim finished the wireless connections for all three dummies as I laced the boots on dummy number three.

"That's not good." My gut churned as I changed the subject, trying to appear as calm as Tim. "Uh, did you ever get a chance to talk to George Stavros?"

"Seems he disappeared two and a half years ago, not long after his mother died and left him their house on Banyan Isle and about 500K in cash assets. His digital footprint ended abruptly, and I couldn't find his death record anywhere. He just vanished."

"Maybe he died as a John Doe." I straightened a dummy's vest. "He wasn't the kind of guy people would miss. After the Korean thing is resolved, I'll look for his old school buddies and see if they know anything."

"Hold on a sec." He spoke into his headset mic, calling someone on his discrete radio frequency. "The dummy decoys are ready. Come to the ballroom with Bill and help me carry them out."

"I can help." I picked up one.

Tim placed a hand on my shoulder. "Thanks, but I don't want you anywhere near your property's perimeter. We'll take it from here." He paused. "Before I go, I need to ask you about two of your classmates who earned their private pilot licenses after college." He consulted his tablet. "Do you remember Grant Gardner and Harrison Hornsby?"

"Sure, they were linebackers on our football team. I think Grant has done well locally as a financial advisor, and Harry owns a chain of fast-food restaurants all over Florida. Do either of them own an airplane?"

He checked the data. "Yeah, Harry owns a Beechcraft Model 18, and Grant owns a Howard DGA 15-P."

"Whoa." I squeezed Tim's arm. "They're both vintage airplanes. The Howard has a R-985 radial engine like the airplane that dropped the bodies, and the Beechcraft has two engines like that. Either man has the strength, size, and pilot skill, and owns an airplane like the one used by the body-drop killer."

He clenched his jaw. "Would either of them have a motive?"

"None that I can think of, but maybe this has to do with money or revenge for something the victims did to one of them."

He frowned. "I'm sorry your classmates are being killed, but right now the Korean gang poses the greatest threat to your personal safety. Once they're dealt with, I'll focus all my resources on George, Grant, and Harry."

At that moment, two guards entered the ballroom and picked up the dummies. I waved goodbye to Tim and his men and prayed their decoy ploy would keep them safe.

# SIXTEEN

I found my housemates still gathered in the great hall. Swords, spears, and battleaxes from the Viking era decorated one wall, reminding me of my ancestors' violent past. Before I had a chance to sit, the doorbell rang. "I'll get it."

I opened the door in the foyer, and Mike walked in. "Hello, Jett. We need to talk in private, and I'd like to include Gwen. Is she here?"

"She's in the great hall. What's up?"

"I'd rather cover it with both of you together." He walked with me into the spacious room and found her. "Gwen, I need a word in private. Please come with Jett and me."

She looked at me, and I shrugged. We followed Mike down a hallway into the study.

We settled on the cordovan sofa while Mike paced in front of us. "I may have a lead in the case. Do you remember a classmate named George Stavros?"

Mike must have done the same research as Tim. Research he warned me not to do. He would be angry if I admitted I already knew about George, so I kept silent.

Gwen said, "He was a geek. I think he was president of the Audio-Visual Club."

Mike stood with his back to the fireplace, looking down at us, as he told us everything Tim had already told me. Then he asked, "Did he ask out either of you?"

We shook our heads "no."

Mike sat in an armchair. "We found a classmate who remembered George being bullied by football players."

"What's he doing now?" Gwen asked.

Mike frowned. "I don't know. Not long after his mother died over two years ago, he inherited everything and disappeared."

I changed the subject. "What about Ben Aaronson's murder? Was it like the other two?"

"His law firm had a small, three-story office building in a converted home in the downtown area of West Palm Beach. The night of the murder, Ben worked alone late, and his car was found in the parking lot behind the building. All four tires had been slashed, just like with the other victims."

I glanced from Gwen to Mike. "It's been ten years since prep school, so if George is the killer, what sent him on this killing spree now?"

"And why is he dropping the bodies on *your* property, Jett?" Gwen asked.

"I was always nice to him." I glanced from Mike to Gwen. "And we earned an "A" as lab partners in chemistry class, so I can't see why he'd have a grudge against me."

Gwen shrugged. "Maybe Sophia was right, and the killer continued to drop bodies here because of the publicity. It might have nothing to do with Jett."

Mike sighed. "I disagree. Too many coincidences."

I leaned forward. "Have you tried searching the DMV database for a guy with George Stavros's face and a different name?"

He arched his eyebrow and said in a condescending tone, "Of course, we checked."

I glanced at my watch. "Well then, I'm all out of ideas for now, and you might want to leave before the gang attacks." I admit I was curt, but his reaction made me angry.

His face flushed. "If you're expecting the assault tonight, I'll stay and help."

"It might be a full attack, or they might send more scouts first. We're not sure."

He pulled out his cell. "I'll call in some off-duty police officers to help guard you."

I stood and touched his arm. "Thanks, but you'd better talk to Tim first. He has a plan that might not work well with last-minute reinforcements."

"Give me his number." He handed me his phone, and I punched it in.

Gwen and I waited while Mike talked with Tim.

Mike pocketed his phone. "You were right. Tim doesn't want police involvement until he calls in SWAT. He has this planned like a military op, and you have Hunter, Snake, Karin, and Sophia for extra firepower in the house." He clenched his jaw and looked at me. "But I'll stay too if you need me, or wouldn't Snake like that?"

*Another jealous guy.* I glared at him. "I think we're good." I didn't want to add to the tension, but I had to tell him. "Please don't be angry. I learned something that might help you catch the body bomber." I told Mike about Grant and Harry and their airplanes.

His face reddened. "Where did you get that information?"

"Have you forgotten I worked in Navy Intelligence?" I bit my lip when anger flashed in his eyes. "Look, I'm sorry, but I want to know who's killing my classmates."

"Dammit, Jett, I told you to stay out of my investigation." He sucked in his breath. "I'll look into Grant Gardner and Harrison Hornsby." Mike stormed out of the room.

Gwen nudged me. "You were a little hard on Mike, but holy crap. Grant or Harry a killer? What motive could there be?"

"No idea, but it's a possibility." I clenched my fists. "And when Mike talks down to me, he really pushes my buttons."

"Yep, you and Mike sure do crank up the tension." Gwen shook her head. "As if we don't have enough to worry about tonight."

———

A scout landed at one in the morning. The puppies woke me when they heard a guard dog barking. I grabbed my Glock and the night-vision binoculars I'd brought home from the Navy and rushed across my bedroom suite to the west-facing balcony.

A paraglider dangled from one of my massive banyan trees, and the scout hung from his harness under the branches. One of Tim's guard dogs waited beneath him.

Men ran toward the tree from fifty yards away as the gang member drew his weapon and aimed it at the dog. A soft crack sounded nearby a fraction of a second before the man's head snapped backward, saving the brave dog from certain death. Score one for Tim's sniper.

Pratt and Whitney stood beside me, sniffing the air. Soon, Gwen joined us, pistol in hand.

She squinted in the darkness. "What do you see?"

I told her about the guy in the tree. "Everything seems to have quieted down now."

"Are you going back to bed?" She stared at the front yard.

"Not a chance. Let's get dressed and keep watch from the murder room. It has a central view of the backyard and beach, and we can see the boat dock from the balcony."

Two months ago, Gwen and I had found the Mayor of Banyan Isle dead under the bed in the room on the second floor we now refer to as the murder room. It was also the room where Sophia shot an intruder not long after that. And her room was next door.

"Okay, I'll be back in five minutes." Gwen rushed to her bedroom as I dressed.

We met in the hall, headed down to the second floor, and knocked on Sophia's door. She stepped out in PJs, ready for action with a Glock in a thigh holster and her night-vision gear strapped to her head. "I saw them nail a guy in a tree."

I glanced down the hall. "Where's Hunter?"

"He went upstairs to check on Karin." She frowned. "I think he might be interested in her."

"Don't worry." I patted her back. "He'll always adore you."

Gwen grinned. "Whoa, Sophia, where'd you get the night-vision gear?"

"Army surplus. I use it for nighttime potty trips, so I don't need a light." She shook her head. "I never dreamed I'd use the goggles to shoot that late-night intruder a few months ago. That was just a lucky side benefit."

Gwen laughed. "Right, you wore them when you shot that guy your first night here."

I cocked my head. "I don't hear anything. Should we check on Mona and Snake?"

"I wouldn't," Sophia said. "They're staying together. Nobody's sleeping tonight."

My dogs whined and pushed us to Sophia's balcony. We peeked out.

"A guy in a wetsuit is sneaking across the beach toward my back gate." I adjusted the night-vision binoculars. "That guard is looking the wrong way. He doesn't see him."

"Can you warn him?" Gwen asked.

"He just shot the guard. I didn't hear anything. Must've used a silencer. I hope he shot one of the dummies." I adjusted the focus as I checked the fallen man. "Oh, good, definitely a dummy. I can tell because the mannequins we dressed didn't have trident patches on their uniforms."

Sophia nudged me. "Look, the shooter's climbing over your beach gate."

We watched him sneak up to the "victim" who lay on the ground dressed in full combat gear, helmet, and night-vision goggles. He fired into the dummy's head. I guess the lack of blood made him suspicious. A closer look revealed his error.

Tim's men had been hiding in bushes along the beach fence line. They cornered the intruder, but the stupid man raised his weapon, and a sniper took him out. Tim's team turned toward the house and saluted their guy on high.

"Score two for the snipers," Sophia said.

I scanned the dark night. "One from the sky and one from the sea. I wonder if we're done for the night."

Gwen shook her head. "My money is on the boat dock for intruder number three."

"Then let's move to a balcony in the north wing." I headed for the hall.

Gwen and Sophia followed me, and the dogs trotted behind us. We settled on a north balcony watching the empty boat dock.

I pointed. "There's a guard seated in a chair under a banyan tree near the dock."

"He's wearing all black," Sophia said. "Hopefully, an intruder won't spot him. I'd hate for any of Tim's men to get killed."

"Are they all former SEALs?" Gwen asked.

"Yeah, Snake knows most of them." I grabbed her arm. "A boat is approaching. I can't hear it. Looks like it has an electric motor."

"Let me see." Gwen reached for my night-vision binoculars.

Sophia stood. "One guy. He docked the boat and now he's sneaking toward the tree where the guard is hiding."

I squeezed Sophia's arm. "Does the guard see him?"

"He's not aiming his weapon at the intruder, so it's probably a dummy."

Things happened fast after that.

Gwen gasped. "He shot the guy under the tree." She handed me the binoculars.

Sophia pointed. "Now the shooter is sneaking closer to him."

I watched as the intruder shot the guard in the head to make sure he was dead, only to discover he'd shot a mannequin dressed like a guard.

In an instant, the scout was trapped against the tree by Tim's men with their weapons drawn. The fool tried to shoot them and went down in a hail of bullets.

I stood. "Looks like Tim is waiting until the scouts stop coming before he notifies the police."

"He's leaving the bodies where they were shot," Gwen agreed.

"So far, three times as many men came tonight compared to last night," I said. "Maybe they're done now until the main event."

"Think they'll attack tonight?" Sophia scanned the sky.

"Chul Han sent the scouts to gather intel." I gazed across the inlet toward Juno Beach. "I'm not sure what he'll do when he doesn't hear back from them."

Sophia grabbed my shoulder. "Look over there along the seawall about sixty yards west of the boat dock. Two guys in an electric-powered boat just tossed several big sacks onto your grounds."

I focused my night-vision binoculars on the boat. "They're driving away now."

"Forget the boat. Look at the burlap bags. They're moving." Sophia pointed.

An eighteen-foot king cobra slithered out of one of the sacks. My breath caught. I focused the binoculars on the other bags. More king cobras worked their way out. "Holy crackers! Those cobras are huge, and they're coming this way." An involuntary chill ran down my back.

I pulled out my cell and called Tim. "King cobras tossed near the seawall just west of the boat dock. I spotted five. Could be more." My voice sounded high and squeaky.

"Calm down, Jett. We're on it. Stay in the house." He disconnected.

Gwen and Sophia looked at me, wide-eyed.

"Tim said they're handling it." I sucked in a deep breath. "What if they don't find all of them? One of those snakes could kill my fur babies."

Gwen rubbed her arms, like she'd just felt a chill. "One could kill us too. I hate snakes, and cobras are the scariest of all, especially giant ones."

Sophia put one arm around me and the other around Gwen. "Don't panic, girls. Tim's men will kill them." She sounded tough, but her arms were shaking.

Gwen pulled away from Sophia's arm and faced us. "This is really scary, but it's good they chose big snakes. They'll be easier to find and shoot."

"She has a point." Sophia patted her pistol in its holster. "My laser sight will paint a red dot in the middle of a huge, hooded head if Tim's men miss it."

I tried to hold my binoculars to my eyes, but my hands were shaking. "Why did it have to be giant snakes? I'm not afraid to face armed men, but snakes, any snakes, big or small—they freak me out, especially venomous ones."

"I'll see what I can find out about them." Gwen pulled out her cell and Googled king cobras. "They average between ten and fourteen feet with the largest one a little over nineteen feet, and … they like trees." She shuddered and almost dropped her phone.

"Oh, great, they'll love my banyan trees." I sucked in a breath, trying not to panic.

Tim called my cell.

"Did you shoot all the snakes?"

"Meet me in the great hall." He disconnected before I had a chance to ask more questions.

I led Gwen, Sophia, and the pups downstairs to where Tim waited.

He was all business until he spotted Sophia in her PJs and night-vision gear. That brought a hint of a smile. "Have a seat."

Once we were settled, he said, "My men nailed four king cobras. The fifth one escaped into a huge banyan tree. It doesn't show up on our infrared scopes because it's cold-blooded. It's too dark to find it tonight, but don't worry, we'll get it tomorrow."

My voice shot up two octaves. "No, no, no, no! It might get away. Set up spotlights and burn down the freaking tree."

Tim looked at me like I was a wild-eyed nutcase, and maybe I was. The thought of a king cobra hiding in one of my trees was too much for me. Wait until daylight? I don't think so. A wave of nausea swept over me.

He sat beside me on the sofa and turned my shoulders toward him. "Jett, you need to calm down. It's just one snake, and it's afraid of people. That's why it's hiding in the tree. The Korean gang is a far deadlier threat. I'm not about to light up your grounds with a huge tree fire, especially when we don't know if more attackers are coming tonight."

He held my face in his hands and looked straight into my eyes. "You can trust me and my men. I promise we'll keep you safe."

I bit my lower lip and spoke in a soft, squeaky voice, "Okay, don't burn down the tree, but please ensure all my first-floor doors and windows are closed and locked."

# SEVENTEEN

An hour later, Tim asked me to gather all my housemates in the great hall. Before everyone had walked in or we'd had a chance to discuss anything, the doorbell boomed Wagner's "Ride of the Valkyries." The Viking tune seemed appropriate with so many men dressed in combat gear. A guard opened the door for Mike.

Mike strode in and focused his bloodshot eyes on me. "Is everyone okay?"

Hunter sauntered in with Karin, and they seemed to be making a supreme effort not to smile. Hard to believe on a night like this. They were the only ones who didn't look tense.

Mike cleared his throat. "Let's recap. We've got four dead Korean gang members and three dead locals who attended prep school with you. Did I get the body count right?"

I shot a look at Tim. His facial expression gave away nothing. Back to Mike. "Your tally is accurate for the humans, but you left out something just as deadly."

"What?" He glanced from me to Tim.

Tim answered for me. "She's referring to the five king cobras set loose on her grounds. We killed four, but one escaped into a banyan tree. We'll find it after sunrise."

Mona and Snake had just rolled in.

Mona's face paled. "There's a king cobra hiding outside?"

Karin's eyes widened, radiating fear. "One bite and you're dead."

Tim sighed. "Relax, ladies. We'll kill the snake. The Korean gang is the real threat."

"What's your latest intel on the gang activity?" Mike asked Tim.

Mona interrupted, "Expect a full-on assault tonight. My uncle is not a patient man. He won't waste time on another spy mission."

"That was my assessment too," Tim agreed. "We're ready for the attack. All three watch teams are here. We'll take turns sleeping on the premises in six-hour shifts."

"Wait." Mike stood, hands on hips. "Don't you think we should evacuate the women?"

"No." Tim glanced around the room at us. "We can't protect them if they leave. The gang could be waiting nearby to grab them the minute they drive off the property."

I stood. "I appreciate your concern, Mike, but we're staying right here."

He shrugged. "The CSU team is almost finished with the shooting scenes. I'll warn them to watch out for the snake." He strode out.

My dogs nudged me.

"Pratt and Whitney need a run outside. I'll take them on leashes out front and hope the snake is still in that tree in the backyard." I headed for the room where I kept their harnesses and leashes.

Hunter checked his handgun. "I'll go with you."

The dogs sensed our tension and took care of business as quickly as possible. No snake in sight.

I nudged Hunter. "I don't think I can live here if they fail to find that giant snake."

"An eighteen-foot cobra should be easy to spot once it's daylight. They'll nail it."

"Don't be so sure. It can easily blend in with the many branches on a banyan tree." I stopped and looked around. "I might be able to handle searching for a huge python. They aren't venomous, but a king cobra? It looks scary and it's full of deadly venom."

Hunter put his arm around me. "Look at the bright side. Cobras eat other snakes."

"I've never seen any snakes on this island, so then what will it eat?"

He pulled out his cell and consulted Google. "Lizards, rats, and slow birds."

"Let's talk about something else." I squeezed his arm. "What's going on with you and Karin?"

He smiled. "She's an amazing woman. I really like her."

"And earlier tonight?"

"A gentleman never tells." He ushered me and the puppies through the front door. "Better get some sleep."

Tim sauntered over to me. "I never thought any client would top the dangerous missions I've fought for Danger Magnet, but I think you're giving her some real competition."

"That's not a distinction I wanted to earn." I patted his back. "I know it's your job, but I'm sorry to put you and your men through this. I couldn't manage without you."

Tim took my arm. "Come and sit with me. We have things to discuss." He cleared his throat to get everyone's attention. "I just want to remind the civilians to hunker down in the panic room when the attack starts. I'll let you know when it's safe to come out." He handed out tactical radios. "Questions about anything other than the snake?"

No one spoke.

"Good." Tim glanced at his watch. "It's three in the morning and there's no moon. They'll probably come before daylight."

Tim's radio crackled. A male voice announced, "A speedboat is coming in hot at the boat docks. Two tangos aboard dressed like ninjas and carrying machine pistols."

"Copy. As soon as they enter the grounds, take them out." Tim stood and said to his men. "Go to your assigned posts." He rushed to his command center in my study.

I stood. "I'll put the puppies in my bedroom and grab some extra mags. It's probably too soon for a full-on assault. Where are Snake and Mona?"

"They went back up to Mona's room on the third floor," Sophia said.

Hunter stood. "I'll warn them and then run back to my room and get my night-vision gear and extra mags."

"Good idea," Sophia said. "I'll get extra ammo too." She turned to leave.

Hunter glanced at Karin. "Get what you need from your room. I'll meet you there, and we'll go down to the safe room together."

Gwen grabbed a sack of water bottles. "I'll bring these."

Everyone rushed out of the great hall. The puppies ran after me up the stairs.

I closed the curtains in my room, set the dogs on my bed, and gave the command, "Stay."

They didn't look happy when I left, but they remained on the bed. I reasoned two bad guys in a boat hardly seemed like a full-on assault. Tim's men would make sure they never reached my home alive. I wasn't eager to be shut inside the indoor shooting range/panic room for hours, and I knew my dogs wouldn't like it either. Better to wait until a real emergency. For now, they would be safe and comfortable in my bedroom.

The radio Tim gave me crackled to life on my last few steps down to the ground floor.

A man announced, "Garbage truck crashed through front gate. One man inside."

I recognized Tim's voice as he said, "Take him out."

Another man said, "Sniper One has him. Driver down. Truck is slowing."

My gut churning, I paused in the foyer near the south staircase and gazed through the floor-to-ceiling windows flanking the entry door. It was too dark outside for me to see any action with the outdoor lights off per Tim's instructions. Inside, recessed overhead lights were set on dim.

Another man reported, "Men on motorcycles behind the truck. They're headed for the house."

Tim announced, "Attention: All civilians to the safe room. Repeat: Civilians to the safe room now!"

A salvo of gunfire drowned out his next words. I turned toward the staircase, intent on saving my fur babies. Just as I reached the bottom step, a hail of bullets preceded a motorcycle crashing through one of the floor-to-ceiling windows flanking the front door.

Fragments of broken glass peppered my back and legs, like tiny razor blades fired from a machine gun. A large shard stuck in my left biceps, and another one lodged in my left thigh a second before the motorcycle rider knocked me down. I fell against the bottom step and yanked out the largest shards before I spun around.

My heart raced as blood soaked my clothes. My right hand was slick with blood as I reached behind me for my weapon, only to discover dart-like glass fragments had pinned my shirt to my skin. Before I could pull away the soaked shirt and reach my handgun, the Korean thug cut his engine and climbed off the bike.

He flipped up his helmet visor and focused his dark eyes on me. "Where's Mona? Tell me now or die." He pointed his Changfeng submachine gun at my chest. "Well? Where is she?"

My heart pounded and my breath caught as I stared up the barrel of his weapon. What happened next was far worse.

Something dark and silent rose behind him.

# EIGHTEEN

The giant snake Tim's men had been hunting had entered through the broken window, its scales glistening with moisture. It must've been in Odin's fountain before the noisy assault began. Its broad hood swayed from side to side as it loomed behind the biker, level with his head.

My mouth went dry, and I tried not to hyperventilate as I croaked, "Okay. I'll tell you, but take one step back first. I-I can't think with your gun so close to my face."

I didn't have to fake my shaky voice or the terror in my eyes.

He grinned and took a step back, sealing his fate.

The biker backed into the enormous serpent. It struck the nape of his neck, its fangs injecting neurotoxin. Unlike most other snakes, cobras have enough venom for many strikes.

I rolled to my right as its deadly fangs sank deep into his neck. The shock of the venomous bite made the gunman pull the trigger, and bullets sprayed the stairs, pinging off the marble steps inches away.

The stricken man turned and tried to shoot the monster as its fangs struck him again and again. In seconds, his knees buckled from the lethal venom. His right hand remained locked on the trigger, but the bullets sprayed my front door, missing the giant reptile.

My worst nightmare loomed a few feet away. I was trapped against the stairs, and my body responded to primal instinct and froze.

I had to do something fast.

The snake's attack on the man took only a few seconds, but I seized the opportunity and drew my Glock. Aiming at the cobra's head was difficult because it moved so fast, and the gangbanger was in the way. My hands shook as I sucked in quick breaths. The man crumpled to the floor, dropping his heavy machine pistol.

I struggled for control, but my body trembled as I aimed for the creature's huge, hooded head.

The monster didn't need movement to locate me. It could smell my blood. It hissed at me and then checked the fallen Korean as my heart skipped a beat.

Seizing the moment, I held the trigger on semi-automatic, firing again and again.

Bullets tore into the king cobra from the front and sides. More bullets than my gun fired. Its body undulated as its hooded head struck at me. I kept shooting and rolled to the side, avoiding the venomous fangs. Its scary head rose again, its beady eyes fixed on me. I fired several rounds at close range into its hissing mouth.

Bullets kept coming even after my pistol was empty. That's when I noticed Gwen and Sophia, crouched beside the staircase. They emptied their entire magazines into the eighteen-foot monster, and it finally collapsed in a heap.

Sophia eased up beside me and stared at the twitching serpent. The raging gun battle outside almost drowned out her words when she asked, "Is it dead?"

"I hope so. The head is barely attached to the body. Th-thanks for the help." I almost hugged her but stopped myself so I wouldn't get blood all over her.

Gwen ripped off her sleeve. "You're bleeding everywhere. Let me take care of the deep wound on your arm." She wrapped the cloth around my left biceps. "Oh, no, your leg looks bad too." She tore off the other sleeve and tied it around my thigh.

"Thanks. Now get into the safe room. I'm right behind you." I replaced my magazine with a full one while they rushed away.

As soon as they were out of sight, I hurried up the steps to rescue my puppies on the fourth floor. A moment of panic hit me when I opened my bedroom door and didn't see the dogs.

My radio blared, "More bikers attacking. They're using ballistic grappling hooks to climb up to the balconies."

"Pratt, Whitney, where are you?" I closed the door and locked it. I was about to check the bathroom when their little heads peeked out from under the bed.

I crouched beside them. "Good doggies. Stay under there where it's safe."

They licked blood off my hands, but I kept them away from the parts where I still had tiny pieces of glass sticking into me.

The radio crackled. "Paragliders landing on the roof."

I ducked when a man climbed onto my west balcony and opened fire, shattering the glass French doors. I dove under the far side of the bed and watched him unhook himself from the climbing gear and enter my suite.

"Come out, Mona. I know you're in here." He sprayed the bed with bullets from his submachine gun.

I looked across from under the bed and aimed at his shins. A round in each leg sent him crashing to the floor. Leaping up, I put a round in his head before he had a chance to shoot under the bed and maybe hit my dogs.

Then Tim crashed through my bedroom door. His eyes locked on my blood-soaked clothes. "Jett, are you hit?"

I pulled the dogs to me. "No, I'm good. Is it over?"

"Not even close. We're defending multiple fronts." He keyed his radio. "I found Jett and the dogs. They're in her room. Report in."

I was too far away from Tim to understand the responses he received amidst loud gunfire.

I shouted, "Tim, how are my housemates and your men?"

"Sophia and Gwen are in the safe room. Hunter, Karin, Snake, and Mona are missing."

"Hunter and Karin might be pinned down in her room at the north end of this floor, and Snake is probably in Mona's room on the third floor." I moved closer. "We have to save them."

Tim grabbed my good arm. "Too many shooters. Stay here and I'll protect you and your dogs."

"What about my uncle and the others?"

"I'll send men to them." He squeezed my shoulder. "Hunter and Karin are former Navy, and Snake is a Tier One SEAL. He'll protect Mona." He spoke commands into his radio as a motorcycle roared down the hall toward us.

Tim slammed the door and shoved my dresser in front of it. "Jett, you and the dogs, under the bed, now!"

I grabbed a lipstick off my dresser, dropped to my knees, and drew pink lines around his ankles. He looked at me like I'd lost my mind.

I gazed up at him. "So I don't shoot the wrong guy." I dived under the bed, my puppies following me. They huddled against the back wall under the headboard with me blocking them like a protective mama bear. I aimed toward the door and waited.

Tim was crouched by the far side of the bed when the motorcycle crashed through my bedroom door, knocking over the dresser. He jumped up and took out the bad guy with one head shot.

In the next instant, a man slipped through my open west balcony while another one shattered my south balcony doors with his machine pistol.

Adrenaline surged through my veins as my heart pounded my chest so hard it almost drowned out the deafening gun battle raging around my home.

Tim took out the man on the south balcony while I nailed the other guy in both ankles, making his shot at Tim go wide as he fell to the floor. Tim turned and put a bullet in his head. One shot, one kill—the SEAL mantra. I definitely hired the right guy.

Above and below us, staccato bursts from automatic weapons pierced the night, and then … nothing.

Tim checked in with his men on the radio. He leaned down and glanced under the bed. "You can come out now. Judging by the number of dead gangbangers, I doubt there will be more attacks tonight."

I crawled out from under the bed, and my doggies followed. "What about our people? Is everyone okay?"

"Your people are safe. I have three men down with serious GSWs and a few others with minor flesh wounds." He glanced at his watch. "County SWAT will be here in five minutes. Once the grounds are secure, ambulances can come in and transport the wounded."

I kissed his cheek, and my dogs covered his hands with kisses. "I'm really sorry about your injured men, but I have some good news for you."

"Really?"

"Yep. The missing cobra is dead. A bunch of us shot its head off. That's one problem solved." I noticed his wounded shoulder. "You're bleeding."

He seemed surprised when he glanced at his wound. I pulled out a shard of broken glass, grabbed a scarf from my dresser, and bandaged his shoulder.

"That should hold you until you get stitches." Feeling guilty, I kissed his cheek again. "I'm sorry to put you through all this combat."

"No worries, Jett. I'm just doing my job. We'd better head downstairs now."

He noticed I wobbled a little after we climbed over the motorcycle, so he put an arm around my shoulder as we walked down the hall. "By the way, you've officially surpassed the woman we call Danger Magnet as our most dangerous client."

"Lucky me."

The pups stuck by my side.

We ran into Hunter, Karin, Mona, and Snake in the foyer. They were staring at the dead reptile, its head barely attached thanks to all the bullet holes.

Tim looked at it and smiled. "Nice job, Jett."

"Gwen and Sophia helped me." I glanced around. "Where are they?"

"Right here," Sophia answered as she rounded the stairway with Gwen.

The dogs sniffed the dead snake while I greeted everyone. When I hugged Hunter, I noticed his shoulder wound. "You're bleeding."

Hunter looked me over. "Not as much as you. Looks like we both need stitches."

"Aw, geez, I forgot about the broken glass on the floor." I nudged Sophia. "Help me check their paws."

By some miracle, the dogs hadn't stepped in the glass.

"Please keep the dogs with you while Hunter and I go to the local E.R." I glanced at my watch and back to Sophia. "We'll leave as soon as Tim says it's okay."

# NINETEEN

I wrapped a beach towel around me so I wouldn't bleed on the McLaren, and Hunter drove us to the small Banyan Isle Hospital in the wee hours of the morning. Tim accompanied his wounded men to a larger hospital on the mainland and left the rest with the SWAT team to guard my people.

As we walked toward the E.R. entrance in the dark, I glanced up at Hunter. "My house sure is a mess, but I'm glad our people got through the attack okay."

He put his good arm around my shoulders. "Your house isn't as bad as you think. It's mostly broken glass and bullet holes. That can be fixed quickly." He stopped and looked into my eyes. "You're shaking. Are you cold?"

"No, I still haven't recovered from the terror." I shuddered. "You saw that monster snake, and lots of men were trying to kill us. This was far scarier than anything I ever faced in the Navy."

"I'd have to agree with you on that." He kissed my forehead. "I'd hug you, but I don't want to deepen your cuts with all the glass slivers in your back."

"I sure hope the Korean gang is done attacking." I shivered. "Nobody wants to go through this again."

"We should ask Mike if the police know how many were in Chul Han's gang. Maybe Tim's men took out all of them."

"I doubt Han sent the entire gang here from L.A. He probably hired local thugs to help his men." I paused. "I hope Chul Han is dead, otherwise, this isn't over."

We were the only patients when we checked in. Noting my blood-soaked clothes, an orderly ushered us into the inner E.R. and seated us in an exam room. A stocky, large-breasted nurse about five-ten with shoulder-length blond hair bustled in. She smiled at us and introduced herself as RN Grace Simms.

"Please, call me Jett." I dropped my towel and turned around. "My wounds are on my backside with deep ones in my left arm and thigh. You'll need to tweezer out all the glass fragments."

"How did this happen?" she asked.

"A violent gang attacked my home with submachine guns. Gunfire shattered a huge window and peppered me with broken glass."

"Wow, that must've been scary." She looked at Hunter's shoulder. "I guess that's how you got the gunshot wound."

He nodded.

"Looks like you'll both need stitches." She glanced from Hunter to me. "Do you want separate exam rooms? You'll need to strip to your underwear, and he'll have to remove his shirt."

I shot an anxious look at Hunter. "Don't leave me."

"Relax, sweetheart. I'm staying right here." Hunter unbuttoned his shirt and slipped it off.

For most women, the sight of a shirtless Hunter was enough to take their breath away. Nurse Simms didn't seem to notice his broad shoulders, hard pecs, and killer abs.

"Doctor Brooks will be right in." She grabbed a pair of scissors. "Your clothes are shredded anyway, Jett. Let me cut them off and make this process as painless as possible."

"Thank you." I lifted my hair out of the way.

She touched my arm as she started snipping away fabric. "Allergic to any meds?"

We both answered, "No."

A handsome young doctor with dark skin and hair breezed in. He introduced himself and read our charts.

"Jettine Jorgensen and Hunter Vann." He glanced from Hunter to me. "We don't normally treat patients together. Are you two related?"

"He's my uncle, and please, call me Jett." I gave him my best smile and tried to stop shaking. "Do you know Doctor Warner? He patched me up here two months ago."

"Warner died last month." He furrowed his brow. "Are you cold, Jett?"

"No, I'm shaking because I'm pumped full of adrenaline. We just survived a major attack by armed assailants. It was terrifying."

The doctor stiffened. "Should we prepare for multiple GSW patients?"

Hunter shook his head. "The bad guys didn't survive. Long story."

I interrupted. "What happened to Doc Warner? He was only thirty-four."

"Heart attack. Dropped dead right here in the E.R. during his shift." The nurse nudged me. "It was awful. I was working that night and found him in an exam room."

The doctor checked me over. "You have two deep puncture wounds, and your uncle has a minor GSW on his shoulder. I'll take care of you first so the nurse can pull out all the glass shards while I stitch your uncle." As he began stitching my wounds, he glanced over at Hunter. "I hope you understand we're required by law to report gunshot wounds."

"The cops already know about this, but go ahead," Hunter said.

"Also, you'll both need tetanus boosters." He turned to the nurse. "Prepare the injections, please."

She prepared the shots while the doctor finished stitching my two deep wounds.

"Nurse, please give me the shot in my wounded arm. That way, I'll only have one sore arm." I turned my left side toward her as the doctor started working on Hunter.

When she gave me the shot, she stood very close, and I noticed her manicured fingernails were polished with glossy pink polish.

"Climb onto the exam table now, Jett, and I'll start pulling out the glass slivers." She picked up tweezers.

Wearing only my blue satin bra and matching bikini panties, I lay on my belly on the table. To my surprise, the nurse snipped open the back of my bra.

"Hey, you could've just unhooked it. And keep those scissors away from my panties."

"Believe me, the back side of your bra isn't worth saving. It's mostly shredded."

The nurse changed the subject by asking my uncle, "Are you the same Hunter Vann who lives in Aerodrome Estates and flies a red Staggerwing Beech?"

"I am, but how did you know that?"

"Last week, Doctor Trish Jordan gave me a ride in her four-seat airplane out at Aerodrome Estates, and I asked her who owned the beautiful cabin biplane we saw."

Surprised, he asked, "Are you a pilot?"

"No, but I enjoy going up in private planes when I get a chance. The view is spectacular, and last time, I saw some sharks when we flew over the beach."

Hunter smiled. "Would you like a ride in my airplane?"

She beamed. "I'd love a ride in your vintage biplane. It's a beauty."

He pulled out a business card and handed it to her. "Call me and we'll schedule it."

"Thank you." She tweezed out more slivers of glass and asked, "What about you, Jett? Are you a pilot too?"

"Yes, Hunter taught me. I have a commercial pilot license and a flight instructor certificate. Sometimes I fill in for him at his flight school."

"Why don't you work there full-time?"

"I have other plans, and I've been away in the Navy."

"Oh, how long until you ship out again?" she asked.

"I decided not to re-enlist." I sucked in my breath during a painful shard extraction. "I'm home for good now."

The doctor left after he finished with Hunter, but he returned just as the nurse pulled out my final sliver. He said, "I brought these surgical scrubs for you to wear home."

"Thank you, Doctor. And thanks to my nurse too. I feel a lot better without all that sharp glass poking into me."

"Just stay put a minute while I cleanse the cuts and apply antibiotic ointment," Nurse Simms said. "Then you can get dressed."

Now braless, I felt a little self-conscious when I donned the cotton scrubs.

Before I left, the nurse said, "I'd love to go flying with you too, Jett."

"Sure." I nodded and waved.

It was still dark when we walked back to Hunter's sportscar. I squeezed his arm. "Better be careful not to give that nurse false hope. She's probably smitten with you."

He laughed. "You're the one she's interested in." He nudged me. "I think she plays for the home team. Besides, I'm into someone else."

"I noticed. Please tread lightly. I'd hate to lose my new chef."

"If vicious gang attacks and bodies dropping from the sky haven't scared her off, she's not going to leave because of me."

I took his arm. "Before we go back, there's something I want to ask you. It's about a woman pilot at your airline who everyone calls Danger Magnet."

"Oh, you mean Captain Samantha Starr, also known in the UK as Sir Lady Samantha. What about her?"

"Tim keeps comparing me to her, and now he says I've surpassed her as his most dangerous client."

"Sorry, honey, that's not a reputation you'd want to live up to."

———

FBI agents were waiting for us when Hunter and I strolled in. They had all my house guests gathered in the great hall, and someone had swept broken glass and debris away from the seating area. The recessed ceiling lights still worked, illuminating the vast room.

A tall man in his thirties waved to us. "Have a seat, Miss Jorgensen and Mr. Vann. I'm Special Agent Taylor, and this is Special Agent Barnes." He indicated a shorter man on his left.

I noticed a stack of grisly photos on a coffee table in front of Mona.

Agent Taylor followed my gaze and said, "Miss Wang has identified eight Korean gang members among the dead. The rest were local thugs."

"Is Chul Han dead?" I hoped he was.

"No, he wasn't here." Agent Taylor checked his tablet. "Han left L.A. a few days ago, but we don't know his current location. The logical assumption is he came to South Florida to kidnap or kill his niece."

Hunter cleared his throat. "Does this mean we should expect more attacks?"

"Several of Chul Han's men were killed. He'll want revenge on Miss Wang and Miss Jorgensen." Taylor's eyes met mine. "We're not sure if Han will import more of his gang from L.A., or if he'll hire local thugs to finish the job. But you can count on another attack."

Agent Barnes said, "You two are lucky Han didn't send a hit team to the hospital. He might wait for you to leave the house and have hitmen pick you off one at a time."

Sophia jumped up and pointed a finger at Barnes. "Sounds like you know what Han has planned, so what are you doing about it?"

"The FBI has been surveilling him for eight months, building a case, but we need evidence he's behind these attacks before we can arrest him."

Sophia crossed her arms. "Kinda hard to arrest the man if you don't know where he is." She pulled out her cell and called her son. "Marco, can your people locate a Korean gangster from Los Angeles named Chul Han? We think he's here in South Florida." She paused. "I know it's before dawn, but this is important."

Mike rushed in and stopped in front of me. "I just missed you at the hospital." He stared at my bandages and clenched his jaw. "I'm sorry you were wounded, Jett. I should've stayed with you even though you asked me not to."

I smiled. "I'm okay. Just a lot of cuts from broken glass."

He sighed. "I saw the dead snake in the foyer. I heard it almost bit you."

"That cobra has more lead in it than a medical-grade radiation shield." I smiled at Gwen and Sophia. "They helped me kill it."

Ten minutes later, Sophia pocketed her phone and smirked at the feds. "Chul Han rented an oceanfront condo owned by a Russian mobster. It's in the Beach Towers near the south end of Banyan Isle, and he rented it under the name Charles Hunt."

Agent Taylor jotted down the info. "Not sure how he slipped past us, but we'll handle this."

"Like you handled it so far?" Sophia asked. "Fuhgeddaboudit."

Mike glanced from the feds to Sophia and smirked. I guess he didn't like the Special Agents either.

Agent Taylor frowned. "You people are skating on thin ice. We have fourteen dead from this night alone. I'm warning you not to interfere."

I glared at the agents. "Fine, then *do* something to resolve this or expect a call from your director. He and my boss from Navy Intelligence go way back."

*That* got their attention.

As he headed for the door, Agent Taylor said, "We'll be in touch."

# TWENTY

At 9:00 a.m., Marco DeLuca and two large men with no necks rolled up in a full-size Hummer and parked in front of the entrance door. The three wore expensive-looking suits with slight bulges where their shoulder holsters held handguns. Tim had notified me of their arrival at the gate, and I opened the bullet-riddled door to welcome them.

They seemed unfazed as men in full combat gear unloaded their luggage and accompanied them inside. One of Tim's men parked the rental Hummer in my garage after commenting, "I hope you guys signed up for the full insurance coverage."

The mobsters froze and stared at the giant snake in my foyer. We hadn't had the time or energy to deal with it, but we'd swept aside all the broken glass.

Sophia rushed over with open arms. "Marco, give your mama a big hug."

"What the hell happened here? This place looks like a war zone ... and that huge snake." He searched his mother's eyes.

"Watch your language, *il maschio*." Sophia grabbed him and gave him a long hug. "We had some trouble last night, but we're good now." She thumbed at the snake. "It's not usually like this here."

His two gorillas stood by, waiting and sizing me up. The dogs sensed Marco was family, but they seemed unsure of the goombahs with him. I kept them close on leashes.

"You look tired, Ma." Marco pulled back from the hug. "I've missed you."

"You're looking as handsome as ever." She straightened his tie. "When are you gonna settle down and give me some grandchildren?"

"Give it a rest, will ya? I haven't met the right woman, speaking of which, who is this raven-haired beauty?" He gave me a million-dollar smile.

"Marco, meet the lady of the house, my dear friend, Jettine Jorgensen."

I offered my hand. "Welcome to Valhalla. Sorry for the mess, and please call me Jett."

He looked into my eyes, kissed my hand, and held it a little longer than necessary. "Thank you for inviting us to your home, Jett. Meet my colleagues, Sal and Joey."

I tentatively slid my hand into Sal's giant paw and received a surprisingly gentle squeeze. Joey did the same when it was his turn.

"And these are my four-month-old Timber-shepherds, Pratt and Whitney, named after my favorite aircraft engine manufacturer."

Marco chuckled as he reached down and ruffled their fur.

Sal said, "You can tell by their feet they're gonna be huge."

Joey stood with a blank look on his face, and the dogs edged closer to me.

I had arranged before they arrived to put Marco in a room beside Sophia, but not the room where the mayor was murdered. Sal's room was beside Marco's, and Joey would be across the hall.

"Security guards will take the bags to your rooms. Would you like to go upstairs and freshen up, or will you join us in the great hall and meet everyone?" I gestured toward the east side of the house.

Marco placed his hand on the small of my back. "We're good. Let's go."

Sophia took his left arm. "Things are a little crazy right now, but this is normally a very relaxing place. I love it here, and wait until you taste Karin's cooking. She's a professional chef."

"Ma, you haven't explained what happened here." Marco stepped around a shattered urn.

"The short answer is a Korean gangster from L.A. named Chul Han sent a bunch of thugs to attack us last night. They're all dead now, but Han is still at large."

"Isn't he the guy you asked me about? The one who's staying in a beach condo here?"

"Yeah, that's him."

"Want me to take care of him?" Marco patted his weapon.

"We'll see. The FBI claims they're handling it."

We strolled into the great hall, and Hunter, Karin, Gwen, and Mona stood to greet our guests. Snake remained seated in his wheelchair. Then Tim strode in. Introductions were made, and everyone settled in for a serious discussion.

Marco and his men remained quiet while Tim explained the situation involving the gang from L.A. and all the precautions in place to protect the household.

Tim ended with a question for Marco. "Any intel on who sent Sophia the note?"

"Carmine DeLuca's daughter, Gina, adored my father and blamed my mother for his hit. We think she might be taking advantage of the body bombings to mess with Ma's head."

"So, there's no real danger from this Gina?" Tim asked.

"Carmine swears he isn't holding a grudge over his brother's execution, but Gina is his personal assassin, and she hates Ma." Marco glanced at Sophia.

Sophia stiffened. "Little Gina's a hitwoman now?"

"The best in the business, and she's not little anymore." Marco adjusted his cuffs. "We have reason to believe Gina's here in South Florida, which is why I want you to come home with me where you'll be safe."

Sophia patted her pistol. "I can take care of myself."

Marco sucked in his breath. "Ma, I came here because I'm a good

Italian son who loves his mother. Even without Gina, you've got bodies dropping out of the sky and a violent gang trying to kill everyone. How can I possibly let you stay in such a dangerous place?"

I broke in, "Maybe Marco has a point, Sophia. I couldn't bear it if anything happened to you."

Sophia glanced around at us. "I feel the same way about all of you and our precious doggies. I won't abandon you." She elbowed her son. "Marco, take Sal and Joey and go home. Straighten things out with Carmine and Gina. We'll handle things here."

Marco jumped up and burst into an Italian-language tirade, waving his arms and pacing in front of his mother.

Sophia crossed her arms. "Your tantrums didn't work when you were a child, and they won't work now. I'm staying."

He glared at her. "Then we're staying too." He looked at Tim. "I suggest we come up with a plan to avoid accidentally shooting each other's men."

My cell rang. Caller ID displayed FBI. "What can I do for you, Special Agent?"

"This is a courtesy call. We raided Chul Han's condo this morning, but he'd already left. We're checking all the airports in case he's trying to fly back to L.A."

"So, what you're really saying is you have no idea where he is or what he'll do next. Thanks for the update." I pocketed my phone, wishing the FBI had caught Chul Han.

Gwen squeezed my arm. "Han got away?"

Mona gasped and hugged herself.

Snake put his arm around her. "Don't worry. We'll get him."

Marco had been listening. He pulled out his cell. "I'll make some calls. See what I can find out about this Chul Han." He stepped away.

Gwen was standing beside me when her cell rang. She glanced at it. "It's Clint. I'd better take it." She stepped away to talk to her boyfriend.

When she returned, she said, "Clint is taking me to dinner tonight at the Banyan Harbor Inn. He wants to make amends for being a jealous jerk last night."

"Is it safe for you to go out with Chul Han on the loose?"

"Don't worry, Jett. I'm not on Han's radar. He's after you and Mona." She patted her pistol. "Besides, I'm always armed, and so is Clint." She yawned. "I'm going home now for some sleep."

Marco came back right after Gwen left. Everyone looked to him for answers.

"My people in New York have connections here and in L.A. They're sure Han's still in South Florida, but they don't have a lock on his new digs yet." He gave his mother a stern look. "They'll call when they have something, but I still think you should come home with me, Ma."

"I'm staying here." Sophia yawned. "And right now, I'm going to bed. We've been up all night, and I'm tired." She headed for the stairs.

I approached Marco. "Have you and your men had breakfast?"

"We're good. You should get some sleep. We'll talk later."

I thanked him and started up the stairs with the dogs.

# TWENTY-ONE

G wen entered the elegant bar in the Banyan Harbor Inn to meet Clint for drinks and then have dinner at the waterfront restaurant. A piano player in the corner sang soft jazz tunes as she scanned the room.

Dressed to impress, she wore an emerald-green cocktail dress and her Aunt Liz's antique brooch pinned to a sash at her waist. The ancient jewelry was a secret weapon known as Guinevere's Lance. It had been forged by Merlin at King Arthur's request for Queen Guinevere's protection. The gold and crystal brooch with rubies and sapphires and a matching ring had been passed down to women in the queen's bloodline for centuries. Now the weapon was Gwen's responsibility. The brooch made her feel close to her late aunt, the Duchess of Colchester, and it had helped Gwen get closure for her parents' murders in an unsolved carjacking years ago.

Clint wasn't there yet, so she settled at the bar and waited. Her cell phone vibrated, and she answered his call. "Hello, darling, are you on your way?"

"Sorry, sweetheart, I got called out to a suspicious death in one of the old-money mansions near the north end of Palm Beach. I'm afraid we'll have to reschedule."

"Need help? I can change clothes and join you."

"I'd love that if you're not too tired. I'll text you the address."

"I'll be there in thirty minutes." She slipped the phone into her purse and sensed someone close behind her.

Something sharp pricked her bare upper back as a man with a Korean accent whispered in her ear, "Make no sound. Come with me or I kill you."

Gwen tensed and slid off the barstool. *Who is this guy, and what does he want with me? I'd better wait until we're away from the bar before I make a move. Don't want anyone here to get hurt.*

He guided her out of the dark bar to the hotel elevators. No one was near as he eased her inside and pressed the button for the top floor. She seized the moment and jabbed both elbows into his ribs, then stomped her stiletto into his right instep.

He ignored the pain and kept her back pinned against him. Moving the knife to her neck, he made a shallow slit across her throat. "Try that again, I slice throat to bone and leave you to bleed out."

Her heart raced as blood trickled down onto her chest. The elevator door opened, and he herded her down the hall to a room on the inlet side of the hotel.

He opened the door and kept her close to him as he shoved her into the room, his knife pricking her back.

She passed a curved sword on the dresser as he pushed her toward the bed.

"Turn around."

She slowly turned, terrified. A middle-aged Asian man with wild, dark eyes grinned at her. *Oh, God, he must be Mona's uncle!*

He shoved her onto the bed, held the knife to her neck, and leaned close to her face. His breath reeked of stale coffee and tobacco.

Gwen's heart hammered in her chest. "You must be Chul Han."

He sneered. "Good guess. Do as I say, or I carve you up, chop off arms, and watch you die." He poked her lower lip with the knife tip and licked her blood. "Umm, redheads taste good."

Déjà vu hit her like a gut punch as terrifying memories flooded her mind—lying helpless while her parents' murderer tried to kill her in an abandoned warehouse. Guinevere's Lance had saved her. Maybe it would save her again.

She squirmed under his weight, trying to ease her right hand to her waist with her shoulders pinned to the bed. Her fingers crawled over the large brooch and paused. She pressed the center ruby, paused again, and ever so slowly slid out the crystal syringe.

Distracting him, she asked, "What do you want?"

Inches from her face, he said, "Call Jett. Tell her bring Mona to room 420. Say you have nice surprise, but is secret, and tell no one." He grabbed the room phone and set it beside her head. "Her phone number?"

"Jett will be suspicious if I call from a hotel phone." She inched back the plunger with her right hand, filling the wide syringe with air. "My cell phone is in my purse." She glanced down to her left, drawing his attention to her left side.

Her purse had hung from her left shoulder and now lay beside her waist. He kept his left hand on her right shoulder as he set the knife next to her left cheek and fished inside the purse.

*He'll kill me right after I make that call. It's now or never.* She sucked in her breath and steeled her nerve.

The instant he glanced down to his right, she stabbed the short gold needle into his left carotid artery and pushed the plunger to the stop, injecting him with a lethal dose of air.

"Arrghhh!" He clutched at his neck, an air embolism shooting into his brain and causing a massive stroke as he collapsed onto his right side.

She yanked out Guinevere's Lance and slid it back into the brooch.

Chul Han gasped and reached for the knife. Gwen snatched it up and plunged it into the exact spot where she had injected him, thereby protecting her aunt's legacy. No one could ever know about the secret weapon or those who had been executed with it.

Blood soaked his shirt and the bed seconds before his heart stopped. Chul Han stared at Gwen through vacant eyes.

It had all happened so fast.

Her stomach churned as the coppery scent of blood filled her nostrils.

She scooted off the bed and circled him. Reaching under him, she pulled out her purse and grabbed her phone. Her hands shook as she called Mike.

"Gwen? What's up?"

In a shaky voice, she said, "Room 420 at the Banyan Harbor Inn. Come right away. You'll need a CSU and the medical examiner."

"Who was murdered?"

"It was self-defense. Chul Han abducted me, and I killed him with his own knife." She paused. "Please hurry." She shoved the phone into her purse and rushed into the bathroom. Leaning over, she retched into the toilet. When the spasms stopped, she rinsed her mouth over the sink and dried her face.

She stared into the mirror at her bloody neck and lip. *That's twice Guinevere's Lance has saved my life. And now Jett and Mona will be safe from Chul Han.*

---

Mike and Gwen arrived together at my house at 10:00 p.m. He was somber, and she seemed shaken. I noted her bloody lip, the bandage on her throat, and the blood on her dress.

I leaned my broom against the doorjamb. "Gwen, what happened?"

She licked her swollen lip. "Chul Han abducted me, and I killed him."

I hugged her. "Thank God you survived. Where was Clint?"

"He got tagged for a murder investigation in Palm Beach." She gazed into my eyes. "You might not have to worry about that gang anymore."

Mike touched my shoulder. "Where's Mona? I need her for a positive ID."

"She's helping sweep up all the battle debris in the great hall." I turned and led them through the foyer.

Everyone stopped what they were doing when they saw Gwen.

Sophia hurried to her. "Is that your blood?"

Gwen held up a hand. "Don't worry. I'm okay, and Chul Han is dead."

Marco strode over. "Who killed him?"

She blew out a sigh. "I did. Stabbed him with his dagger."

Snake rolled his wheelchair close and squeezed her hand. "Well done, Red."

Hunter stepped in and hugged Gwen. "Good job. I'm glad you're safe."

Sal elbowed Joey. "Imagine that. The broad took him out."

Joey looked at Gwen with his usual blank stare.

Mike turned to Mona. "I need you to ID the body."

Mona's eyes darted around the room. Panicked, she said, "What if it isn't him?"

Just then, Tim arrived looking badass in his black combat gear.

*He's the perfect man to make Mona feel safe.* I tapped his shoulder. "Tim, Mona needs you to protect her while she goes with Mike to identify Chul Han's body."

Tim's jaw dropped. "Han is dead?"

"I killed him when he attacked me at the Banyan Harbor Inn," Gwen explained.

Tim glanced from her to Mike. "Does the FBI know?"

"I called them," Mike said. "The feds contacted their gang informant in L.A., and he told the remaining gang members that Han had died. That triggered a power struggle for the top spot. Turns out Han was more feared than liked. The feds don't think anyone wants to avenge his death. They're probably grateful to be rid of him. They blamed Han for their dead gang members."

"Good. We'll remain vigilant, but it sounds like the gang attacks are over." Tim took Mona's arm. "I'll be happy to escort you. Let's go."

"Thanks." Mona clung to him and took a breath. "I'm ready."

Mike said over his shoulder, "They'll be back soon. The body's still at the hotel."

I put my arm around Gwen. "You look like you need a drink."

"Yes, and maybe some cannoli or something. I missed dinner." She slumped onto the sofa.

Sophia squeezed her hand. "You need wine and comfort food. How about a grilled cheese sandwich with cream of tomato soup?"

Gwen nodded.

Karin stepped in. "Sophia, you warm up the soup, and I'll make the sandwich."

"I'll open the wine. I think everyone needs a soothing drink." I headed for the temperature-controlled wine storage room.

Hunter said, "I'll bring in some beer too." He headed for the kitchen.

Soon we were all gathered together, sipping drinks and staring into space.

"I just called Joe Caldarelli for a rush job on repairing the battle damage." I took a sip of merlot. "And tomorrow I'll hire an army of cleaners to help clear away the debris from the attack. We have to stay on schedule for the charity ball."

Hunter paused mid-sip and set down his beer bottle. "You're still having the ball?"

"Why not? The danger from the gang is over, and my ball will bring in a lot of money for the women's shelter."

He sighed. "I knew I couldn't get out of wearing a tux that easy."

Sophia said, "You'll need three new mannequins for the ball decorations."

"Right. I forgot about that." I chewed my lip. "Lots to do, but we'll manage."

I looked up when Tim returned with Mona. She settled beside Snake.

"Good news," Tim said. "Chul Han is definitely dead."

"Thank God that's over." I patted Mona's back. "You must be relieved."

"I've lived in fear for so long, it's wonderful to finally be free of him." Mona snuggled against Snake.

Sophia leaned into Marco. "You and your boys can go home now that the gang issue has been resolved. That is, unless you want to stay and help us put the house in order."

"We'll stay another day. I have meetings set for tomorrow with our Florida connections. I won't feel comfortable going home until I know what Gina is up to." He swirled his red wine.

Sophia shook her head. "It's hard to imagine Gina all grown up and wanting to kill me. What does she look like now?"

I listened in, eager to hear his answer.

"She's five ten, has long, dark-brown hair, and is super fit. I wasn't kidding when I said she's Carmine DeLuca's top assassin."

I gasped. "Sounds like the woman I spotted several times on my beach."

# TWENTY-TWO

The next day brought a flurry of activity. Joe Caldarelli was in his jeans and tight T-shirt, providing eye candy for us ladies as he worked with his crew. Marco and his goombahs were somewhere off the island meeting with colleagues.

By 6:00 p.m., we had accomplished most of the first-floor cleanup, but we were too tired to contemplate a dinner that required any effort. I ordered a variety of large pizzas from Luigi's Italian Ristorante, which they delivered.

We gathered on the back terrace and passed around all the pizza boxes. I was on my second slice when Marco and his men returned. Sal and Joey lit up when they smelled the pizza. They were easy to please.

Marco pulled up a chair between Sophia and me. I handed him a plate and poured him a glass of Chianti Classico.

After he devoured a slice of pepperoni pizza, he said, "The family swears Gina is in Rome now, shopping before she visits relatives in Sicily. And a check with our guys in L.A. confirmed the Korean gang has no interest in coming here. So, it looks like you're in the clear, Ma." He took a sip. "That is, except for bodies falling from the sky. Nobody has a clue about that."

"There haven't been any body drops for a few days, so maybe that's finished too." I drained my glass. "At least I hope so."

Marco put an arm around his mother. "I'd still like you to come home with me, but if you won't, then please stay inside at night. We're leaving in the morning."

———

Construction workers continued restoring broken windows and repairing damaged walls and doors every day. True to Joe's promise, Caldarelli and Sons would have Valhalla in top shape well before the charity ball.

Sophia and I took turns hugging Marco and bidding him goodbye. Hugging Sal and Joey would have been like hugging refrigerators, so we didn't attempt it. Light kisses on their cheeks brought smiles.

As we watched them drive away in the Hummer, Sophia said, "Would it be okay if I take a run into the Gardens Mall and stop at Bloomingdale's for some Estee Lauder stuff? I'm running low on makeup and moisturizer."

"That sounds like a great idea. Mind if I join you?"

"I'd love that. It'll feel good for us to do something kinda normal after all the craziness we've been through."

I asked Karin and Mona if they needed anything and then grabbed my handbag. "Let's go."

We strolled through the mall, window shopping before we ducked into Bloomingdale's and bought what we needed at the cosmetics counter.

On our way back to the car I said, "Once or twice in there I thought I saw a woman matching Gina's description."

"There are probably hundreds of women who look like her—five-ten with long brown hair." She patted my back. "You're just paranoid because of all the crap we've been through lately."

I blew out a sigh. "You're right. I've had my guard up for so long, it's hard for me to relax now, but we'll have loads of fun at our ball and forget all about the scary stuff."

# TWENTY-THREE

I took the dogs for a run the following day and then checked on the workmen's progress. Repairs were going well, and Hunter had gone home. Except for some custom glass orders, Joe Caldarelli's men had repaired almost all the damage from the gang's attack.

Sophia strolled up to me wearing a one-piece bathing suit and shorts over it. "Let's try our luck at catching dinner off the end of your floating pier."

"Sounds like fun. I keep all the fishing gear in the garage. Give me a minute to change into my bikini, and I'll help carry everything out there."

Soon, we were sitting on the end of my pier with our feet dangling in the water while we held fishing rods and faced the inlet between Banyan Isle and Juno Beach. The dogs were curled up behind us, and Sophia had a zippered bag with a few food items for bait in case the lures didn't work.

After thirty minutes with no bites, Sophia shoved a chunk of sausage onto her hook. "I'll see if this gets the fish excited."

Her line wasn't in the water more than a few seconds before a fish took the bait.

"Whoa! I hooked a big one." She struggled to hang onto the rod.

I set my rod aside, wrapped an arm around her waist, and helped her hold the rod with my other hand. "I've got you. Reel that big guy in."

The heavy fish put up a hard fight, jumping and diving. When she finally reeled it in close enough to see it, it was a four-foot cobia.

"It's too big to fit in our little scoop net," I said. "We'll have to pull it beside the pier and drag it up onto the beach."

Straining on the rod with both hands, Sophia glanced over her shoulder at me. "If I try to stand up, I'll get yanked into the water."

"Hang on. I'll get up first and take the rod while you stand." I kept a firm grip on her waistband and eased up to a standing position.

I grabbed her rod with both hands. "Okay, you can get up now." I managed to reel the fish in another five feet before handing the rod back to Sophia.

What happened next was a complete surprise. The fish flopped up onto the floating pier and smacked into Sophia. It was dark brown with a serrated dorsal fin preceded by nine sharp spines.

"Argghh! Grab that devil. Don't let him get away." Sophia whacked the writhing fish with her rod.

Then the cobia smacked its tail into my shins, cutting my skin, and I yelped.

The dogs weren't sure what to do. They tried to bite it, and it whacked them with its tail, knocking them into the water. They surfaced snorting salt water.

"My fur babies!" I jumped in to help my puppies get to shore. Grabbing their collars, I kept their heads above water. I looked back just as Sophia tried to grab the shark-like fish.

"Ha! Got ya." It slipped free and smacked her in the face with its powerful tail. Her split lip bled as the fish flopped into the water.

"Oh no you don't!" She grabbed the rod and started reeling in the slack.

Just then the fish reached the end of the line and yanked her into the water. She surfaced, sputtering, and clung to the rod as the cobia towed her toward deep water.

A speedboat zoomed up to her, and a woman with long brown hair leaned over, zapped her with a Taser, and hauled her into the boat. Sophia collapsed onto the boat's deck as the driver sped toward the ocean.

Mafia assassin Gina DeLuca.

I pulled my puppies to shore and then sprinted to where I'd left my cell on a terrace table. I called Tim.

"Hey, Jett, what's up?"

"Gina DeLuca just abducted Sophia in a speedboat and headed out to sea. I think she means to put her feet in concrete-filled buckets and drown her like she threatened in that note. Pick me up in your helicopter and bring a sniper. I'll be ready with my dive gear on the back lawn." I hung up and rushed to the house before he had a chance to respond.

I bolted inside and yelled for Karin to help me. "Gina took Sophia. I keep dive gear and twin scuba tanks in the garage. Grab a big lift bag, a mask and fins, and my double 80s. I'll meet you on the back terrace."

Snake rolled up. "Your shins are bleeding."

"A fish smacked me." I ran upstairs and pulled a pink one-piece nylon dive skin over my swimsuit and zipped up the front. I donned neoprene booties to protect my feet, grabbed my buoyancy-compensator vest, and shoved a Glock into the vest pocket. Then I strapped a dive knife to my right calf and slipped my cell phone into a waterproof sleeve and shoved it into my other vest pocket along with my dive gloves.

Snake and Mona waited with Karin. She had gathered everything I requested, plus two beach towels.

"Will one large lift bag be enough?" Karin held up the limp sack.

"It has to be," I said. "I can inflate my BC vest if I need more buoyancy to bring her to the surface, but I hope we'll have enough air. I only have two full tanks, and that lift bag isn't the kind with an inflation cartridge."

"What can we do?" Snake asked.

"Keep the dogs inside and don't tell anybody about this. If the New York Mafia finds out, this could start a Mob war." I mounted the twin air tanks to my BC vest, so it was ready to slip on when the time came. "Karin, please help me carry this stuff."

We hurried into the backyard, and I searched the sky. I prayed Tim would arrive in time to save Sophia. In the meantime, I Googled quick-setting concrete. It would take twenty to forty minutes for it to harden before Gina could drop her into the ocean. Ten minutes dragged by before thundering helicopter blades and the high-pitched whines of twin Pratt & Whitney turboshaft engines echoed off the water. Fortunately for me, his Bell 429 Global Ranger had floats.

Tim landed near me, and Karin helped me climb into the cabin with my dive gear. I waved goodbye to her and closed the cabin door. Then I slipped on my BC vest with the tanks mounted on the back and pulled on my fins as we took off and sped east at 170 mph. Last, I pulled on my stretchy dive gloves.

A man I didn't know sat in the left cockpit seat, holding a scoped, light-weight Sig Sauer Cross Sniper/Hunter Rifle on his lap. I scanned the horizon as the helicopter raced over the water at fifty feet. We spotted a small speedboat about five miles from shore.

Edging against the door, I yelled, "That's the boat. The woman with long brown hair is your target."

The sniper checked his rifle as we closed in. Sophia's feet were already encased in concrete-filled buckets. Had to be the quick-drying kind, like I thought. Her hands were tied in front of her, and Gina crouched behind her under a sunroof covering the center console. One bucketed foot hung over the side as Sophia struggled, twisting and trying to hit Gina with her bound hands.

The sniper had no shot because Gina was hidden under the boat's central roof.

As we hovered, Gina lifted Sophia's other bucketed foot onto the side rail. Sophia glanced up, spotted the sniper, and realized her gyrations made it difficult for him to isolate his target. She ducked her head and froze, but the helicopter was too high for the sniper to spot Gina under the roof. Tim had to land on the water to give his shooter the best angle, but that also made us easy targets for Gina.

I screamed, "Hurry! She's about to push Sophia overboard."

Tim landed with the chopper's left side facing the right side of the free-floating boat, and we bobbed alongside it in the current. The sniper had the front left cockpit door open, and I sat behind him by the open cabin door. Gina crouched behind her boat's center console and shoved Sophia into the ocean using the handle on a long boat hook.

Tim turned and yelled, "Jett, wait until we take out the shooter."

"I have to save Sophia." Struggling with heavy tanks on my back, integrated weights, and flippered feet, I climbed down onto the pontoon. Three-foot swells jostled me in the salty breeze. I would have to turn backward to drop in without banging into the float.

I was so anxious to jump in, I didn't think about getting shot. Gina was only twenty feet away. I drew my pistol and fired several rounds in her direction to keep her pinned down. Then I tossed the handgun onto the back seat and turned.

Gina was so determined to drown Sophia that she aimed at me instead of taking out the sniper first. When she popped up to shoot, the sniper's rifle barked at almost the same instant she fired her pistol. Her head snapped back, and her bullet went wide, barely grazing the inside of my left arm close to my heart. Blood ran down my inner arm as I rolled backwards into the water, pressing my mask against my face. I had to reach Sophia in time.

The cool water eased my stinging wound. After adjusting my mask, I searched for a bubble trail. Sophia would drop almost straight to the bottom with the heavy concrete dragging her down. I prayed the water wouldn't be too deep.

The saltwater was clear but only a few miles from the Gulfstream. A strong current swept me north as I descended. I fought against it as I raced to the bottom, kicking my flippers hard toward Sophia's rapidly vanishing bubbles. Desperate, I could barely see her dark shadow in the distance.

*Can't bear to lose her. How many more seconds can she hold her breath?*

Sophia landed twenty feet south of me amidst sand, coral, and rocky protrusions. It may as well have been twenty miles as I battled against the powerful current. My depth gauge read one hundred feet.

Adrenaline drove me as I swam hard, struggling to reach her. Barely making headway, I hugged the bottom and inched along, pulling myself from one rock to the next. Every second brought her closer to drowning as the clear river of current pummeled me, trying to sweep me away.

*Please, God, help me save her.*

She squinted, the saltwater stinging her eyes as she extended her tied hands toward me. The next rock I grabbed pulled free. I lost precious ground when I turned my head, and the current dislodged my mask. I hugged a rock protruding through the sand while I repositioned the mask and cleared it.

Critical time lost. I dug my hands into the sand and pulled myself to the next rock.

Although I was an experienced diver, the exertion made me use more air than normal. Mustering all my strength, I dragged myself the final five feet, clawing at the rocky bottom and kicking hard. Her outstretched hands were within reach, and I grabbed them and pulled myself to her.

Good thing she had taken a deep breath before she went overboard. After clearing my spare regulator, I shoved it into her mouth. She closed her eyes, breathed in the compressed air, and exhaled. A faint blood trail spiraled upward from her ears. Sophia wasn't a scuba diver, and the rapid descent had burst her ear drums.

But she was alive.

I hugged her.

After cutting her hands loose, I checked the concrete-filled buckets in case they were loose and might drop off. No luck there. I secured the lift bag's line around her and took a deep breath so I could use my mouthpiece to inflate the bag enough to make her neutrally buoyant. This type of bag required manual inflation so the diver could control the buoyancy. Inflating it used a lot of our air.

Clearing my regulator, I took another breath and then released my integrated dive weights. Curious lionfish loomed nearby, their beautiful spines hiding painful venom that ironically was similar to cobra venom.

We slowly ascended together, my left arm around her. She kept her eyes squeezed shut, which was good because then she couldn't see the blood from my wounded arm clouding the water around us. Occasionally pressing against her abdomen, I reminded her to exhale. The rule was to never rise faster than your bubbles.

Judging by her massive bubble stream, Sophia was on the edge of panic, gulping air. I hugged her, trying to calm her.

Rising too fast wasn't a problem at first, but as our depth decreased, so did the surrounding pressure. The air in the lift bag expanded, and we began ascending too fast.

Sophia clutched me with an iron grip, making it difficult for me to reach the relief-valve cord, which dangled under the bag. Reaching up, I grabbed it with my right hand, and it came off, severed in two. At least ten years old, it must've gotten frayed.

Our ascent accelerated to a dangerous rate that could be fatal. If I didn't slow us down, air embolisms might cause strokes, or we might suffer lung ruptures.

Sophia was too panicked for me to ask her to briefly give up the spare regulator attached to my tank so I could rise above her and reach the release valve on top of the lift bag.

Every second brought us closer to death. I drew my dive knife and stabbed the bag once, releasing enough air to stop our rapid rise. Then I hugged Sophia to reassure her as we paused for a safety stop. I pinched the knife hole to stop more air from escaping.

What happened next sent my heart rate into the danger zone. A sixteen-foot tiger shark homed in on us. I tried not to panic when I spotted its tell-tale stripes. It must've smelled the blood from my wounded arm and her burst eardrums. The huge beast flashed past us and circled back.

We were in the shark's domain, and the apex predator was on the hunt.

# TWENTY-FOUR

My dive knife was no match for this monster almost three times our size, but I unsheathed it anyway. As the beast circled ever closer, I clutched the knife and concentrated on keeping my breathing slow and steady.

It was so close on its next pass, that the tiger shark almost brushed against me. I wondered if Sophia could feel my heart pounding as I tightened my grip on her.

*She survived a top assassin and almost drowning. She's come too far to lose her now.*

The denizen of the deep dived below us and vanished. My eyes strained to locate it in the shadowy depths. Just when I thought it had gone, it zoomed up and chomped down on Sophia's left bucket, shaking it from side to side. Her eyes popped open, and she gurgled and almost choked on her mouthpiece.

Struggling to avoid getting tangled with the lift bag amidst the thrashing, I bent over and grabbed Sophia's left shin above the bucket, barely reaching it while stretching the limits of our regulator hoses. Determined to save her, I stabbed the beast's massive head as it shook the bucket back and forth with such violence, I feared it would break her leg.

Its jaws were clamped firmly around her left bucket as I clung to her and stabbed the shark with the ferocity of a pelagic incarnation of Jack the Ripper. My survival instinct was secondary to my drive to save Sophia. No way would I let this monster drag her away. The only good thing was this huge predator had scared away other sharks.

Our vicious battle raged on. If it didn't let go soon, we'd run out of air, and the lift bag would steadily lose air where I'd punctured it.

The solid concrete must've been an unappetizing surprise coupled with my blade jabbing its head and right eye, because the beast finally released its prey. Luckily, it had bitten a concrete bucket instead of soft flesh. I prayed it wouldn't return.

A long-time diver, I knew sharks were necessary to maintain the critical balance in ocean ecology, and they rarely attacked humans. Blood in the water triggered them. Our fault this time, but I still had to defend us. I hoped the tiger shark would survive.

I checked our air gauge. With my earlier exertion, Sophia gulping air, the air used to fill the lift bag, and the shark battle, the tanks were almost empty. Adrenaline hummed through my veins, and my chest pounded so hard, I didn't think my heart rate would ever return to normal.

We still had fifty feet to go, the height of a five-story building, but we couldn't risk rising faster even if it were possible. The remaining air in the tanks would be easier to breathe as we ascended, but I wasn't sure if we'd have enough. I'd have to inflate my BC vest manually at the surface so it would become a life preserver.

Conserving what little air I could, I eased us upward and checked for predators. Time seemed to stand still, and our air-pressure gauge read close to zero. The sun reflected on the surface, sparkling like a million diamonds, so close and yet so far.

We surfaced with the tanks reading empty. Spitting out my mouthpiece, I took in a deep breath, choking on salt spray. I pulled the lift bag under Sophia, and she draped herself over it, spit out her mouthpiece, and gasped for air. Saltwater splashed our faces as I blew into the manual inflation tube, inflating my BC vest.

Tim's helicopter bobbed on its floats alongside the speedboat sixty yards away. I waved and yelled, kicking hard and struggling to hold up Sophia as the current swept us north.

Tim and his sniper sped to us in the boat and cut the engine. They reached over the side and hauled up Sophia as I shoved her upward. Even though she was a slender four-foot-ten, the solid concrete encasing her feet probably made her weigh close to two hundred pounds.

I tossed my mask into the boat, slipped off my vest, and handed it up to Tim, tanks and all. The other guy easily lifted me into the boat, grabbed a first aid kit, and wrapped a gauze bandage around my wounded arm.

"We have to get Sophia home and free her feet before she loses circulation," Tim said. "Do you have an electric drill at the house?"

"Yes." I yanked off my fins. "I can take her back in this boat and meet you at my dock."

Sophia poked me and shouted, "No! Use the helicopter. Bind Gina to the outboard motor and scuttle the boat. Make sure it sinks. She has to disappear forever, or there'll be a Mob war with us in the middle. *Capiche?*" Her bloodshot eyes, irritated from the saltwater, searched our faces.

I assumed she was shouting because she couldn't hear well with her broken eardrums. "She's right. Do what she said and then fly us home staying close to the water."

Tim parked the boat beside his helicopter. "By the way, this is Kelly Mahone, SEAL Team Alpha's best sniper back in the day. He also flies helicopters and airplanes."

Like Tim and all his men, Kelly was fit and ruggedly handsome. I shook his hand. "Thanks for saving my life and bandaging my wound."

He smiled. "My pleasure."

Sophia hugged him and shouted, "Thanks for protecting Jett."

The three of us lifted Sophia into the chopper and wrapped her in a beach towel.

Tim and Kelly did a thorough job binding Gina's body to the engine, using the anchor line. Then they slashed her flesh in several places to make her more appetizing to the sea life. Meanwhile, I jumped in the water and pulled out the boat's drain plug.

Gina DeLuca, top assassin for the Mafia boss Carmine DeLuca, would sleep with the fishes, just like Sophia's husband Vinnie had twenty years ago—a fitting end.

Onboard the chopper, Tim, Kelly, and I opened fire, peppering the boat's hull with bullets. Water gushed into the cabin, and the boat slipped beneath the surface as we took off and raced back to Valhalla.

I leaned close to Sophia. "How are your feet?"

"Can't feel anything below my shins."

We landed on the back lawn, and the men carried Sophia onto the terrace where Snake, Mona, and Karin fussed over her. I ran to the garage and grabbed a hammer and chisel. Gina must not have allowed enough time for the concrete to properly harden. The temperature and pressure changes in the ocean during Sophia's descent and trip back up helped deteriorate it. A few well-aimed hits on the chisel cracked the concrete into small pieces.

Tim and Kelly wrestled the buckets off. Sophia's tennis shoes were wet and stiff.

"I can't feel anything. Help me get these shoes off." She tugged at them.

We worked on removing her shoes, then massaged her feet. Slowly, the color returned.

"Ow! My feet feel like a train ran over them."

"Thank God you're okay." I hugged her and gently touched her ear lobes. "How are your ears?"

She shouted, "They don't hurt now, but I'm pretty sure my eardrums are broken. I can barely hear." She looked at my arm. "You might need a few stitches."

"Forget it. How would I explain a gunshot wound?"

"Let me see." She unwound the bandage. "We'll say we were fishing, and I accidentally scraped your arm with a gaff hook." She turned to Tim. "That'll work, right?"

He checked the wound. "After being in the ocean so long, there's no gunshot residue. It looks like it could've been made by any sharp object. Go with the fishing story."

Sophia asked, "How am I supposed to explain my busted eardrums?"

"Tell the ENT doctor you fell into deep water at the end of the pier while fishing and couldn't clear your ears," Tim suggested. "We don't want it on record that you've been in the ocean."

"Right," Sophia agreed, "but I'd better shower and change first."

"Me too. Do you need help?" I asked.

"I don't think I can walk yet." She reached for Tim.

Tim scooped her into his arms. "Where to?"

"Just a minute." Before we headed upstairs, Sophia looked at everyone. "This thing with Gina never happened. *Capiche?*"

"We get it," Tim said. "Nobody wants a Mob war."

———

Tim drove us to the Emergency Room in my SUV, while Kelly flew their helicopter back to their base of operations. Banyan Isle Hospital was the closest. Their ER was rarely busy, and today was no exception.

Nurse Grace Simms greeted us. "Hi, Jett. What happened to your arm?"

"Fishing mishap with a gaff hook, but we landed a four-foot cobia. Sophia fell off the deep end of the pier and wasn't able to clear her ears. We think she may have burst her ear drums."

Grace picked up the phone. "I'll page an ENT doctor. Have a seat, Sophia." She made the call and turned to me. "Let me check if you need stitches." She led me to an exam room, while Tim waited with Sophia.

I unwound the bandage. "Had any plane rides lately?"

"Nope. Think you could take me for a ride in your uncle's Staggerwing sometime?"

"I'd love to once I get caught up on a few things."

She cleaned my wound, then checked the old cuts on my back.

"Not bad, Jett. That narrow groove will only need a few stitches, and your glass cuts are almost healed. Does your arm hurt?"

"It stings a bit, but it's not bad."

"The doctor will be here in a moment. Any news on who dropped those bodies on your property?"

"Not a clue, and I'm busy getting my house ready for a charity ball. The gang attack caused a lot of damage." I paused. "Would you like a free ticket? The ball will be Saturday night at seven."

"I'd love to come, but I have to work that night. I hope it turns out great for you. Which charity?"

"The West Palm Beach Women's Shelter. They take in battered women and help them get a fresh start. We're planning to add college scholarships for those who'd like to prepare for a career."

"Good idea. Here's Doctor Brooks." She prepared a tray for him to stitch me up.

When I walked out, Sophia and Tim were waiting.

Sophia said, "The doc said my eardrums will heal in a month, and he gave me some antibiotic pills to prevent an infection. I'm good to go. How about you?"

I smiled. "I'm ready to roll. Only needed a few stitches."

"Good." Sophia smiled, her eyes looking red and tired. "Now we can go home and pass out."

Tim drove us home and walked us in as he took a call. He pocketed his phone and said, "Your grounds are secure, and all the damaged security cameras are back up and running. I have four men patrolling the grounds at night until the body bomber is caught. The FBI confirmed again that you have nothing to worry about from the gang in L.A., so you can rest easy."

"Thanks, Tim. What about your wounded men? How are they doing?"

"They survived surgery and should be back to work in a month or so."

"And your shoulder?"

"It's no problem. The stitches come out next week."

"Look, I know you guys were just doing your jobs, but I think you all deserve bonuses. I really appreciate how fiercely you and your men protected me and my people. Please distribute the money equally." I handed him a check I'd been carrying in my purse.

"Thanks, Jett, but this isn't necessary."

"Yes, it is. You and your men literally bled for me. I won't let that go unrewarded." I kissed his cheek.

He smiled. "Well, okay. Thank you. I'll see to it everyone gets their share." He pocketed the check and bid me good night.

# TWENTY-FIVE

When Sophia's sons called to check in, she told them she caught a cold from all the late nights, that her ears were blocked with congestion, and she couldn't hear well. They bought it. And they said Carmine told them Gina was still in Italy.

Mob war averted.

We all turned in early that night, exhausted from the stressful ordeal. Before going to bed, I checked my back in the three-way mirror. The cuts were scabbed over, but they looked ugly, and my left arm had stitches on two sides. I called Cam and asked him to alter my ballgown with a covered back and three-quarter length sleeves.

I didn't wake until the next morning when the dogs licked my arms. "Okay, I get it. We're going outside."

After watching them run around the east grounds, I had breakfast on the terrace. I finished my last bite of toast when my cell rang. It was the nurse from the ER, Grace Simms, calling. "Hi, Grace, what's up?"

"Just checking in to see how you're doing."

"I'm good, just a little sore. Thanks for asking."

She paused a beat. "Hunter was supposed to give me a ride in his Staggerwing today, but he had to fly an airline flight. He said to ask you. Any chance you're free today?"

"Sure. Flying is just what I need. I can be there in an hour."

"Thanks. I'll meet you at Hunter's hangar."

I popped upstairs, dug out my pilot license and medical certificate, and tied my hair into a ponytail. Here in sunny Florida, shorts, a T-shirt, and sneakers were my uniform of the day.

Sophia and the dogs met me in the foyer. "Going somewhere?"

"I'm taking that nurse from the ER up in Hunter's airplane. I'll be back in a few hours."

"Have fun. I'll supervise the work crew and look after the pups."

"And, please, no fishing today." I grinned.

Sophia rolled her eyes.

———

We flew around Lake Okeechobee, then headed for the beach, and Grace loved every minute. Hunter's airplane had a throw-over control yoke that pivoted on a horizontal arm from a vertical stand in the center and could only be positioned in front of one pilot at a time. Rudder pedals were installed on both sides, and the throttle and engine controls were centrally located.

"Sorry I can't give you a lesson, but as you can see, there's only one control yoke." I glanced at her.

"That's okay. I just wanted a ride in this rare antique airplane, and the visibility has to be about fifty miles today."

After cruising along the beach, we headed back to the runway at Aerodrome Estates.

On the way, I asked, "Do you have family here in Florida?"

"No, I'm from California, but my parents moved to Hawaii three years ago."

"I'm surprised you didn't go with them. Hawaii is so beautiful."

She shrugged. "I'd already enrolled in nursing school in Pasadena and earned my RN. After a three-year relationship ended badly, I decided to make a fresh start here in Florida. I started my new job about three months ago."

"Do you like living on Banyan Isle?" I picked up the mic and announced our entry into the traffic pattern on the UNICOM frequency as we entered the downwind leg.

"It's a charming community, and my apartment is only two blocks from the hospital."

I lined up with the runway and lowered the landing gear. The engine noise decreased when I pulled back the throttle.

As we taxied in, I opened my side window. "I have to be gentle on the brakes. With that heavy engine hanging on the front, it doesn't take much to stand this airplane on its nose." I eased it in front of the hangar and let it roll to a stop as I cut the engine.

"That sure was fun, and you're a really good pilot."

"I'm glad you enjoyed it. Flying is always more fun when you do it with someone." I scanned the panel and checked all the switches.

She reached over and patted my thigh. "Want to grab a drink? My treat."

I glanced at my watch and lied, "Sorry. Gotta run. I've got a hot date tonight."

She frowned. "Oh, I didn't know you were dating anyone. Maybe I'll see you when you come in to get your stitches out."

Pretending not to have a clue about her sexual preference, I winked. "I bet you're dating a handsome doctor." I waved as I headed for my car. "Call me when you're free for another ride."

As I drove home, I thought about Grace. Hunter was right about her being interested in me, and I was uncomfortable fending off advances from a woman. If I *had* a boyfriend, the problem would solve itself.

*I wonder if Mike is coming to my ball?*

When I arrived home, Cam Altman waited for me in the great hall. "Hey, girlfriend. The ballgowns are finished, and they look fabulous." He raised his voice. "Come out, ladies."

Karin and Mona glided into the room, and Sophia limped in behind them. Karin's full-skirted cobalt-blue, satin gown sported a plunging neckline with a corset bodice. The tiara adorned with synthetic sapphires matched her eyes.

True to his word, Cam made Mona look like a goth queen in her slender black satin gown with side slits and vertical black leather and blood-red lace panels. Her tiara sparkled with simulated rubies.

And Sophia was every inch an Italian Contessa in her elegant, champagne silk gown styled with a straight skirt that made her seem taller and more regal. The faux diamond tiara she wore added a little more height.

"Wow! You ladies look like Renaissance royalty. And I love those tiaras." I glanced at Cam. "Bravo to the brilliant designer."

He bowed. "And you, my dear Jett, will be the scandalous lady in red." He pulled out a red silk gown that shimmered in the light. The daring, low-cut corset bodice looked like something a bold princess would wear, and the high back and three-quarter sleeves would hide my injuries. A tiara with faux diamonds and rubies sparkled in the box.

"Perfect. I love it. Give me a sec to grab my heels, and I'll try it on." I trotted upstairs and returned with my formal shoes to be sure of the hem length. I felt like a little girl at her first dress-up party.

I slipped into a bathroom and emerged in the gown to plenty of oohs and ahhs after Cam zipped me up. Twirling around, I noticed Snake sitting quietly in his wheelchair, grinning.

"Jett, darlin', you look amazing." He gazed around at the smiling women. "Y'all do. I won't mind wearing a tux now that I see how sexy y'all look in these gowns. I think I can persuade some of my teammates to come down for the ball."

Cam lit up. "I'll need their sizes so they can radiate a James Bond vibe in their custom-fitted tuxedoes." He grinned. "This'll be so fun."

I couldn't argue with that. "And they'll bring in big bucks at the bachelor auction."

"Saturday will be here in four days," Sophia said in a louder than normal voice, still suffering from her broken eardrums. "Are you still providing horse carriages to pick up the local VIPs on the island?"

"Definitely. I want to create a lot of buzz so the next ball will be a sellout." I smiled at Snake. "And none of the other charity balls feature a bachelor auction. This could be a big selling point with all the rich widows."

Cam arched a brow. "I hate to point out the elephant in the room, but what if another corpse drops in? And what if it lands on someone and kills them?"

"I won't let a serial killer cancel my charity ball. Besides, it's been four days since the last drop. The pattern was a body every two days. Maybe the killer has moved on."

"Just four days?" Karin said. "After all that's happened, it seems more like two weeks."

"That means Saturday will be the eighth day since the last body." Snake shot a glance at me. "Jett's right. Serial killers follow a pattern. He's probably moved on."

"Yeah." Mona blew out a sigh. "That must mean he's done."

"Unless there were more bodies after number three, but they landed in the ocean," Sophia said, looking thoughtful.

———

Mike stopped by while we were still in the gowns. "Did I miss the memo? I thought the ball was scheduled for Saturday night."

"It is. Cam delivered the dresses so we could make sure everything fits perfectly." I twirled around. "How do we look in Renaissance couture?"

Mike gazed at our little gathering. "You ladies look spectacular." He saluted. "Good job, Cam."

"Thanks, Mike. Is your tux good to go or do you need a new one?"

"I'm not going to the ball." He shot a glance at Snake. "Will you be out of the wheelchair by then?"

"Yeah. The stitches come out on Friday morning." He wheeled closer to Mike. "Why would you pass up a chance to dance with all these lovely ladies?"

Before Mike answered, I moved closer.

"I was counting on you coming. Your parents and sister will be here, and besides, I need you for my bachelor auction. The money is for the women's shelter in West Palm Beach." I hit him with my best version of big, sad eyes and pouty lips. "Please come."

He hesitated. "Well, okay. I guess I should be there in case the body bomber strikes again."

"We're pretty sure he's done. He isn't sticking to the pattern anymore," Snake said.

"I hope you're right." Mike shot a glance at me. "Valhalla has seen too much craziness since you came home from the Navy."

My cell rang. "Hey, Darcy, what's up?"

"I have an important case for us. You're certified as a rescue diver, right?"

"Yes, I'm rated through P.A.D.I." I waited to hear the particulars.

"The FBI is looking for a guy with a top-secret flash drive. They think he fell in Diamond Lake while fishing and drowned."

"Don't they have their own divers?" I didn't relish the thought of looking for a dead body in a lake populated with alligators and venomous water moccasins.

"John Jameson's family hired my agency because they think the feds are looking in the wrong place, and they're worried gators will feed on their loved one if he isn't found soon."

"Hold on a sec, Darcy."

Tim knocked on one of the glass French doors on the ocean side of the great hall, and I waved him in.

"Perfect timing, Tim. I need Kelly's sniper skills to protect me while I'm diving for a body in a lake. Is he available now?"

Tim paused a moment, taking in the fancy gowns. He checked his tablet. "If you're in a hurry, he can pick you up in the helicopter in fifteen minutes."

I held up my cell. "Let me check with Darcy." I told her about the sniper and helicopter.

"There's a helipad on the north side of the Garnet Marina. I'll meet you there in thirty." She hung up before I had a chance to ask more questions.

I turned to Tim. "I need Kelly ASAP. Tell him he'll be on sniper duty for gators and water moccasins while I'm in the lake, but we can't totally rule out bad guys."

He stared at me for a beat, then checked his sidearm. "I'm coming with you. How can I help?"

"Good thing I refilled my twin 80s with the air compressor in my garage. Get them, a lift bag, my mask, fins, and a speargun. I'll change, grab my BC vest, and meet you in the backyard."

Mike clutched my arm. "Whoa, Jett, what are you getting yourself into?"

"It's part of my private investigator apprenticeship with Darcy McKay. She needs me to dive for a body recovery in Diamond Lake."

"It sounded more complicated than a simple body recovery."

I glanced at my dive watch. "The FBI is involved. Something about a top-secret flash drive. I have to run." I pulled free and headed out.

Snake yelled to Tim as I left. "You probably thought civilian life would be easy. I bet Afghanistan is lookin' better all the time."

# TWENTY-SIX

Kelly landed the helicopter on the helipad in Garnet, and Darcy and her cadaver dog waited for us nearby. Laddie, a yellow Labrador, proudly wore his bright orange work bandana.

Tim had arranged for Kelly to bring two Sig Sauer Cross Sniper/Hunter Rifles and several magazines. I guessed the gang assault had made him wary of missions involving me. His overcautiousness was better than me ending up as gator food.

After meeting the men, Darcy said, "Our boat is at the end of this pier."

Gulls squawked and dived at minnows as we lugged everything down the long pier to a wide pontoon party boat about thirty feet long with a roof covering the rear half of the deck. Bench seats lined the side rails and aft end. A dining table and control console completed the covered half, and a barbeque grill with a portable propane tank stood alone on the bow deck.

Darcy introduced us to the boat captain. "This is Glen. He knows this lake better than anybody, and Laddie can easily move from side to side, sniffing for the body."

The men shook hands.

"Glad to see you guys came well prepared," Glen, a weathered man in his fifties, said. "Wouldn't want gators or snakes to hurt this lovely lady." He tipped his hat to me.

Tim and Kelly checked their weapons as we motored out onto Diamond Lake. The round freshwater lake was the second largest in Florida, and there were no islands to block a clear view of the shoreline on all sides. Paddleboarders cruised close to the town of Garnet along the eastern side and elite Banyan Country Estates along the northern shore. The southern end was heavily forested, and a wildlife refuge bordered the western coast.

Numerous fishing boats dotted the water, except on the western side near the wildlife refuge where federal agents had temporarily blocked public access. Two speedboats towing people on water skis zipped across the lake, avoiding the fishing boats and paddleboarders. Several sailboats glided through the water in the distance.

I gazed around the lake with Darcy's binoculars and spotted several law enforcement boats grouped in a circle around dive flags near the western shore.

Once we reached the center of the lake, away from the marina and its many scents, Glen stopped the boat and waited while Laddie sniffed the air after taking scent from one of Jameson's soiled shirts. A light breeze from the south carried scents of fresh water and jasmine bushes mixed with occasional whiffs of marine fuel.

Laddie barked once, and his nose pointed toward the southern end of the lake about midway between the western and eastern shores.

Glen turned and slowly headed toward the southern coastline. I slipped on my BC vest with the double tanks attached, checked all my gauges, turned on the air, and tested the regulator. Then I turned off the air and checked my speargun.

Kelly had been watching me. "I guess you know the spear will bounce off a gator unless you shoot its belly."

"Yep, that's why I requested you for guardian angel duty." I held up the speargun. "This is in case I encounter bad guys underwater."

Tim sat beside Darcy. "Miss McKay, I'd like to ask you a few questions so we can best protect you and Jett."

"Don't forget Laddie and Glen." She thumbed at her yellow Labrador retriever and the boat captain. "And please, call me Darcy."

"Okay, Darcy, why is the FBI swarming all over the west side of the lake?"

"That's the best fishing area."

"The feds aren't fishing."

"No, but the guy we're looking for is believed to have fallen in and drowned while fishing. He's a defense contractor with top secret info about a new weapon that's stored on a gold flash drive he always wears on a chain around his neck. The feds want to get that flash drive before it falls into enemy hands."

"I see." Tim glanced across the lake to the west. "Do they suspect foul play?"

"They think his death was accidental." She paused. "That's assuming he drowned, but it's been forty-eight hours, and no one has found his body. His family is worried they're looking in the wrong place. They hired me to find him before a gator eats him."

Tim frowned. "Sounds like maybe he was snatched, and his empty fishing boat was left to misdirect law enforcement."

"Anything's possible." Darcy turned to me. "Our primary job is to find and retrieve Jameson's body, but if you spot the gold drive, grab it and zip it into your BC."

Tim and Kelly surveyed the lake with binoculars.

Kelly shook his head. "We don't have much cover if bad actors wanting that flash drive come in hot in a speedboat."

Tim frowned. "He's right. If we get in a firefight, you three should jump overboard, get under the deck between the pontoons, and use the boat for cover. Chances are, the battle won't last long."

Darcy shot a nervous glance at me. "There are men in boats everywhere."

"And you can bet some of them are watching us," Kelly said. "If they see us bring up a body, they'll come in hard and fast."

Darcy held up a radio. "Should I call the FBI and tell them we're about to dive for the body?"

"No. Anyone could be listening," Tim said. "Wait until Jett finishes searching below." He turned to me. "If you find him, bring him up under the deck where no one can see you, and then we'll call the feds for backup."

"Okay." I petted Laddie. "Where is he, boy?"

The dog ran from side to side, sniffing the water as we glided along at 3 knots. After twenty minutes, he barked and pointed his nose at a spot on the water.

Glen cut the power and eased back twenty feet. Laddie sniffed, wagged his tail, and barked again.

Darcy looked at me and pointed. "That's the spot. Laddie can smell the oils and gasses expelled by the body." She studied the water. "Be careful down there."

We were a hundred yards from shore in the shallow end of the lake. The water was clear enough that I could see submerged tree branches when I peered over the side. I pulled dive gloves from my vest pocket and tugged them over my fingers.

Glancing at Tim and Kelly, I asked, "Ready for gator patrol?"

They shouldered their weapons as I rolled backward over the side into the warm lake.

Visibility was about twenty feet as I eased downward toward the branches, assuming the body might be caught underneath. Either that, or a gator had shoved the body in there to let it decompose for a later meal.

The lake depth in this area was thirty feet, and the branches were clustered five feet from the bottom in cooler water. I eased down to avoid disturbing the bottom silt and almost swallowed my mouthpiece when I encountered a hideous, bloated face under the tree debris.

I backed away, exhaling a cloud of bubbles, and got my breathing under control. This had to be John Jameson.

Steeling my nerve, I eased closer. Fish had nibbled out his eyes, and a large-caliber-bullet hole in his forehead led to a much bigger exit wound in the back of his head. Looked like a .50 caliber round from a Barret sniper rifle had done the deed. A small fish exited the gaping head wound and darted away.

I gulped air as my heart pounded. Taking a deep breath, I exhaled slowly, calming myself.

The body was caught inside a debris nest, feet first. Jameson couldn't have drifted under there on his own. Something had shoved him in there, and I prayed it wouldn't be back any time soon.

A glint of gold caught my eye, hanging from his neck as he floated face down. I grabbed the flash drive, pulled the chain over his head, and zipped it into a pocket on my BC vest.

*Jameson was murdered, so why didn't the killer take the flash drive? He must've shot him from a long distance, Jameson fell into the water, and the current carried him away before he could retrieve the prize. That means he could be watching our boat.*

I dreaded the gruesome task ahead—moving the body.

It appeared to be bloated enough that it would float if I freed it from the branches. The job required two hands, so I clipped the speargun to my vest and tugged on Jameson's shoulders. I had him about halfway out when a branch caught on his belt. After easing along his side, I pulled away the branch, and a six-foot water moccasin zipped past me. Could this *be* any scarier?

I glanced around, looking for the venomous snake, and felt a disturbance in the water. A ten-foot gator dived down and clamped his jaws around the bloated torso, releasing a flurry of gas bubbles from the punctured body and obscuring my view for a moment.

Suddenly face-to-face with fierce reptilian eyes, I almost swallowed my regulator.

# TWENTY-SEVEN

Would the gator leave me alone if I swam off and called for help? I backed away, hoping for the best, and felt a disturbance in the water behind me.

A spear flashed past me.

I risked a half-turn to look and spotted an even bigger gator with an unknown scuba diver in its jaws. The diver must've been sneaking up behind me when it attacked him. A fountain of bubbles burst from the man's severed air hose as the huge reptile dragged him away by the head.

*I need to get away from here!*

I unhooked my speargun and turned around. The big gator let go of Jameson and charged me. I was too deep for the snipers to save me. My only chance was to climb onto its back, avoiding its teeth, claws, and powerful tail. I held both ends of my speargun horizontally in front of me like a barrier.

The gator chomped down on the speargun and shook me from side to side as I tightened my grip. The angry beast tried to spit out the speargun, but it was caught between its teeth.

This was my chance.

I let go and tried to climb onto the gator, but it turned and whacked me with its powerful tail, sending me tumbling backward.

Just as I recovered, it charged me again, the speargun still wedged between its teeth. This time, I grabbed its neck and swung myself onto its back, wrapping my arms and legs around the fearsome reptile.

It rolled over and over, trying to throw me off, but I held on. Our struggles stirred up the bottom silt, and visibility went to zero. My world became a spinning, dark-brown nightmare.

I tried not to panic as I clutched its hard scales with all my strength and waited for a chance to grab my dive knife. I dared not reach for it while the alligator rolled and gyrated. I hoped he'd tire soon and stop. Thank God I still had plenty of air because I couldn't help gulping it. Adrenaline surged through me as I clung to the beast.

My armor-plated adversary tried a new tactic and burst onto the surface, splashing and thrashing twenty feet from the boat.

I didn't know if Kelly or Tim could shoot it in the head amidst all the violent gymnastics and with me hanging on. The gator turned and charged the boat, probably intending to knock me off on a pontoon. Trusting my snipers, I let go and rolled off the gator.

Two loud shots echoed off the water, and my stomach twisted into a knot. The gator stopped moving, and I pulled up my mask and peered at its head. Both eyes had been shot out.

I definitely hired the right guys.

Tim yelled, "Better get in the boat before more gators come."

I swam to the boat, and they hauled me up. Tim pulled off my BC vest, and Kelly took off my mask and fins. My hands were useless, the muscles in spasms from gripping the gator, but I managed to hug each man in turn.

"Th-thanks for saving me."

Tim wrapped a towel around me. "You're shaking."

"Terror will do that. And you didn't see the bloated body, the big water moccasin, another huge gator, or the scuba diver who shot a spear at me."

"Where's the enemy diver?" Kelly scanned the water with his scope.

"A twelve-foot gator chomped down on his head and dragged him away."

Tim checked me for injuries. "You okay, Jett?"

I looked behind him. "A speedboat is headed this way, and it doesn't look like a Law Enforcement boat."

Kelly checked his scope and yelled, "Hug the deck."

I blurted, "Darcy and I are qualified with firearms."

"But can you shoot *now*?" Kelly asked.

I looked at my shaking hands. "Maybe."

"Not good enough." Tim pushed me aft. "Hide under the dining table."

Darcy, Laddie, and Glen hid beside me. Darcy held her handgun.

Law Enforcement boats sped toward us from the northwest, several miles away.

Kelly said, "Looks like the bad guys will beat the feds here by about five minutes."

Tim and Kelly crouched behind the side-rail seats on the port side and aimed at the approaching speedboat. Bullets peppered our boat as the attackers raced toward us. When they were twenty yards away, they slowed to a few knots and kept firing.

Kelly and Tim waited until the enemy was close enough to sight on without missing, then returned fire.

Not long into the firefight, Laddie growled at the starboard side of our boat near the boarding gate. I peeked out as a guy in scuba gear surfaced with an assault weapon.

Darcy spotted him too. We opened fire before he had a chance to aim his rifle.

I yelled, "Hey, guys, we've got your six."

Another boat full of shooters raced up to our starboard side. Tim and Kelly retreated to the aft section for more cover, and Darcy and I joined the firefight. Someone shot the barbeque grill's propane tank on our bow. A loud explosion peppered the boat with shrapnel from the metal tank, and a blazing inferno engulfed the bow.

Pinned down under the covered deck, we crouched behind seats, the control console, and the dining table. Bullets buzzed all around us. I prayed the feds would arrive soon.

The men in the enemy boats weren't just shooting at us. They also fired at each other. Apparently, they were rival factions vying for the flash drive.

Then the boat on our starboard side exploded. Someone must've shot the gas tank. It blazed beside us as flames from our burning bow crept ever closer.

Tim yelled, "Jett, put on your scuba gear. You and Darcy can jump in and buddy breathe under the boat."

Just as I donned my BC vest, Law Enforcement boats surrounded us, and a man with a megaphone ordered the shooters to surrender. The feds soon had the scene under control.

I noted Tim and Kelly were bleeding from grazes to their shoulders. Glen looked worse with a through-and-through wound in his left thigh. His pant leg was soaked in blood.

Darcy pulled open a compartment in the console and grabbed the first aid kit. "I've got you, Glen. Sit over here." She helped him onto a seat and began wrapping his wound.

"You guys are bleeding." I grabbed a towel and dabbed at Tim's and Kelly's wounds.

Tim squeezed my hand. "You're bleeding too. Give me that towel."

"I'm so pumped full of adrenaline, I didn't even feel it." I glanced at my grazed right shoulder and bit my lip. All the trauma of the past two weeks caught up with me, and my eyes flooded with tears. I sobbed, "I just wanted to look pretty at my charity ball."

Tim shook his head. "We just survived a massive shootout, and you're worried about how you'll look at the ball?"

I took a deep breath and recovered. "It's important. Mike will be there, and I was hoping—"

"You'll look extra crispy if that fire gets any closer." Kelly grabbed me and lifted me over the side into a waiting FBI boat.

Embarrassed by my emotional outburst, I stared at the deck and shrugged off my BC vest and tanks.

Tim and Darcy helped Glen board, and Kelly lifted Laddie into the nearby boat as Darcy climbed aboard. Tim was the last man off.

I peeked down to where the diver we shot had slipped beneath the surface. A dark cloud of blood marked the spot where he sank. "There's a dead diver down there."

"And several bodies from the exploded boat," a fed said. "Our diver will retrieve them."

"Looks like our pontoon boat will sink before it burns up," I noted, the pontoons were dotted with bullet holes and rapidly taking on water.

Local Law Enforcement pulled alongside us, including Garnet Police Chief Joe McKay, Darcy's father.

Chief McKay jumped aboard and hugged his daughter. "Thank God you're alright."

"Yes, thanks to Tim and Kelly. And Laddie and Jett found Mr. Jameson."

The tank on the dead diver's back bumped against the boat, and a fed glanced down at it. "Where's the missing body, and who's the dead guy?"

"He arrived in that boat with the other shooters." I pointed at the boat on the port side of the burning pontoon boat, then scanned the water nearby. "Jameson is stuck under some branches down … never mind." The body bobbed to the surface. "He's right there." I pointed.

One of their boats idled up and pulled him in. A black body bag lay unzipped on the deck. Several men searched Jameson and then placed him in the vinyl bag.

A man yelled, "No flash drive."

I glanced around at all the feds. "Who's in charge?"

"I am." A man in a white shirt with a navy tie held out his credentials. "Special Agent McKenny. Show my divers exactly where you found the body."

"That won't be necessary." I unzipped the pocket in my BC vest and pulled out the gold chain and flash drive. "Here it is." I handed it to Agent McKenny.

He smiled, looking relieved. "Good job. The FBI could use another skilled diver like you. Interested?"

"No, thanks, but there's something you can do for us."

"You just saved me a world of trouble. Name it."

"Any chance you can reimburse Glen for his pontoon boat?" I

pointed as the burning bow rose out of the water, and the boat slipped beneath the surface.

"I'll include it in our expense report, no problem," the agent agreed.

On the way back, Darcy said, "I've never worked a case like this before. That was a scary shootout."

Tim laughed. "Better get used to it if you intend to keep working with Jett."

I socked his good arm. "That's not fair. The bad guys had nothing to do with me."

"Maybe not, but I'm beginning to think you're a lot like the other Danger Magnet we've worked for." Tim grinned. "You know, the one you recently surpassed as our most dangerous client?"

I sighed. "Well, at least you know working for me is never boring."

Kelly patted my back. "Want to know a secret? We like working for you. It's like being back in the SEALs but with way better pay and fewer rules."

"Good to know." I kissed his cheek. "Thanks for saving my butt."

Kelly said, "Tim and I landed our gator shots simultaneously."

I hugged Tim. "You've saved me so many times, I've lost count."

He grinned. "Just doing my job, and you and Darcy saved us too."

"In any case, you both qualify for hazardous duty pay again. I hope your jobs will be safer from now on."

"We still have to deal with the body bomber. I've got people looking into your former classmates, Grant Gardner and Harrison Hornsby. Either one could be our guy. They both have airplanes that fit the profile, but we have to find a motive."

"I need to sharpen my private investigator skills. I'll check Banyan Isle gossip at the Dye to Be Beautiful Hair Salon and the Upper Crust Bakery. You'd be surprised what those women know. And Delores Delgado, owner of Fit and Fabulous, owes me a favor. She probably hears lots of gossip at her health club."

"Fine, but steer clear of Gardner and Hornsby in case one of them is the killer."

# TWENTY-EIGHT

The following morning, I walked into Dye to Be Beautiful at nine to have my ends trimmed and get a wash and blow dry. Donatella DaVinci, owner, and hairdresser extraordinaire, waved me to her chair.

Before settling in, I greeted her flamboyant business partner, Renaldo Ortiz. "Hey, Renaldo, what's new?"

"You tell me, girlfriend. You're the one with men raining down on your property and gangbangers shooting up your house." He struck a pose, hands on hips, eyebrows arched.

"That's all finished. The gang leader is dead, and although the body drops had nothing to do with him, they, too, have stopped." I turned to Donatella. "The thing is, I wish I knew who killed my friends from prep school and why." I hesitated. "Do either of you know Grant Gardner or Harrison Hornsby?"

"Why?" Donatella turned my chair. "Do you suspect them?"

I explained what I knew about them and their airplanes. "Any thoughts?"

"Grant told me all three murdered men were his clients." Donatella snipped my ends. "He's a financial advisor, you know. Gets his hair cut here every three weeks."

"Oh, then I guess killing his clients wouldn't benefit him." I adjusted the hair bib.

Renaldo quipped, "Unless he stole their money and didn't want to get caught."

"Good thinking," I said. "Lots of murders are either about money or sex."

Renaldo sashayed over to my chair. "I just remembered a juicy tidbit. Ben stole Harry's longtime girlfriend, Marissa Southerland of the Philadelphia Main Line Southerlands."

"Okay, but that's just a possible motive to kill Ben. What about Roger and Chad?"

He paused with a finger on his lips. "If he only killed Ben, he'd be a prime suspect. But if he also killed two guys he had no reason to kill, then it would look like some crazy serial killer did it."

"I don't recall Harry being that diabolical. Hard to believe he'd kill three men just because one stole his girlfriend."

"Well, you know what they say." He checked his nails. "Everyone is capable of murder under the right circumstances."

"Food for thought. On another subject, has a nurse named Grace Simms ever been in here?"

Donatella said, "She comes in twice a month to get her nails done."

I hesitated. "You two have finely tuned gaydar. Do you think she plays for the home team?"

Donatella shrugged. "Maybe, but she's difficult to read. Why do you ask?"

"I took her up for an airplane ride, but I sensed she might be interested in more than flying. I could be misreading her. Hunter and I first met her in the ER, and afterward, he suggested she might be hot for me."

"Jett, honey, your uncle is a god," Renaldo said. "If Grace didn't swoon over *him*, then she's definitely gay."

"Time to lean back over the sink." Donatella tilted my chair and began spraying warm water on my head.

A male client came in for a cut from Renaldo, and our speculations came to a halt.

Before I walked out with smooth, glossy hair, I reminded them about the at-home appointments Saturday at noon for Gwen, my roomies, and me. My next stop was the Upper Crust Bakery two doors down.

It was almost ten-thirty, and there was a lull between the breakfast customers and the lunch crowd. The bakery was deserted.

Perfect timing.

I greeted the owner, Maggie Burns. "Hey, Mags, what's good today?"

"If you're shopping for yourself, then anything chocolate." She chuckled. "Two dozen chocolate caramel brownies just came out of the oven."

"Ooh, sounds yummy. I'll have a brownie and a small glass of low-fat milk. Have you got a minute to join me and catch up?"

"Give me a sec to check the oven timers." She disappeared in the back.

I took a window seat, and she brought a plate of brownies and two glasses of milk.

"I do love the ones with caramel. So moist and chewy," she said. "I heard things have been exciting at Valhalla the past several days."

"Everything has calmed down now, and I'm trying to figure out who killed my three classmates from prep school." I explained about Grant and Harry. "Have you heard anything that might make you think one of them could've done it?"

"Well, you know how they say it's always about sex or money? Christy Carrington represents both."

Her answer surprised me. "You think Christy killed them?"

"No." She patted her lips with a napkin. "Could be Grant killed Roger because Roger stole Christy from him, and they got engaged. Grant was counting on marrying into all that money."

"Interesting."

She lowered her voice. "Rumor has it Grant lost a ton of cash gambling. Christy was the perfect solution to his problem until Roger swooped in."

"That's a possible motive for killing Roger." I arched an eyebrow. "But what about Chad and Ben? Where would they fit in all this?"

Maggie took a sip of milk. "Maybe Grant read about Chad's murder and decided to copy it so no one would suspect him killing Roger."

"But that doesn't explain Ben's murder." I took another bite of the delicious brownie.

"Ben's killer could be the same guy who killed Chad." Her eyes widened. "Ooh, what if Harry killed Chad and Ben, and Grant killed Roger, and neither one knows what the other did? I think I saw a Hallmark movie like that."

"That's an interesting theory, but then what were Harry's motives?" I sighed. "I think we'd better leave that to Hallmark."

Maggie thought a moment. "Maybe you should talk to Dolores Delgado. Grant and Harry workout in her club." She smirked. "Dolores is a licensed masseuse and likes to give free rubdowns to the hot guys. She calls it a perk for VIP members."

*I'll keep that in mind when I talk to her.*

Three customers came in, and Mags jumped up to wait on them. I finished my brownie, paid my bill with a generous tip, and left.

Next stop: the Fit and Fabulous Health Club.

Dolores rushed over when I walked in. "Jett, how nice to see you. Thinking of joining?"

"May we talk privately in your office?" I scanned the main floor, not expecting to see Grant or Harry, but checking anyway. They weren't there.

Dolores took my arm. "Come with me. My office is on the second floor where I can observe most of the main exercise area." She led me up a curving staircase to her glass-enclosed office.

I settled in a chair across from her desk. "Here's the thing—I'm hoping you can help me figure out who's been killing my prep-school classmates and dropping them on my land."

"Me?"

I told her everything I knew about Grant and Harry. "But Harry only seems to have a motive for killing Ben, and Grant for killing Roger."

Her face blanched. "Okay look, I know I owe you after that fiasco with the mayor, but you didn't hear this from me."

"Go ahead." I pretended to zip my lips.

She glanced down at the main floor. "Harry came in one day and worked out like he was beating the machines to death. I said he seemed tense and suggested a deep massage. While I worked the knots out of his back, I coaxed him into telling me why he was so upset."

"Was it something one of his old classmates did?"

"Turns out Chad, Roger, Ben, and Grant voted Harry down when he was up for membership in the old, prestigious Banyan Isle Men's Club. The vote was supposed to be kept secret, but Harry's father is a member and told him who voted against him. He said it only took four nay votes to be rejected," Dolores explained.

"Hardly seems worth killing over."

"Harry told me the Banyan Isle Men's Club is as exclusive and influential as the Skull and Bones Society at Yale. Membership practically guarantees business success and high social standing."

"But he owns a chain of fast-food restaurants. Doesn't sound like he needed the membership."

"He wanted something more prestigious. They humiliated him, and he missed out on a chance to own a chain of high-end steak houses. The seller wouldn't close the deal when he heard Harry's membership had been rejected."

"I can see how he'd feel angry and betrayed and want revenge, but murder is so extreme."

She sucked in her breath. "Not when you consider he also lost the love of his life to Ben Aaronson. All on the same day. Can you imagine?"

I leaned forward. "Do you recall if all this happened before the first murder?" Could this be the lead I'd been looking for?

"Hold on." She checked her ledger. "I keep records of all my massage clients. He was on my table the same day he had all the trouble, and that was one week before the first victim, Chad, was dropped into your tree." She pulled out newspaper articles she had in a drawer. "I know because I kept clippings about all the murders."

I glanced at her news collection. "Dolores, this is important. You have to share this information with Detective Mike Miller, only please don't tell him I was here asking about it. He'll be angry if he finds out I've been looking into the murders."

She frowned. "I remember Mike from when he questioned me about the mayor's murder back in January, but how am I supposed to explain what made me think Harry might be the body-drop killer?"

"Just say you were looking through your clippings and you remembered that day Harry was at your club. Ask Mike to look into whether Harry is a pilot. That way you won't seem to know too much, and Mike will take a close look at whatever alibis Harry gives him."

She chewed her lower lip. "I'll do it, but only if Mike keeps my name out of it. I don't want to lose club members over this."

"I understand, but it all depends on whether the evidence indicates Harry is the killer. If he is, you don't want a murderer in your health club. Besides, you could be in danger if he remembers he told you about his motives. That's why you should go to the police right away."

She sighed, checked her smartwatch, and gathered the clippings. "I'll go over there now."

I stood and patted her back as we walked out. "Dolores, you may have solved the murders. I hope this puts an end to the killings. Thank you, and please remember, don't mention me to Mike."

I drove home wondering if Harrison Hornsby was the killer.

# TWENTY-NINE

Sophia and the puppies greeted me when I walked through the front door. As I fussed over the dogs, she asked, "Did you learn anything about the murders?"

"Boy, did I ever." I checked my watch. "I might know who the killer is. See what you think when I go over everything at lunch." I noted she'd stopped limping. "Looks like your feet are back to normal."

"They're still a tad bit tender, but no problem walking now."

The doorbell boomed Wagner's famous tune, and we let Tim in.

"I have a lot to tell you." I led him out through the great hall to the terrace and greeted everyone.

Once we were settled around the table, I shared everything I'd learned from my friends at the beauty salon, the bakery, and the health club.

I gazed at all the surprised faces. "That's all of it. What do you think?"

"I'd like to check if Harry's airplane was flown on the nights the bodies were dropped," Tim said.

Sophia joined in, "We need to find out what he was doing when the men were killed."

Snake cleared his throat. "Have you told Mike about this?"

"I asked Dolores Delgado to tell him and leave me out of it. Maybe he'll bring Harry in for questioning today." I glanced at everyone. "Remember to act surprised if Mike shows up and tells us he arrested him."

Mona broke in, "So that nerdy guy at your school had nothing to do with the murders?"

I thought about it. "What if the reason nobody can find George Stavros is that he's wearing concrete overshoes on the bottom of the ocean?"

Karin weighed in, "I thought you said George disappeared over two years ago. That would mean Harry killed him long before the others."

"Okay," Sophia said, "but what was his motive?"

I shrugged. "It's just a theory." A terrible thought hit me. "What if he's been killing since prep school, and he killed Mike's younger brother, Matt?"

"How was Matt killed?" Snake asked.

My voice broke as I answered, "He was strangled with a wire garrote, just like Chad, Roger, and Ben."

———

That evening, Mike stopped by and asked me to invite Gwen over. I called her, and she drove next door and joined us.

"Do you want to meet in the study like last time?" I asked Mike.

"This time, I'd like to include everyone." He strode into the great hall and settled on a leather chair in front of the wall covered with Viking weapons. My parents gazed down on us from the painting above the fireplace mantel, their eyes radiating kindness, contrasting with all the weaponry.

As soon as my roomies were seated, Mike revealed, "I received new information today on a possible motive for the body-drop murders." He told us about Harrison Hornsby.

"Were you able to find out if he flew his airplane on the nights in question?" Snake asked.

"He flew it all three nights, but he claimed the flights were to deliver various items to his restaurants." He paused. "And it turns out Grant Gardner flew his airplane those same nights too."

"But Grant didn't have a motive to kill all of them, did he?" Gwen asked.

"Grant has a serious gambling problem, and all three victims were his primary clients. I got a court order for a forensic audit of his accounts. If he stole their money, that's a strong motive."

Sophia asked, "What about that geeky guy from prep school, George Stavros? Any chance one of them killed him too?"

Mike arched a brow. "Why would you ask that? Neither man had a motive for George, and he disappeared over two years ago."

Sophia shrugged. "Could be the killer started years ago and has been killing anyone who got in his way. We don't know if George did something that earned him a garrote."

Mike's face paled. "If that's true, one of them might've killed my brother ten years ago. Both suspects were in the same class with him, and Matt was killed with a garrote just like Chad, Roger, and Ben."

I jumped in. "Grant and Harry weren't pilots back in prep school. That would explain why Matt's killer, if it was one of them, didn't drop him from an airplane."

Mike's jaw tightened. "When I was looking into George, I discovered that two months after he was fired from Bright Investments, Harold Bright was murdered. He was killed with a garrote. That was around the same time George disappeared. I suspected George, but what if both were killed by Grant to clear the way for his financial business?"

"I guess you'll have to go back and see if Grant and Harry have alibis for the night Bright was killed," Gwen said. "It'll be harder to dig up a motive for killing George."

Mike sighed. "Gwen, I need you and Jett to think about your sophomore year in prep school when Matt was killed. Can you recall any bad blood between my brother and Grant or Harry or any beefs one of them might've had with George?"

I thought hard. "Matt was the second-string quarterback, but he played a lot after the starter was injured. There might've been some jealousy since Grant and Harry rarely played that year."

Gwen interrupted, "And I think they were interested in the same girls, but Matt always won out."

A memory popped into my head. "George was responsible for including some unflattering photos of Grant and Harry in the yearbook. I remember they got teased a lot over that."

Gwen said, "None of that would be enough to cause a normal person to kill a classmate, but a person with psychological issues might think he had ample reasons to murder a rival or a perceived enemy."

Mike glanced around the room. "This conversation took quite a turn from my original premise. I had a hunch including all of you would pay off."

Snake asked, "What's your next move?"

"I'll bring both men in for questioning again and see if I can get one of them to crack." He shook his head. "That probably won't work because they retained expensive lawyers. Plan B is a deep dive into their years at Banyan Isle Prep."

"Is there anything we can do to help?" I wasn't sure if he wanted us in the hunt.

"I don't want to put any of you at risk, but if you happen to hear something through the grapevine, let me know."

Mona added, "You might want to check with hair salons, bakeries, health clubs, bars, you know, places where your suspects go on a regular basis. Those places are great sources of gossip." She shot me a quick glance, knowing I wanted Mike to have all the info without realizing it came from me.

He nodded. "In the meantime, stay vigilant. We still don't know why the killer is dropping the bodies on Jett's land." Mike looked from me to Gwen. "You two could be targets. There are too many coincidences stemming from your prep school days."

After Mike left, we put our heads together and tried to devise a strategy to catch the killer.

Mona volunteered, "I can hack into their business records and see if anything raises an alarm."

Sophia offered, "I'll call Marco and check if the Mob has anything on Grant or Harry."

"You could ask the FBI to put surveillance teams on both men," Snake suggested.

Gwen frowned. "The feds won't get involved without more evidence."

"I'll visit the airports where they keep their airplanes and see what I can learn."

"You're not going alone." Sophia patted her pistol. "I'm coming with you."

Snake grinned. "Good idea. Our little dead-eye diva never misses."

"Who are you calling a diva?" Sophia said, fists on hips.

Snake rolled his chair over and gave her a hug. "I meant that in the most flattering way possible. You know I adore you."

She smiled. "Well, okay then."

I went to bed feeling like we might be closing in on the body-drop killer.

# THIRTY

I drove with Sophia out to Aerodrome Estates right after breakfast. The plan was to borrow my uncle's cabin biplane and fly into the airports where Grant and Harry kept their airplanes.

I decided to check Grant's Howard DGA 15-P first at Naked Lady Ranch, a pilot community near Stuart, and then head back to North County Airport where Harry kept his Twin Beech cargo plane. Grant's Howard, a vintage airplane that comfortably carried four passengers, was tall and muscular with a high wing, radial engine, two main wheels, and a tailwheel that resulted in the airplane sitting nose high on the ground. It had the same engine and cabin size as my uncle's Staggerwing. I looked forward to admiring its beautiful design.

When we settled in the cockpit of Hunter's plane, I glanced at Sophia and realized she'd need a seat cushion so she could see out the windshield. I grabbed one from behind the bench seat aft of the two front seats.

She held up her huge purse. "I've got extra mags in here. Where should I put this?"

"This is supposed to be a fact-finding mission. I'm not expecting a shootout."

"Don't forget what happened in Miami back in January. You can never have too many bullets," she said with a smile.

"Good point." I returned her smile. "Put your purse behind your seat and buckle up."

On the taxi out, I pointed at the hand crank for rolling down her side window, like the ones in old cars, to cool off the cockpit while we were on the ground. We'd close the side windows before flight because the air sound would be too noisy.

"I love this." Sophia rested her arm on the windowsill. "It's like riding in a grand old Cadillac."

I laughed. "You look like you belong here."

I checked her seatbelt and pulled onto the east/west runway. "Staggerwing November One Hotel Victor is taking off on runway niner," I announced on the common UNICOM frequency for the uncontrolled field. Pilots tuned to that radio frequency to announce their movements at airports without control towers.

We flew east, then turned north and headed up the coast, enjoying the view of the ocean and beaches. It wasn't long before we entered the traffic pattern for Naked Lady Ranch. I made a smooth landing on 9, the east/west grass runway, and taxied to the clubhouse.

Sophia turned to me. "Why is this airport community called Naked Lady Ranch?"

"It was once a nudist colony."

She hopped out and glanced around. "Think we'll see naked people?"

I laughed. "Not anymore."

Two fully dressed men met our airplane. One said, "Welcome to Naked Lady Ranch. That Staggerwing sure is a beauty."

"Thanks, my uncle keeps her in top shape." I smiled and introduced us. "We were hoping to catch Grant Gardner here and check out his Howard."

"He keeps it in that hangar over there by his house." He pointed at a house about halfway down the runway. "His airplane's in pristine condition."

The other man seemed more cautious. "Do you know Grant?"

"We were in the same class at Banyan Isle Prep School all four years."

"Is he home?" Sophia asked.

"Afraid not," the more talkative one said. "Saw him drive away about an hour ago."

"That's too bad. Does he fly much?" I asked, glancing around.

"Hardly ever during the day," the tight-lipped guy said.

Mr. Talkative said, "He likes to fly at night when it's cooler and there's not much flight traffic."

"Makes sense. How often does he go up?" Sophia asked.

Mr. Talkative rubbed his chin. "At least one night a week, but more recently he flew every other night."

"Yeah, that's right. I live near Grant, and I heard his airplane return late several nights," the other guy agreed.

"I'd love to fly in his beautiful plane sometime," Sophia said. "Does he ever take passengers?"

Tight-lip shrugged. "Hard to say. When he pulls out of his hangar and heads for the runway, it's too dark to see into the cockpit."

I glanced at my watch. "It's been nice chatting with you guys. Tell Grant we stopped by, and if you ever get to Aerodrome Estates, visit Hunter Vann's Flight School and Maintenance Shop. It's owned by my uncle."

We hopped back into the airplane and headed to North County Airport. Our aerial view showed the airfield covered a lot of ground with many rows of private hangars. Our best bet to find Harry's airplane would be to talk to mechanics at the aircraft maintenance shop located beside the main operator on the field.

To save wear on the tires, I landed on grass runway 8L and parked near the terminal. We hopped out and glanced around.

A man in coveralls met our airplane. "Hey, there."

"Hi." I pointed at the building. "Is that the maintenance shop for the field?"

"Sure is." He thumbed at a big, open hangar. "Mighty fine airplane you've got here. They don't make 'em like this anymore."

"Thank you." I introduced us. "We're looking for Harry Hornsby. He keeps a Beech 18 in a hangar here. Do you know him?"

"Yep, I maintain his airplane." He scrutinized us. "How do you know Harry?"

"I went to prep school with him, and I live down the street from his parents on Banyan Isle." I gave him my best smile. "I just love old airplanes, especially ones with Pratt & Whitney R-985 engines, and Harry's has two."

"Yep, that Twin Beech is a real workhorse. He uses it to deliver stuff to all his restaurants around the state."

"Must keep you busy."

"Harry puts a lot of hours on his airplane, but it mainly just needs lots of oil." He paused. "Lucky for me, he does most of his flying at night, so that gives me all day to work on his plane when it needs it."

*Ah ha!* I gazed toward several rows of hangars. "Do you know which hangar is Harry's? As long as we're here, we'd like to stop by and say hi."

"He always taxis the plane here when it needs work." He turned and pointed. "I think he's in the middle of one of the farthest rows. If he's there, the main door will be open."

"Thanks. We'll give it a shot. Nice meeting you." I waved as we walked away.

Sophia and I wore holsters that hooked on the inside of our waistbands at the small of our backs. Our shirts hung outside our shorts, concealing the weapons.

She adjusted her shorts and unzipped her purse. "Don't forget I have extra ammo if we need it."

"You're too much." I chuckled. "I'm not worried. This airport is probably monitored with security cameras, and it's a sunny morning. He's not going to try anything." We headed down the road that led to the last row of hangars. "We'll start on the farthest row and work our way back."

I was surprised there weren't any CCTV cameras as we walked past each row of hangars. The deep rumbling of two radial engines caught my attention. I turned as a Beech 18 disappeared past the far end of the nearest row, probably taxiing in from the runway. The polished aluminum airplane had two pilot seats and could hold six to eight passengers, but Harry's probably had the passenger seats removed for cargo space. The tailwheel aircraft stood nose-high during ground operations.

"Darn! I didn't see the tail number, but it must be Harry's airplane. There are only about fifty Beech 18s still flying commercially worldwide."

"Hurry, let's see which hangar he parks in." Sophia trotted to the next row with me rushing to catch up.

Again, we just missed a good look at the airplane as it passed a building on the far end. Sunlight reflected off its shiny silver skin. We rounded the corner on the last row just as a big hangar door finished closing midway from the end.

Sophia pointed. "He parked in there. Let's check it out."

I stopped and smoothed my hair. "How do I look?"

"Lovely, like always." She smiled. "If it's Harry, he'll be happy to see you."

We strolled over like we didn't have a care in the world. When we got close enough, I tried the handle on the side door. Unlocked. I peeked inside.

"Looks like Harry's airplane, but I can't see the tail number from here. Let's go in and say hello." I led her inside.

We left the glare of the sun, and it took a moment for my eyes to adjust to the dark hangar before I realized my mistake. Men armed with submachine guns stood in the shadows near a van, and it looked like they were unloading drugs from the airplane.

My heart rate skyrocketed, and I grabbed Sophia's arm. "Wrong hangar."

We tried to back out, but they spotted us.

"What are you doing here?" An angry looking guy pointed his weapon at us.

"Sorry, we're looking for a friend's Twin Beech." I eased backward with Sophia at my side, our hands up.

"Stop right there. You two aren't going anywhere."

"You're not the boss of us, dirtbag." Sophia yanked me behind two big oil drums.

"Crap," I whispered, my heart pounding as I crouched down. "Did you see those weapons?"

A quick nod. "And the drugs."

One of the men shouted, "We're within our rights to shoot trespassers, but if you come out now, we won't hurt you."

"Sure, and then we can all go to church together on Sunday," Sophia yelled.

I poked her. "Why are you antagonizing them?"

She whispered, "I'm stalling so you can plan our escape."

I glanced at the open man door twenty feet behind us. "If we run for it, they'll have clear shots at us."

"Last chance before we ventilate you," a man warned.

I sneaked a quick peek as the gunmen moved in our direction, aiming at the oil drums and moving with confidence, probably assuming we were unarmed. *Crap!*

My stomach did a flip-flop as I drew my Glock and sucked in a deep breath.

In the next second, bullets peppered our metal oil drums, the staccato sound deafening in the metal hangar. Dense oil prevented bullets from passing through the back side of the barrels.

Sophia crouched low and peeked out just long enough to shoot the guy who told us to come out. One round into his head. Her trademark.

No turning back now. Bullets whizzed past us, some ricocheting off the walls.

I seized the moment and fired at another shooter, hitting him in the chest. He went down with his finger on the trigger, creating a metal storm that sounded like we were in a live war zone.

Resisting the urge to cover my ears and curl into the fetal position, I kept firing to stop the gunmen from advancing on us.

Thick oil pooled on the concrete floor, leaking from bullet holes in the oil drums, and more shots pinged into the metal wall behind us. Our bare knees and lower legs were inches away from the ever-widening black puddle. I glanced over at Sophia, whose eyes were wide. She kept firing, despite her fear.

The remaining shooters crouched behind the airplane and van.

"We need a diversion. Cops will be here soon." I slid my empty magazine to her.

She dropped it in her handbag and handed me a full one. "Aim for the van's gas tank."

We both knew we had to escape before the cops arrived. I inserted a full mag and fired at the van. Calling 9-1-1 wasn't an option. We couldn't risk the cartel getting our names from a police report.

Sophia slapped in a fresh mag. "Run outside. I'll cover you." She fired a salvo.

Some of her bullets must've hit the plane's fuel tank. A deafening explosion rocked the hangar, followed by searing heat and flames. The blast knocked over the heavy barrels and blew us backwards into a corner close to the open man door.

I grabbed her hand. "Hurry!"

We scrambled to avoid burning oil and ducked out before the smoke and fire reached us.

"This way!" I led Sophia between hangars onto a different row. We holstered our pistols and sprinted across the access road, ducking behind closed structures as sirens blared. I didn't see any security cameras covering the mid-sections of hangar rows.

Out of breath, we sat on shaded grass behind a metal building.

"Whew, that was a close one." Sophia pulled out a tissue and wiped her forehead.

"Those drug dealers must have someone from airport security on their payroll, but I'm surprised there were no CCTV cameras near any of the hangars, which is good for us." I checked my pistol in the holster under my shirt.

Sophia said, "I didn't notice any security cameras either."

"We'd better leave quietly while everyone is busy dealing with the fire."

She glanced back at the rising black smoke. "We don't want drug dealers after us."

"The intense heat will melt the bullets we fired, so we can't be tied to the gun battle." My hands shook as I took a moment to improve our appearance. "Let's go."

We strolled back to Hunter's airplane, climbed in, and taxied out. In minutes, we were airborne. I circled around the traffic pattern, and we watched the fire department fight the raging fire. Engulfed in flames, the hanger roof had buckled.

"Someone's valuable drug cargo burned up, and we don't want to be blamed." I banked the airplane. "I'll land at Okeechobee Airport on the north side of the lake, and we'll order lunch at the Landing Strip Café and take some time to recover."

"Good idea." Sophia glanced back at the billowing black smoke. "It'll take a while for the adrenaline to wear off." She looked at her shaking hands. "Outings with you are never boring."

"Right back at you."

# THIRTY-ONE

My hands still shook as we sat at an outside table under a sun umbrella. We watched airplanes come and go while we ordered sandwiches and iced tea.

"Uh oh." I pointed at an airplane making a low pass over the runway. "Are they looking for us?"

"You're being paranoid." Sophia watched the airplane fly away. "It's too soon for the cartel to know about the hangar fire. Besides, we got away clean."

"You're right. I guess my nerves are spooking me." Once my heart rate returned to normal, I said, "Seems like either Grant or Harry could be the killer. We need more evidence."

"I have an idea that'll guarantee no bodies will drop on our ball." Sophia smirked. "Call Harry and Grant, apologize for the last-minute invitations, and explain two men withdrew from the oh-so-important bachelor auction. Ask them to fill in."

I thought it over as I nibbled my sandwich and took a sip of iced tea. "That could work. They can't drop a body on us if they're at the event."

"And the place will be swarming with armed guards." She grinned. "Problem solved."

"Unless the killer backs out."

"Right," Sophia agreed.

"I'll get them drunk at the ball, and maybe one will slip up and reveal something to help us solve this." I drained my iced tea.

Sophia grabbed a handful of my long hair and sniffed it. "Uh oh." She sniffed her shirt. "We smell like smoke. How do we explain this?"

"I have a key to Hunter's hangar apartment. We can take showers while our clothes are in his washer. Then we'll arrive home squeaky clean."

"And if he comes home while I'm wearing nothing but a towel, I'll be okay with that." She grinned.

———

Sophia wore Hunter's green T-shirt with Antique Aircraft Association stenciled on the front. It looked like a baggy dress on her, hanging six inches below her knees. I wore his U.S. Navy T-shirt, and it covered me down to about eight inches above my knees.

When the dryer's timer dinged, I retrieved our clothes, and we headed for Hunter's bedroom.

I froze when I walked through the door, and Sophia bumped into me. Hunter must've just returned home from work. Dressed in his airline captain uniform, he was seated on his bed, holding one of my sneakers and one of Sophia's.

Her jaw dropped. "Whoa, you sure look sexy in that pilot uniform. Yowza."

He stood and arched an eyebrow. "Just when I thought I'd run out of surprises in my bedroom, I walk in and find two pairs of women's sneakers reeking of acrid smoke and engine oil. It's obvious you just washed your clothes. What's going on here?"

"Um, uh, we'll get changed in your guestroom, and then we'll meet you in the living room and explain." I rushed out, and Sophia followed me.

After dressing as fast as possible, Sophia said, "Shoot, we left our sneakers in Hunter's bedroom."

"He's probably changing out of his uniform. We'll get them in a few minutes." I led her to the living room.

Hunter had changed into shorts and a T-shirt and was already seated on a sofa. Our shoes were on the hardwood floor in front of him. He looked at me. "Jett, did you fly my airplane today?"

I bit my lip. "I hope that was okay."

"You're always welcome to fly it, but why does it smell like it's been in a fire?" He paused. "Where did you go?"

"We, um, uh." I glanced at Sophia.

He crossed his arms and arched his eyebrows. "Did you fly into North County Airport earlier today?"

Sophia sighed. "Face it, Jett, we're busted. May as well tell him everything."

Hunter struggled to keep a straight face. "Did you two have anything to do with that hangar fire?"

"We sort of blew up the hangar," Sophia confessed, "but in all fairness, the bad guys shot at us first. We were just defending ourselves."

I jumped in. "The thing is, no one can know we were there because drug dealers own that hangar, and they lost several men and a lot of drugs today."

Hunter sighed. "Tell me everything."

We did.

"Sounds like you got away clean. We'll keep this between us, but please, no more dangerous snooping missions." He gave us his most serious look.

"Right. We'll let the cops sort this out." I glanced at Sophia. "I've had more than enough excitement this week anyway."

"Tell him about the shootout on Diamond Lake," Sophia prompted.

He rolled his eyes. "Really, Jett? What the heck?"

"It was part of my apprenticeship with Darcy." I told him all about it and added, "I doubt anything like that will ever happen again."

"Well, it's a good thing Snake set you up with those retired SEALs. They're doing a great job. Keep them on duty, even if the body-drop killer is caught soon." He paused. "I almost forgot—Samantha Starr is coming to your ball. She called me and said she's home from Scotland for a week, so I invited her."

I laughed. "Oh, good, I'll finally get to meet the other Danger Magnet."

"Right, you two have a lot in common in that regard." He stood, pulled me up to him, hugged me, then did the same with Sophia. "Stay safe. I'll keep your secret."

I chewed my lip. "What if Mike stops by and checks if our weapons were fired recently?"

"No worries. I'll clean them before you leave, and we'll replace the rounds you fired." Hunter led us to his workshop.

Thirty minutes later, we were on our way home with clean Glocks, full magazines, clean clothes and bodies, and sneakers that had been wiped clean and treated with odor-eliminating spray.

Problem solved.

———

The moment Sophia and I walked through the front door, the puppies smothered us with wet doggie kisses.

Karin hurried over and whispered, "Mike's waiting for you in the great hall. He doesn't look happy."

Sophia and I exchanged glances. "We'd better get our story straight before we go in there." I paused, thinking. "Tell him we went for a flight in Hunter's Staggerwing, and when we stopped at North County Airport, we heard an explosion, got scared, and left. Then we flew to Okeechobee Airport for a sandwich. After we returned the plane, we visited with Hunter. End of story."

Karin's jaw dropped. "You didn't blow up that hangar, did you? It's all over the news."

Sophia put her finger to her lips and nodded. Then she said in a loud voice, "No, absolutely not," and grinned.

Mike appeared in the foyer. He leaned in close and sniffed my hair. "Where have you two been?"

"Out flying around in Hunter's biplane," I said. "The view along the beach was fabulous. Saw a bunch of sharks too."

"Uh huh, and did you land at North County Airport?"

Sophia gave him our agreed-upon story and then asked, "So what happened there?"

"It looks like somebody shot a bunch of drug dealers and blew up everything in their hangar." He gave us a hard look.

"How do you know they were shot if everything got blown up?" I asked.

"The cops recovered lead blobs from several bullets. Too bad they're too damaged to do a ballistics match." He looked us over. "Are you armed?"

We reached behind our backs and pulled out our pistols.

He held out his hand. "Let me see those." He sniffed each weapon and checked the magazines. Relief flooded his face. "I can't tell you how glad I am your weapons haven't been fired today. I'd hate to see you pulled into that hornet's nest with the FBI, DEA, ATF, and Colombian drug cartel. Looks like somebody in Airport Security was dirty, but they don't have a clue who attacked the drug dealers."

"Have you learned anything new about Grant or Harry?" I asked, changing the subject.

"Let's sit down and talk." He led us into the great hall and told us everything I already knew from talking to friends at the beauty shop, bakery, and health club.

The dogs snuggled between Sophia and me on the sofa. She ruffled Pratt's fur and asked, "Are you going to arrest Harry?"

Mike frowned. "I don't have enough evidence. We're waiting for him to make a mistake. Meanwhile, keep your guards up. There's a reason all the bodies were dropped here. We just haven't figured it out yet."

"Sophia has an idea that might keep everyone safe at the charity ball." I glanced at her. "She suggested I invite Grant and Harry and ask them to participate in the bachelor auction. They can't drop bodies on us if they're at the event."

"Inviting them is a good idea," Mike said. "Plenty of armed

security. But auctioning off dates with potential murderers? I don't think so."

Sophia shook her head. "Didn't think about that."

I jumped back in, "I'll invite them and explain we need to even out the ratio of men to women so everyone can get a chance to dance."

"That sounds good," Karin agreed.

Mike sighed and looked at me. "My job was a lot easier before you came back."

"Easier or boring?" I smiled. "You have to admit life on Banyan Isle isn't dull now."

"Right. Keeps you on your toes." Sophia grinned.

Snake walked in with Mona.

Sophia stared. "Where's your wheelchair?"

"Don't need it anymore." He patted his leg. "Stitches come out tomorrow morning."

"Good." Sophia grinned. "Save a dance for me, sugar buns."

# THIRTY-TWO

F riday was a flurry of activity with last minute preparations for the ball. All the house repairs had been completed, and the decorations were in place. Snake's stitches were removed that morning, and his SEAL buddy arrived mid-afternoon. Handsome with killer abs, green eyes, and thick black hair, Six-Pack would be a big hit at the ball.

Moments after he arrived, another hot guy rang my doorbell. I opened the door to Justin Newton, early thirties, six-four and fit with brown hair and blue eyes. A P.A.D.I. Tec Deep Instructor, he helped me two months ago with a deep dive on my parents' crashed jet.

"Hi, Justin. Thanks for agreeing to participate in the bachelor auction tomorrow night. I really appreciate it." I thumbed at my SEAL friends and introduced them. "They'll be with you in the auction."

Everyone shook hands as Cam rolled in. He had their tuxedoes ready. I don't think I've ever seen him look so excited about fitting clients. He seemed disappointed everything fit perfectly on the first try.

Cam checked them over in their flawless tuxedoes. "You guys will bring in a fortune at the bachelor auction."

I grinned. "Thanks for bringing the tuxes, Cam, and thanks for coming, guys. The auction is for a good cause, and I'm sure you'll have a fun time at the ball."

"Yes, we will." Cam gave me a kiss on the cheek and departed.

Justin changed and slipped his tux into a clothes bag. "I'll see you tomorrow night."

I waved goodbye and turned back to my new houseguest.

Six-Pack hugged me. "Good to see you, Jett." He glanced at Snake and back to me. "Has your wounded patient behaved himself?"

"Of course not, but Mona is keeping him out of trouble." I smiled at Snake and Mona. "It hasn't been all fun and games for him. Poor guy had to help us in a big shootout with a Korean gang."

It was obvious Snake and Mona were a couple, and he politely took her hand.

"You forgot to mention the five king cobras and all the bodies fallin' from the sky." Snake shrugged. "We still aren't sure who's droppin' them."

"What bodies?" Six-Pack asked.

"Change out of your tuxes and come out to the terrace. We'll get everyone cold beers and fill you in." I waited and led them outside.

After listening to our tales of giant snakes, gang attacks, and falling bodies, Six-Pack chuckled. "Sounds like your ball might be a lot more exciting than I thought."

"All the guys on my security team are retired SEALs. They saved my butt several times already, and they'll be on duty tomorrow night. Should be fine."

"Hah!" Snake laughed. "You actually believe that after everything that's happened since you returned home from the Navy?"

"Things have quieted down a lot in the last few days." I arched an eyebrow.

"*Really*? What about the shootout on the lake and your adventure with Sophia yesterday?" He smirked.

"You aren't supposed to know about yesterday. We have to keep that a secret, unless you *want* a drug cartel after us." I arched an eyebrow. "Haven't you been in enough gun battles recently?"

"Not as many as you." He grinned. "Who blew up the hangar, you or Sophia?"

"She did, sort of, but it was an accident. The shootout was intense." I waved my arms for emphasis. "Bullets flew everywhere, and some hit the plane's fuel tanks. There was already a lot of spilled oil from bullet-riddled barrels, and a van was parked close to the airplane."

Sophia strolled in and added, "When the airplane exploded, it blew up the van and set all the leaked oil on fire. Lucky for us, we were close to an open side door and got away clean."

Six-Pack grinned at Sophia. "You must be the little Mafia spitfire Snake told me about." He pulled out a chair for her. "He said you never miss with your Glock, and you make awesome cannoli."

Sophia smiled. "That's me."

"An honor to meet you, Sophia." He hesitated. "I'm curious, how many guys have you shot since you moved in here?"

She shrugged. "I lost count after yesterday. Why? You checking if my gun belt has more notches than yours?"

He laughed. "Woman, you're one of a kind. We're gonna get along just fine."

She grinned. "I love Navy men."

I cleared my throat. "Sophia's date for the ball is headed this way."

Karin ushered John Caldarelli onto the terrace. He looked dapper in a navy suit. I introduced the men to our new arrival.

John shook their hands then leaned over for a quick peck on Sophia's cheek. "You look lovely, my dear. Are we still on for the ball tomorrow?"

"Count on it, handsome. The house is ready, I have my gown, and I'm looking forward to our first date."

John took my hand. "Jett, sorry I turned you down for the bachelor auction. I want to lavish all my attention on Sophia—you understand."

"Of course." I sent a smile her way. "She deserves it."

Six-Pack nudged me. "I assume you expect the men in the auction to fend for themselves."

"Is that a problem?"

He arched an eyebrow. "What if the winner thinks she's entitled to more than dinner?"

"It's your decision, but handle it like a gentleman." I glanced at the SEALs and chuckled. "Studs like you can manage frisky women."

Snake and Six-Pack tapped their beer bottles together and grinned.

John kissed Sophia's hand. "I'll see you tomorrow night." He smiled at us. "Until tomorrow, ladies, gentlemen."

———

Saturday afternoon, Donatella and Renaldo brought their salon tools to Valhalla and styled our hair for the ball.

Renaldo gave me the once-over. "Jett, darling, you look positively ravishing. I hope you have a sexy gown to complete the picture."

"Cam made me a saucy red gown with a plunging neckline." I bit my lip. "He had to include a full back and long sleeves to hide all my ugly wounds."

He posed, hands on hips. "Well, I hope you won't let a few scabs and stitches stop you from bidding on Mike."

"Don't worry, I'll win his bid, no matter what the cost." I sighed. "We were so close when I was in college. Then not a word from him during my six years in the Navy. I guess I just want closure whether we end up together or not."

He smiled. "Good. Somebody has to make the first move, or you two will be senior citizens before you get around to dating again."

Donatella finished Sophia and twirled her for our approval. Her updo included a matching hairpiece to add height and a few curls cascading down her back. Her tiara would fit perfectly.

"You look regal and about a half foot taller," Karin said.

Gwen grinned. "Ladies, I think Donatella and Renaldo outdid themselves." She glanced at Mona. "And your Goth hairstyle makes you look sexy and dangerous."

We all loved our fancy Renaissance hairstyles and thanked them.

Gwen waved goodbye. "See you in a few hours. Fingers crossed Clint will show up and all will be well with us."

"He'd darn well better come," I called to her. "He's in my bachelor auction."

Gwen turned and yelled, "And he'd better be attentive, or I'll let Mimsy Farnsworth outbid me."

"Something tells me tonight could end up a free-for-all at that auction." Sophia checked her hair in the mirror and chuckled. "Our security team might have their hands full."

"It's an elite bachelor auction, not a male strip show. I'm sure everyone will behave like ladies." I petted Pratt and Whitney.

Mike walked in as the beauticians were leaving. He took in our fancy hair and makeup. "You ladies look lovely. I hope tonight goes well." He took me aside. "Did Harry and Grant accept your invitations?"

"They both agreed to come and dance with all the single women." I noticed Mike stood very close to me. In seconds, my temperature shot up, and my heart raced.

"Good. That should eliminate any worries about another body dropping in." He glanced around. "Did Snake's SEAL buddy show up?"

"Yes, and Snake is fully healed and able to dance. Thanks to you and the other guys, we should have enough dance partners for the single ladies. I'm hoping my first charity ball will be a success and pave the way for a bigger event next winter."

Mike stared into my eyes for a long moment. "See you tonight." He turned and left.

I lingered, savoring the intensity of his brief gaze.

Tim tapped my shoulder. "Earth to Jett."

"Oh, hi, Tim. Sorry, my mind was elsewhere."

He asked me the same question Mike had asked about Harry and Grant. My response brought a nod.

"Good. One less thing to worry about. My men will keep a close eye on them."

"Uh, you may need to referee the bachelor auction if some of the ladies get into a heated bidding war. Remind them it's for charity and keep them from pulling out each other's hair extensions." I grinned.

"You can handle that, right?"

He arched an eyebrow. "You're joking."

"Nope. We have several wealthy single women who'll be bidding against each other for some seriously hot men. Tempers might flare. I'm counting on you and your team to handle things as diplomatically as possible."

He clenched his jaw. "I'd rather be outnumbered in a shootout with the Taliban."

"And if some ladies drink too much, don't let them rip off any clothing on my auction bachelors." I chuckled. "This is supposed to be a dignified event."

"No way, Jett." He crossed his arms. "I'll protect you with my life, but the guys in the auction can fend for themselves." He shook his head. "Seriously?"

"The way my life has been going lately, nothing would surprise me. And stuff like that happens in Vegas all the time." I failed to mention I'd participated in said "stuff" in a Thunder from Down Under show in Vegas with some of my gal pals from the Navy.

"This is Banyan Isle. They have higher standards here."

I laughed. "I forgot you weren't in charge of my security a few months ago when the Mayor of Banyan Isle and several married women participated in a sexual free-for-all in one of my guest bedrooms while I was overseas. Of course, that ended when I came home and found the mayor's body under a bed."

Tim paused a few beats before responding, "I'll brief my security team to keep a close eye on the auction participants."

"Oh, one more thing—Samantha Starr is coming to the ball."

His eyes widened. "What? Two Danger Magnets in the same place? I might not have enough men for this."

"Don't be silly. I'm looking forward to meeting her." I chuckled. "What could possibly go wrong?"

"Don't ever ask that." He left, shaking his head.

# THIRTY-THREE

P ratt and Whitney entered the elevator with me, and we rode down to the ground floor. I worried they would step on my full-skirted gown, but they kept their distance and seemed wary of the rustling petticoat as we headed to the ballroom.

Larger than a basketball court, the elegant room covered the first floor at the north end of the castle. Three sides had access to the outside through tall, glass French doors that opened onto a wraparound Italian-tiled terrace. The doors were flanked by fifteen-foot-high windows draped in red velvet and spaced every six feet along the outer walls.

Magnificent crystal chandeliers reflected their many lights on the polished oak floor. A large stage stood between French doors on the north side, and the inside wall opposite the stage held an elaborate hand-carved bar, a serving station, and doors to men's and ladies' restrooms. A lighted infinity pool bordered the terrace on the ocean side and ran beyond the length of the ballroom to the wider central terrace.

The indoor security team assembled in the ballroom at 5:45 p.m. Everyone stopped talking when I walked into the room with my dogs.

The ruby red, low-cut gown with a push-up corset bodice made me look voluptuous.

*Hope I'll have this effect on Mike.*

The dogs chased each other around the huge room, their puppy feet skidding as they darted between circular rows of round, red-linen-covered tables bordering the central dance area. I glanced in their direction. "Let them wear themselves out. I'll put them in my bedroom before the guests arrive."

Tim and Kelly stepped forward, looking dashing in their tuxedoes. Whiffs of musky men's cologne wafted over me.

Tim smiled. "You look beautiful in your gown, Jett. Not a wound in sight."

"See, all that worry for nothing," Kelly said. "You'll be the belle of the ball."

"You're very kind, but I'd be lucky to place in the top five." I glanced at Tim's team. "Too bad I can't put you guys in the auction. You'd bring in a fortune."

"That reminds me," Tim said. "We have pictures with the names of all the single women, so we'll know who's who during the auction. Hopefully, they'll behave."

"You could increase the odds of a civilized event by holding it during the first hour, you know, before everyone drinks too much," Kelly suggested.

I grinned. "Silly man. Charity auctions are always held after everyone is snockered so the bids will skyrocket. That's Rule Number One."

Kelly arched an eyebrow. "Are the women going to behave like starving waifs at a meat market?"

"Probably, but don't worry. If they get handsy with you, remind them you aren't in the auction and move away." I smiled. "You guys can handle that, right?"

My question was answered with several groans.

―――――

The eight auction bachelors arrived on time, all looking dashing in fitted tuxedoes. My heart did a flip-flop when my eyes met Mike's. Long-standing, unrequited love fueled my emotions.

I sucked in a breath and greeted everyone, "Gentlemen, thanks a million for coming tonight. I promise this'll be fun. You'll each wear a red-rose boutonniere for easy identification as an auction participant, and here are photos with the names and table numbers of all the potential bidders. Dance with as many single women as possible and charm them into bidding high. My foundation will cover the expenses for the dates. If two women bid big for the same bachelor, we'll offer them each a date. Questions?"

"So, we should schmooze the ladies and let them cop a feel as long as they don't get too frisky on the dance floor?" Six-Pack asked.

The men laughed.

"Guys, just play along and let the women have their harmless fun." I grinned. "I'm sure you can handle them. And be mindful of potential murder suspects Grant Gardner and Harrison Hornsby." I showed them their pictures. "They'll probably be here sometime after the ball starts, but we don't think they'll try anything. Right, Mike?"

"Jett's private security team will keep a close watch over them." Mike shot a warm smile at me. "Shouldn't be a problem."

Light floral scents accompanied Gwen, Mona, and Karin as they strolled in. Gwen's full-skirted emerald gown accentuated her robust cleavage, and Karin's cobalt-blue gown did the same for her. Sparkling tiaras completed their ensembles. Goth Queen Mona's straight-skirted black gown with side slits and red accents blended perfectly with her spiked black hair and faux-ruby tiara.

They helped me pin boutonnieres on the men.

"Alright, gentlemen, our guests will arrive any minute." I gave them my best smile. "Please make the single women feel welcome as you escort them to their tables."

As usual, Hunter looked drop-dead handsome, the SEALs radiated testosterone, Darcy's boyfriend Scott looked sexy, and Jeff, the airline pilot Hunter invited, could have passed for a movie star. Justin, Mike, and Clint looked like they were auditioning for roles as James Bond. The bidders would be very happy indeed.

A thirty-piece orchestra filled the room with classical music as Muffy Murdoch, Kitty Kensington, and Bunty Berenson, three attractive twenty-something socialites from Palm Beach, arrived in Renaissance couture dripping with diamonds. My bachelor squad swarmed them, and their haughty demeanor transformed into radiant smiles.

Soon several couples from Banyan Isle, Palm Beach, and the mainland filled many of the tables, but my focus was on the single ladies I hoped would bid big at the auction.

The men stopped talking when Samantha Starr, who I recognized from photos Hunter had shown me, strolled in wearing a form-fitting navy silk gown with a side slit that showcased her Barbie-Doll figure. Five-inch stilettos like mine raised her to over six feet. Twenty-seven, her long blond hair shimmered under the crystal chandeliers as she offered me her hand.

"Hi, I'm Sam. You must be Jett. Hunter showed me your picture. He brags about you all the time." She smoothed her gown. "Sorry, I couldn't find something in a Renaissance style on short notice."

I looked into her brilliant aqua-blue eyes flecked with dark blue and green—such an unusual color. "It's a pleasure to meet you, Sam, and I love your bracelet with that large marquise diamond."

"It's twelve thousand years old." She held out her right arm. "I found the bracelet in an ancient underground chamber in Africa."

"No kidding? I've never done anything like that, but according to Tim Goldy, you and I share the nickname, Danger Magnet." I laughed. "In fact, Tim claims I've surpassed you in the most dangerous client category."

She grinned. "I'm happy to pass that baton to you." She glanced around. "Your ballroom is spectacular, and I couldn't help noticing all the hot guys you brought in for the auction. Should be a fun night."

I spotted a big diamond sparkling on her left hand. "Uh oh, I may have made a mistake. I thought you were single and gave your name and picture to the auction bachelors."

"I got engaged last summer, but no worries. My fiancé is somewhere downrange on a SAS mission. He won't mind if I contribute to your charity auction." She glanced around at the men. "Which one are you bidding on?"

"I have a thing for that guy." I thumbed in Mike's direction. "Over there—the one with the dreamy brown eyes."

"He's quite a hunk."

"What's your fiancé like?" I tried to imagine the man who'd won Sam's heart.

"Tall, dark, and Scottish. He's a captain in the UK's Special Forces." She glanced at her ring. "He lives in a castle near the North Sea."

"He sounds awesome." Changing the subject, I said, "Looks like your airline buddies are headed this way."

Hunter and his airline boss, Captain Jeff Rowlin, took turns hugging Sam.

"Hello, stranger, may we escort you to your table?" Jeff said.

"Of course." She kissed his cheek. "Good to see you guys." She said to me, "Nice meeting you, Jett."

I waved. "We'll chat more later. You're at my table."

Darcy and her girlfriends waltzed in with the Calder twins, Molly and Mary, who were wealthy seniors from Banyan Country Estates in Garnet. I greeted them, and Darcy's boyfriend, Detective Scott Logan, led them to their table.

Horse carriages began arriving at the outside entrance to the ballroom at 7:30, after the off-island guests had valet-parked and entered via the castle's main door. This allowed the Banyan Isle women, grand entrances seen by everyone in the ballroom.

Vibrant fifty-something Mimsy Farnsworth was the first to disembark. Her pale-pink Renaissance gown shimmered as she strolled into the ballroom, her ample bosom barely contained in the low-cut bodice, as her pink-topaz tiara sparkled under the glinting chandeliers.

I welcomed her at the ballroom door. "Thank you for coming, Mimsy. We have a fun evening planned."

She glanced around. "I'm ready. Bring on the hot men."

Hunter stepped up and offered his arm. Mimsy's jaw dropped as he guided her to a table near the on-stage orchestra. He pulled out her chair, and a waiter appeared and took her drink order.

Hunter kissed her cheek and brushed his lips against her ear as she said in a loud voice, "Hurry back, handsome."

The orchestra played romantic music that encouraged slow dancing.

I sucked in a breath. *So far, so good.*

Marjorie Wentworth arrived next. She was the widow of murdered Mayor Phil Peabody, but she used her maiden name to distance herself from the scandal. The grand dame of Banyan Isle, she was sixty but looked more like mid-forties with perfect curves. I waved as she accepted Justin Newton's arm, and he escorted her to a seat beside Mimsy. She gave Justin a long, appraising look, smiling as she took her seat.

I noticed most of the women wore gowns created by my flamboyant friend, Cam Altman. He wore a tuxedo typical of the period and a powdered wig to make himself memorable, as if he wasn't already. He fluttered around the room in a state of designer ecstasy as he fussed over each client.

The next carriage brought Mike's parents and his beautiful younger sister, Priscilla—blond, curvy, and long-legged in a low-cut, corseted blue gown.

When Prissy strolled in, she was swarmed by auction bachelors and accepted Six-Pack's arm, much to her brother's chagrin. A bit spoiled, she stuck her tongue out at Mike when he gave her a disapproving look. I grinned, amused by their sibling interaction.

Last to arrive was exotic bachelorette Cleopatra Bentley from exclusive Jupiter Island. I don't know how she managed it, but she rolled in on a gold chariot pulled by two white horses. She handed the reins to the man beside her dressed like a Nubian warrior, and he drove away as she strolled to the entrance.

Cleo's father was a wealthy English anthropologist and Egyptologist who had named his daughter after his favorite Egyptian queen. She wore a gold silk Egyptian gown and a gold snake headpiece. Her radiant hazel eyes were lined in a charcoal color like ancient Egyptians, and her glossy black hair was styled like her namesake. When she strolled in, her gown shimmered under the sparkling chandeliers.

Chief Pilot for Luxury International Airlines, Captain Jeff Rowlin, escorted Cleo to a table. She seemed pleased with his tall, Nordic good looks, and he couldn't take his eyes off her. This was shaping up to be a very good night indeed.

Waiters swarmed the tables carrying silver trays laden with a variety of delicious hors d'oeuvres. Champagne, wine, and whisky flowed. The orchestra played slow dances so the single women could get close to the auction men and assess their choices.

Brenda Carrigan of Treasure Chest Antiques agreed to be the auctioneer. She was one of the naughty married women who had misbehaved with Mayor Peabody in one of my guest bedrooms. But I decided to let bygones be bygones. Newly divorced, Brenda had paid dearly for her transgressions, and the mayor's widow was so focused on potential bachelor bids, she didn't seem to care either.

# THIRTY-FOUR

I circulated around the busy dance floor, alternately searching for Mike, Harry, and Grant. I noticed Sam dancing with Justin. They seemed to be enjoying themselves. Lots of women grabbed Mike for dances, always right before I could get to him, but no matter how hard I looked, I couldn't find Harry or Grant.

*Uh oh. Where are they?* I continued searching.

Sophia looked like an Italian countess in her slender champagne silk gown and faux diamond tiara while gliding around the dancefloor in John's arms.

Snake snagged me for a dance. "Hey, Jett, how goes the ball?"

"So far, so good. I hope you managed a dance with Mona amongst all the potential bidders."

"Of course, but those randy single women keep cutting in." He gazed over my shoulder and laughed. "Sophia should've been in the Navy. She's a master at repelling boarders."

I turned just in time to see her give Marjorie Wentworth the evil eye as she approached them, probably intending to cut in. Marjorie backed away.

"Ah, yes, Sophia tends to be very possessive when it comes to men." I waved goodbye to him when Kitty cut in.

As I headed for my table, I spotted Mimsy getting handsy with Tim. A bit tipsy, she squeezed his buns.

He stiffened, and his face reddened as he tried to back away.

I grabbed Six-Pack, swooped in, and led him to Mimsy.

"Excuse me, Mimsy. Tim is my head of security, and I need to borrow him. Six-Pack will take his place. Thanks!"

I took Tim's arm and led him out a French door by the infinity pool. When we reached the far side of the pool, I stopped. "Take a deep breath."

He sighed. "I'm fine. Is there a problem, or are you just rescuing me?"

"Um, actually, there might be a big problem. I can't find Grant or Harry. They never showed up." I shot a glance around the grounds.

He pulled out his cell and handed it to me. "With your eidetic memory, I'm guessing you know their phone numbers."

I punched in Grant's number first, and it went straight to voicemail. Next, I tried Harry. He answered on the third ring, and I heard airplane engines in the background.

"Who is this?"

"Hi, Harry. It's Jett. Are you coming to my ball?"

"Sorry, but my Tallahassee restaurant had a freezer failure, and they need me to deliver supplies. Reservations are filled tomorrow. You understand."

"I do, but we'll miss you. Have a good flight." I tapped off and handed the phone to Tim. "He's in his airplane. Claims he's flying to Tallahassee for a restaurant emergency."

Tim groaned and called the Flight Service Station. "I'm checking on a friend's airplane. Do you have a flight plan on file for a Beech 18, November Bravo One Eight Hotel?" He paused and listened. "Good, when is it due in Tallahassee?" Another pause. "Thank you."

I searched Tim's eyes. "Well, I guess this means Grant can't kill Harry, and Harry really is flying to the state capital and won't be dropping Grant on us."

"Or Grant is with him right now with his feet stuck in concrete buckets." He looked up at the black night sky dotted with stars.

Not an airplane in sight.

I turned back toward the ballroom and spotted Mike in an open French door, gazing across at us. "We'd better tell Mike."

By the time we'd walked around the pool, Mike had vanished inside. I found him dancing with Muffy Murdoch and cut in. "Excuse me, Muffy. I hope you don't mind, but I need a word with Mike."

She grabbed Clint as Mike said to me, "Wouldn't you rather dance with Snake?"

"Why would I do that? He's Mona's boyfriend."

His eyes widened. "I thought you and Snake—"

"They've been sleeping together ever since he arrived." I looked into his eyes.

Confusion clouded his face. "All this time I thought you two were together."

I rolled my eyes. "That explains a lot, but we'll have to discuss that later. Right now, we might have a bigger problem. Grant is MIA, and Harry is in his airplane, supposedly flying to Tallahassee."

He stopped mid-dance. "Are you sure?"

I explained why I'd been outside with Tim. "It might be nothing. Harry filed a flight plan for Tallahassee, and maybe Grant found something better to do. Let's face it, most men don't like formal balls."

"I hope you're right. Better start the auction now. That will encourage everyone to stay inside and watch the bidding." He squeezed my waist. "We'll talk later."

My body still tingled from Mike's squeeze when I found Brenda. "Think everyone's snockered enough to start the auction?"

"Oh, yes." She giggled as I followed her to the podium on stage. "Look at them. Potential bidders are sampling the merchandise, you know, squeezing buns and biceps."

"Alrighty. Let's get started." I glanced at her packet. "You have the bidding order?"

"Yep." She pulled out a paper. "First up are the cops, starting with Garnet Police Detective Scott Logan."

I rounded up the bachelors while Brenda announced the auction was about to begin. Darcy's handsome boyfriend bravely took the stage and stood beside Brenda. A bidding frenzy erupted among the younger women and Mimsy Farnsworth.

Darcy let the price run up to twenty-five thousand dollars as she enjoyed watching Scott sweat over the prospect of ending up in Mimsy's clutches. Then she raised her hand and yelled, "Thirty thousand."

Apparently forgetting to offer Mimsy a chance to match Darcy's bid, Brenda announced, "Sold to Miss McKay for thirty thousand."

Gwen's boyfriend, Palm Beach Detective Clint Reynolds, stepped forward to plenty of oohs and ahhs. A young Pierce Brosnan lookalike, he inspired another bidding war. Gwen let him sweat as the senior Calder twins battled the younger women.

Taller Dolores Delgado, owner of Fit and Fabulous, stepped in front of Bunty Berenson, cutting her off.

"I don't think so," Bunty said, yanking Dolores's gown and pulling her to one side.

Kelly stepped in between them. "Calm down, ladies. Plenty of beefcake for everyone."

Bunty huffed and shouted, "Twenty thousand."

Dolores countered with, "Twenty-five thousand."

Gwen stepped up and offered the high bid.

Brenda yelled, "Sold to Gwen Pendragon for thirty thousand," before anyone had a chance to bid more.

I took the stage and pulled Brenda aside. "You forgot to offer two dates if there's a bidding war. Remember that for the rest of the bids."

The object of my desire was next on the auction block. The Palm Beach girls bid against the Calder twins, and the price for Mike ran up to thirty thousand.

I yelled, "Fifty thousand," ending the battle.

Mike stared at me, stunned, as my winning bid was announced.

Luxury International Airlines Captain Jeff Rowlin stepped forward and inspired another bidding frenzy among young and older women. The bidding had reached thirty thousand when Cleopatra Bentley said, "Fifty thousand."

Taken by surprise, Brenda forgot to ask for a matching bid and yelled, "Sold to Cleopatra Bentley."

Brenda continued, "We have two United States Navy SEALs who, for security reasons, use nicknames. Our first SEAL bachelor goes by Snake, and you ladies can use your imaginations as to why. Shall we open the bids at ten thousand?"

The bidding started at fifteen thousand and escalated until Bunty and Muffy were awarded dates for thirty thousand each.

# THIRTY-FIVE

"And here we have Six-Pack, named after his awesome abs," Brenda said with an admiring grin. "Let's open the bids at fifteen thousand."

After Kitty ran the bid up to twenty-five thousand, Mimsy yelled, "I'll pay thirty if he shows me his abs right now."

Several women yelled, "Take it off!" "Woot, woot!" "Show us your abs, handsome!"

Grinning, Six-Pack unbuttoned his jacket and shirt, displaying his magnificent abdominal muscles as he worked his hips, giving the women a show.

The bidders went wild, hooting and whistling.

Mimsy yelled, "Thirty-five thousand."

After rowdy bids and naughty suggestions from the crowd, Mike's sister Priscilla snagged a date for forty thousand as her father looked on in dismay, stuck with the bill. Brenda offered a date to Mimsy for the same price, and she agreed.

Professional scuba diver Justin Newton, a brave man indeed, faced a group of lusty women the SEALs had whipped into a feeding frenzy worse than great white sharks in bloody, chum-filled water.

Senior Molly Calder yelled, "Twenty thousand."

Her twin Mary bid, "Twenty-five thousand."

Mimsy Farnsworth yelled, "Thirty thousand."

Marjorie Wentworth, normally reserved, yelled, "Forty thousand if you take off your jacket and shirt."

"Yeah! Take it off!" several women yelled in unison.

Justin froze, and Sam, using her commanding airline captain voice, said, "Fifty thousand, fully clothed."

The women turned and frowned at her. She responded with an intense, no-nonsense glare.

Brenda seized the moment. "Any matching bids?"

Kitty raised her hand.

"Sold to Samantha Starr and Kitty Kensington for 50K each."

Justin smiled, happy to have dates with two beautiful young women.

"And now, ladies, we saved the most exotic for last—Luxury International Airlines Captain and full-blood Cherokee, Hunter Vann. The bidding will start at twenty thousand," Brenda announced.

Six-foot-three inches of raw masculinity packaged in a flawless forty-year-old body with thick black hair, golden eyes, and golden skin, Hunter radiated a wild spirit every woman longed to tame.

Marjorie waved. "Twenty-five thousand."

Mimsy countered, "Thirty thousand."

The bids escalated as the Calder twins bid against the other women and each other. None of the older women wanted to leave empty-handed, and it was obvious all four women lusted after Hunter. Their bids escalated while nostrils flared and elbows jabbed.

Tim had to step in. "Now, ladies, let's keep this civilized."

When the bids reached sixty thousand, Hunter whispered something to Brenda, and she offered all four women individual dates. They glared at each other, not wanting to share.

"Remember, this is for charity. Shall I close the bids at sixty for each of you?"

The women agreed, and Mimsy and Marjorie stomped outside in a huff, while the Calder twins rushed up and hugged Hunter.

Mimsy and Marjorie stood beside the pool, airing their displeasure at having to share Hunter. Even though the orchestra had resumed playing, I could hear the grand dames of Banyan Isle shouting at each other outside.

I felt a gentle tap on my shoulder and turned.

Mike offered me his hand. "May I have this dance?"

I smiled and took his hand as he pulled me close. We glided around the dancefloor, and he nuzzled my neck, sending tingles down my spine.

Memories of our torrid romance throughout my time as a university student flooded my mind. I had told him all along that I intended to serve my country in the Navy after graduation, but he assumed I'd changed my mind because we were so close. When I enlisted, he shut me out of his life until I left the Navy almost four months ago.

Mike was about to brush his lips against mine when ear-shattering screams interrupted us. We rushed outside to Mimsy and Marjorie.

They turned and faced us. Mimsy's right side was soaked with pool water, and Marjorie's left side was equally drenched. Water dripped from their hair and ran down their faces.

Sophia pushed forward, took in the scene, and said, "Well, you know what they say—it isn't a party until somebody falls in the pool."

"But they didn't fall in." I asked them, "What happened?" as Tim and Sam joined us.

Still in shock and unable to speak, the frightened women turned and pointed at the pool.

A man's head poked out of the water behind them. I looked down and noted his feet were mired in concrete-filled buckets. *Not again!*

Mike leaned down and checked the face. "It's Grant Gardner."

My stomach twisted into a knot as I bit my lip. "Poor Grant."

Mike put his arm around me. "At least now we know Harry is probably the killer. He had the means and opportunity."

"And he was the only one with a motive for all the murders." I leaned against Mike's shoulder. "I guess you'll tell the Tallahassee police to arrest him when he lands."

"Right. Hopefully, this will put an end to the killing."

A hushed silence shrouded the pool as tension knifed through the gathering crowd.

Sam looked down at the body. "I concede the Danger Magnet crown to you, Jett." She patted my back and whispered, "Sorry about this, but your ball just became the most exciting charity event ever. Your next one will sell out."

Hunter and Jeff swooped in and wrapped Marjorie and Mimsy in their tuxedo jackets. They scooped them into their arms and carried them inside. Holding the ladies on their laps, the men ordered hot toddies for the women.

Thanks to the pilots' quick action, the traumatized women felt safe and cared for. Blankets were brought in, and the hot toddies warmed them. Clint and Scott helped Tim's men herd everyone inside, and Mike called for a CSU, the ME, and more cops to secure the scene at the pool.

Then Mike took the stage. "Everyone, remain in the ballroom until we determine that it's safe outside. Everything will be secured and ready for your departure within the hour. In the meantime, you're safe inside and free to enjoy yourselves."

The orchestra resumed playing, waiters swarmed the tables with dessert treats, cognac, and gourmet coffee. Smiling couples danced. Everyone seemed excited, rather than upset. The consumption of alcohol had probably helped maintain the festive mood.

I circulated among the guests, thanking everyone for coming and reassuring them they were not in danger. Comments like, "Best ball ever," "Loved the bachelor auction," and "Never a dull moment," surprised me.

Palm Beacher Edith Pickering said, "Jett, darling, this was by far the most exciting ball I've ever attended, and God knows I've been to plenty of these over the years."

Gwen nudged me. "Looks like you and I are the only ones upset about our fallen classmate. Nobody else here knew him. Women are posting on social media as if they just survived a combat mission."

"I can't help wondering if this last body was intended to ruin my ball." I shook my head. "Harry must really hate me, but I can't think why."

The Palm Beach girls and Prissy gathered around Justin, Snake, and Six-Pack. Everyone was smiling and laughing. No one seemed to mind the body dropping into the pool. I overheard the women bragging about their social media posts going viral.

Thanks to a little gentlemanly TLC from Hunter and Jeff, Mimsy and Marjorie recovered in record time. Wrapped in blankets and sipping hot toddies, they smiled at their rescuers. After a while, two handsome men from Tim's security team replaced Hunter and Jeff. Mimsy and Marjorie clearly enjoyed being the center of attention.

Jeff rejoined Cleo, who seemed favorably impressed with his gallantry, and Hunter danced with Karin. I spotted Justin and Sam smiling and enjoying another dance.

Tim nudged me. "Looks like your ball was a huge success, despite what happened."

"It'll be hard to top this next time." I sighed. "Well, I guess it's safe to go outside now. Everyone on Harry's revenge list is dead."

"Everyone except you." Tim arched an eyebrow. "Why else did he drop all the bodies here?"

# THIRTY-SIX

Everyone slept late the following morning. The dogs woke me at 9:00 a.m., and I led them outside. Yellow crime-scene tape still bordered the ballroom side of my pool, but Grant's body had long since been removed.

Snake sidled up beside me. "I'm in big trouble with Mona, and it's your fault."

"What's wrong?"

"She's upset I'm about to have dates with two hot women."

"Or maybe it's personal. Have you and Mona discussed what will happen when you return to Virginia Beach in a couple days?" I leaned down and petted Pratt and Whitney.

He shoved his hands in his pockets. "Naw, I kinda avoided that topic."

"Why not ask her what she has in mind?" I smiled at him. "You're welcome to visit her here any time you like."

"Thanks, Jett. Guess I'd better talk to her." He paused. "Uh, what do you suppose those Palm Beach girls will want to do on our dates?"

"They'll probably want to go clubbing and wear you out on the dance floor. Those nightclubs stay open until 4:00 a.m."

He groaned. "So even if I behave myself, I'll return exhausted, and Mona will think I cheated."

I grinned. "She won't think you cheated if you jump her bones as soon as you get home."

He shook his head. "My stay with y'all was supposed to be for rest and relaxation. I need to go home to Virginia Beach to recover."

"Good thing you're a tough Navy SEAL." I patted his back and laughed.

"Six-Pack has two dates too, and one's with Mike's sister."

I chuckled. "I'm sure Prissy will want 40K worth of fun."

"And his second date is with that woman in her fifties with the giant boobs." He rubbed his neck. "She got handsy with all of us last night."

"I'm sure he'll soldier through and take one for the team."

Snake smacked my butt. "You're enjoyin' this a little too much."

"Hey, turnabout is fair play. Now you know how we women feel most of the time."

We strolled onto the oceanfront terrace and found Mike waiting for us.

I asked, "Was Harry arrested?"

"He lawyered up and is already out on bail, so have Tim beef up your security."

"Why would he come after me?" I sat at a large round glass table and poured a cup of coffee.

Mike sat beside me. "Why did he drop all the bodies on your land?"

"I don't know. Did you ask him?"

He poured a cup of coffee and grabbed a cinnamon roll. "He claims he's innocent."

Sophia joined us in time to hear Mike's comment. "Of course, the dirtbag claims he didn't do it. That's what they all say."

"All I have is circumstantial evidence." Mike took a bite of the roll.

"Did Harry fly to Tallahassee last night?" I bit into a cinnamon roll, the sweet vanilla frosting melting in my mouth.

"Yes, but he stopped at Palm Beach International first to take on supplies." He paused. "The thing is, he took off from North County Airport and flew straight to the coast before turning south. His flight path brought him directly over your home, which was out of his way. He could've dropped Grant here before continuing on to PBI. The timing fits."

Sophia asked, "How did he explain that?"

"He said he flew east first because the wind was out of the west, and he knew he'd be landing on runway 28L." Mike sipped his coffee.

"That's baloney." I finished my cinnamon bun. "ATC would've routed him south to enter a left-hand pattern for 28L. His way, he had to cross the final approach path for 28R."

Mike shrugged. "He claimed traffic was light, and ATC didn't care that he approached from the north along the coast."

Snake had been listening. "Did you find evidence of Grant and his bucketed feet inside Harry's airplane?"

"No, the cargo bay had been cleaned with bleach before the food supplies were loaded aboard," Mike answered. "Also, he pointed out that his autopilot wasn't working, so he couldn't have pushed a body out."

I thought about that. "Not true. All he'd have to do is position the body bucketed-feet-first by the open door and put the airplane into a knife-edge or side-slip maneuver to make the body slide out. The weight of the concrete would've dragged it out."

Mike paused mid-sip. "If necessary, could you demonstrate that with a dummy?"

"Sure. I can do it in Uncle Hunter's Staggerwing. Is that the proof you need to make the charges stick?"

"It can't hurt. I'll ask the District Attorney." Mike paused a beat. "Maybe if we tell Harry a pilot demonstrated how he could have done it, he'll confess. He has to feel guilty about killing so many of his friends from prep school."

"Not if he's a psychopath." I glanced around the table. "Let's face it. A normal person couldn't have killed all those people."

Mike frowned. "That's what bothers me. Harry seems so normal."

"And he's always been nice to me, even last night on the phone. Didn't seem like he hated me."

Sophia shrugged. "Look how many people Ted Bundy fooled."

"I'd feel better if I could find a storage locker somewhere with cement mix, buckets, and a bloody garrote, all with Harry's fingerprints." Mike drained his coffee.

Sophia shook her head. "Too late. If Grant was Harry's final victim, he won't need that stuff. It'll all be gone now."

"Then the D.A. will have to prosecute Harry with a bunch of circumstantial evidence and the motives Harry admitted to Dolores Delgado." Mike sighed. "There's a good chance Harry's lawyer could get him acquitted."

Sophia stiffened. "What if he intends to finish by killing Jett and dropping her on her own land? Maybe that's why he dropped all the other bodies here first."

We all turned at the sound of Tim's voice. "I'll increase her security and make sure he never gets her." He glanced at Mike. "I heard Harry made bail already."

"I came here to warn Jett."

Tim turned to me. "Don't go anywhere without a security escort. We need time to figure out what his next move will be."

———

I hunkered down at home with my roomies and doggies while the SEALs went on their dates with Muffy and Prissy. A security guard told me neither man made it back to my place before 5:00 a.m.

The guys went straight to bed, and I didn't see them until five that evening, which wasn't long before their dates with Bunty and Mimsy. Their eyes looked bloodshot when they settled across from me at a terrace table.

Sophia nudged Snake. "Hey, sugar buns, how was your date last night?"

He rubbed his temples. "Exhaustin'. Muffy dragged me from club to club, dancin' until four a.m. I don't think she does anything in daylight. Then I had to save some energy for Mona so she wouldn't be jealous."

Sophia patted his back. "One more date with a spoiled young socialite, and then you can go back to easier stuff, like fighting terrorists."

I chuckled and asked Six-Pack, "What about you?"

He moaned. "I have a date with a terrorist tonight. I think Mimsy intends to ravage me."

Snake laughed. "You can handle one horny middle-aged woman." He yawned. "I have a date with Bunty, and she'll probably want to go clubbin' all night."

"I'm sure you'll both soldier through somehow." I smirked, enjoying the turnabout.

# THIRTY-SEVEN

Once again, the men rolled in around dawn. But this time was different. Six-Pack had been picked up in Mimsy's Bentley for their date, but he returned home in a shiny new black Corvette. He showed it to us after he'd had ten hours of sleep.

We gathered on the terrace for a casual dinner at dusk. A light sea breeze freshened the air, but my SEAL friends still looked tired.

Sophia raised her wine glass. "Well, boys, I hope you did yourselves proud and showed those women a good time for Jett's sake."

Snake snickered and tapped his glass against hers. "Looks like Six-Pack took one for the team, judgin' by the new Corvette Mimsy bought him."

"Mimsy hid it in her garage and gave it to me this morning." Six-Pack stared at his plate of lasagna. "She's very patriotic and wanted to express her appreciation for my military service."

"You sure it wasn't for some other kind of service?" Snake asked, chuckling.

"I'm grateful to both of you for helping me with the bachelor auction," I blurted, interrupting. "Despite the dead body dropping in the pool, the ball was a huge success, mostly because of you guys and the other bachelors. I can't thank you enough."

"This was a fun break." Six-Pack grinned. "If you have another ball, count me in."

"Me too, but next time, let me take out Mimsy," Snake said. "I need a new car."

Mona glared at him.

"Just kiddin', sweetie."

"Would you like me to ship your Corvette to Virginia Beach?" I asked Six-Pack.

"Thanks, Jett, but no need. Snake will help me drive it home. We'll leave tonight."

Snake took my hands. "Thanks for takin' me in, Jett."

"It was my pleasure, and thanks for protecting us." I hugged him.

"Never a dull moment." Snake glanced around like he was looking for someone. "Did you set things straight with Mike?"

"We haven't had a chance to talk. He's busy nailing down evidence on the body-drop killer."

"When is he taking you out on the date you bought?" Six-Pack asked. "You should go soon."

"He hasn't said anything about it." I sighed.

"That man needs a good talking to. I'll straighten him out." Sophia pulled out her cell.

"Thanks, *Mom*, but I'll handle this myself."

She crossed her arms. "So, handle it already ... while you're still young."

I picked up my cell and called Mike. "Hi, how's everything going?"

"The D.A. thinks we have enough circumstantial evidence to convict Harry."

"Good. Does that mean you'll have time to take me out on our charity date?"

"Saturday night at seven, if that works for you. Wear something fancy."

"Saturday night at seven. See you then." I pocketed my phone and smiled.

Sophia grinned. "See? That wasn't so hard."

I changed the subject. "When are you going out with John again?"

"We have a date Friday night."

I glanced at Karin. "Have you heard from Hunter?"

"He wouldn't go into detail, but he said Mimsy and Marjorie were the most aggressive women he's ever dated, and he has the claw marks to prove it." She laughed. "And the poor guy still has to take out the Calder twins."

Everyone looked at Six-Pack.

Sophia asked, "Do you have battle scars too?"

His face reddened. "A gentleman never tells."

———

We stood near Odin's fountain and waved goodbye to Snake and Six-Pack as they drove down my driveway in the new Corvette. Mike passed them on his way in. Mona, Karin, and Sophia turned and went inside with the dogs to give us a moment alone.

Mike parked and strode up to me. "Where'd they get the car?"

"It was a thank-you gift from Mimsy to Six-Pack for his military service." I tried to keep a straight face.

He turned for one more glimpse of the sportscar. "Mimsy was quite appreciative."

"Have you wrapped up the case against Harry?" I walked beside him into the great hall.

Mike frowned. "The evidence is strong, but it's all circumstantial, and he insists he's innocent. If we could've found evidence that the bodies had been inside his airplane, that would've clinched it." He perched beside me on a leather sofa.

"What happens now?" I glanced at a Viking broadsword gleaming on the east wall beside French doors leading to the terrace.

"The D.A. is charging him with multiple murders, but his lawyer got him out on a million dollars' bail. He's considered a flight risk, so his passport was confiscated, and the FAA suspended his pilot license."

"But he's a killer." A wave of unease washed over me. "Are you having him followed?"

Mike shook his head. "We don't have the manpower for that. It's possible Harry might come after you, so stay home or have one of Tim's men with you at all times." He squeezed my hand. "Please."

My eyes met his. "Okay, unless I'm with Hunter. He's as capable as Tim's men, and don't forget the Navy trained me for combat."

"I know, but even a soldier needs someone to watch their back." His cell dinged, and he read a text message. "I have to run. Please meet with Tim ASAP, and don't forget our date Saturday."

———

The following morning, a gentle sea breeze swirled my hair as I played frisbee in the backyard with the dogs. I had a hard time relaxing knowing I might be on Harry's hit list. A half hour later, I took a break and had iced tea with Sophia on the oceanfront terrace.

Glancing around, I said, "I hate feeling like I have a target on my back."

Sophia reached behind her and pulled out her pistol. "If Harry sneaks in here, I'll put a hole in his head."

"I'd prefer ironclad evidence against him and a speedy trial." I leaned down and ruffled my dogs' fur. "I don't like having this hanging over me."

"Yeah, but if he tries to kill you, that'll prove he's the body-drop killer, and we can end this." Sophia patted my back.

"There's no way you'll get a shot at him. He'll never get past Tim's security team." My eyes swept the well-guarded grounds. "They'll take him out in a nanosecond."

"Just so long as somebody nails him. We've endured this long enough."

My cell vibrated on the table. I grabbed it and answered a call from Hunter.

"Hey, Jett, I hope you remember you agreed to fly my Staggerwing while I take aerial shots of my flight school and maintenance facility this morning."

"Oh, right, we planned this a few weeks ago. Need help getting the plane ready?"

"I already removed the cabin door so I can shoot photos from behind the wings."

"The thing is, I'd hate to put you at risk." I paused a beat. "There's a chance Harry might come after me. Are you okay with guarding my six?"

"Always. Meet me at my hangar in an hour, and we'll have lunch afterwards."

I dropped my phone into my shoulder bag. "Hunter needs my help with a little project."

"Anything I can do?" Sophia had that same dreamy look every time his name was mentioned.

"Sorry, he wants me to fly his plane while he takes pictures of his business."

"Drat the luck." She paused. "You should invite him back here for dinner tonight."

I grinned. "I'll give it a shot. Karin would like that too."

I finished my iced tea, and then I found my pilot license and pilot medical certificate and shoved them into my wallet, dropped it in my purse, and tied my hair in a ponytail.

It was a perfect flying day—clear skies and gentle breezes. Also perfect for riding my Harley. I entered my garage and donned the teal helmet that matched the bike's cream and teal paint job. Images of Winged Valkyries decorated both sides of the helmet and the motorcycle's gas tank. I was pretty sure Harry had never seen my bike, and the murders always took place at night, so I decided the risk was minimal.

The engine rumbled to life, and the bike came alive beneath me. I rolled up to Valhalla's main gate and stopped to tell a guard where I was going. I ended with, "Nothing to worry about. My uncle will be with me."

# THIRTY-EIGHT

Not two minutes after Jett drove away, a body landed with a massive thud ten feet from the terrace where Sophia sat with the dogs.

Startled, she leaped up and spit out her sip of iced tea.

The fallen body's feet were encased in concrete-filled buckets that cratered the lawn and splattered dirt, grass, and congealed blood onto Sophia. The corpse collapsed onto the buckets in a grotesque tangle of fractured limbs.

She gasped and wiped her mouth as an airplane overhead turned and headed west. Looking up, she noted it had a radial engine like the one that had made all the previous body drops. Sophia yanked out her cell and called Jett.

No answer.

The dogs ran over and sniffed the mangled corpse, and Sophia stumbled onto the lawn and pulled them back. Then Tim's men surrounded the gruesome heap of flesh.

She yelled to the men, "Jett isn't answering her phone. I'll call Mike."

Sophia made the call and then put the dogs inside the house. The Banyan Isle Police headquarters was only five minutes away, and by the time she returned to the body, Mike had jogged around the corner and stopped beside her.

She gripped his arm, her voice shaky. "Who is it?"

Mike pulled on a glove and checked the man's smashed face. Sucking in a breath, he froze. "Looks like Harrison Hornsby—has his hair and eye color." He lifted the left forearm. "Definitely his watch and class ring." He faced Sophia. "Where's Jett?"

"I tried to reach her, but she's riding her Harley out to that pilot community where Hunter lives. She can't hear her phone while she's on that noisy motorcycle."

Mike clenched his jaw. "What time did she leave here?"

"Right before Harry dropped in." She glanced at her watch. "Maybe ten minutes ago."

Mike called Hunter and put it on speaker for Sophia. "Is Jett with you?"

"No. I'm about to depart PBI on an airline flight. I got called out thirty minutes ago to replace a captain who broke his arm in an auto accident on his way to the airport. I sent Jett a text explaining what happened. Is there a problem?"

"Harry Hornsby's corpse just dropped into Jett's backyard."

"Oh crap! That means he's not the killer, and Jett's in danger. Get someone out to my place right away."

———

I pulled into Hunter's hangar and parked my bike in a corner. The hangar was silent. I slung my purse over my shoulder and checked the office.

Empty.

"Hunter?" I called out as I walked over to his Staggerwing. The plane was ready to go, sitting outside the hangar and pointed toward the taxiway. I noticed the cabin door had been removed like he said.

I stuck my head through the doorway for a quick glance inside the plane, then pulled out my phone and found a text from my uncle.

Before I read it, a shadow fell over me, and alarm bells rang in my head. "Hunter?"

Before I could turn around, someone strong grabbed me in a chokehold, and something sharp pricked the back of my neck.

"Stop!" I tried to resist, but everything went black.

I didn't know how much time had passed. I woke with my hands tied behind me, belted into the front right seat of Hunter's airplane. The throw-over control yoke was positioned on the left side, and I was shocked to see nurse Grace Simms flying the plane.

She grinned. "Good. You're awake. Otherwise, this wouldn't be nearly as much fun."

A quick peek at the instrument panel showed us airborne at six thousand feet and headed east toward the Atlantic Ocean.

I shook my aching head. "What is this, Grace, some kind of sick joke?"

"No joke, Jett. Lucky for me, I bumped into Hunter yesterday, and he told me about his plans to photograph his facilities today with you at the controls. He even invited me to ride along. That was plenty of time to put the rest of my plan into action."

"But why are my hands tied?"

"This is my final act of retribution for all the bullying I endured at Banyan Isle Prep School."

"What? You were never in school with me or my friends."

"You really don't recognize me, do you?" Grace pulled off a blonde wig and tossed it behind her, revealing a brown crewcut. "You knew me as George Stavros."

My jaw dropped as I turned and stared at his face, altered by feminine makeup.

He frowned. "I assumed my life would be easier posing as a woman, but Doctor Warner treated me like dirt when I started working at Banyan Isle Hospital." He smirked. "He's dead now. I killed him."

"Wait. You murdered Doc Warner just because he wasn't nice to you?"

"It was ruled a heart attack, but he died from an insulin injection in his scalp. I did the same thing to my classmates and then garroted them before their hearts stopped. That way, cops thought a man choked them, and no one looked for a needle mark in their hairlines or suspected a woman did it."

"That's diabolically clever." My heart raced. "Insulin would never show up on a toxin screen because everyone has it in their bodies."

He grinned, and his wild eyes sparkled with a glint of crazy.

*He intends to kill me, and we're only minutes away from my house. Must talk him out of this.*

I tried to get inside his head. "Transitioning to a woman is a drastic move. Did you have the full gender reassignment surgery?"

"No, silly, I had a minor operation so I could change my identity and kill my enemies. My Adam's apple was shaved down, but I kept my man parts. All I have to do to change back is stop taking estrogen, and wearing the wig, padded bra, and makeup."

A shiver shot down my spine. *I'm dealing with a crazy man.*

"I understand you were angry with the guys who bullied you, but murder? That's pretty drastic."

"How would you feel if Matt Miller shoved *your* head into a toilet? Huh, Jett?" Smug, he said, "I felt vindicated when I garroted him behind the bleachers."

I glanced through the windshield and spotted Banyan Isle, our plane drawing closer to Valhalla with every passing second.

*Oh, God!*

I kept stalling. "So, Matt was your first kill?"

"I enjoyed it, but I realized I'd have to be patient if I wanted to kill all my enemies and get away with it."

My stomach churned. "What about your boss at Bright Investments?"

A sinister smile. "Oh, yeah, he died same as Matt. He deserved it. Bastard bullied me at work and then fired me when I complained to HR."

I studied his face, trying to recognize George under the makeup. "When did you have your throat surgery?"

"I needed money, but after Mom died and left me a sizeable inheritance, I had more than enough for a new look. It was soon after I killed Bright." He looked at his chest. "I was never pretty as a woman, but these big falsies made up for it."

"What I don't get is why you came back. You had a new life as a nurse. Why risk returning for petty revenge over school pranks done ten years ago?"

"It was all part of my master plan. I had my commercial pilot license and flew for a sky-diving club while I was in nursing school in California. They had a Beaver jump plane like the one the skydiving club has at Aerodrome Estates. I volunteered to fly for the parachute club here so I could get access to their airplane."

"And you decided all the popular jocks in our class did things worthy of death sentences?" My stomach churned.

Another quick peek out the windshield revealed time was running out for me.

"You don't understand, Jett. You're beautiful and were popular in school. You had a great social life. Nobody picked on you." He chewed his lip. "But me? I suffered all four years. Those bastards made my life a living hell and enjoyed doing it."

"Look, I'm sorry you went through that, but I don't understand what you have against me. I never mistreated you. In fact, I liked you, even though you never talked to me, except in chemistry class." That last part was a lie, but I was desperate.

"Hah!" He stabbed a finger at me. "You … our pretty little prom queen, you dated those monsters. That proves you were okay with what they did to me."

"George, I swear I had no idea they were harassing you. How could I possibly know?"

"Oh, I'm sure they told you all about the mean things they did, and I bet you laughed, like it was a big joke. Well, now the joke's on you. You'll die in a ball of fire, and your precious puppies and roommates will die with you."

Trying not to panic, I glanced over my shoulder. "I don't see any buckets or cement mix. Are you planning to die too?"

"Oh, no, I've got a parachute stashed behind the bench seat. You'll be crashing solo, sweetheart." He chuckled, opened a wet wipe, and rubbed off his makeup and lipstick.

*He's made his decision, and I can't reason with a psycho.*

"Since you intend to kill me, at least answer a few questions first."

He unbuckled his seatbelt and turned toward me. "Make it quick."

"Why put their feet in concrete-filled buckets and drop them on my land, instead of in the ocean where they'd never be found?"

"Oh, that—the buckets confused the issue, but their real purpose was to make it easy to dump the bodies without me having to leave the pilot seat. I positioned them with the heavy buckets close to the open door and then tilted the plane into a sideslip. The buckets dragged them out, easy peasy."

"But why drop them on my land?"

"So you would know what it felt like to suffer constant attacks." He laughed. "The national publicity was an added bonus."

"You put a lot of thought into this. If you had quit after you dropped Grant, you probably would've gotten away with everything and pinned it on Harry."

"You don't know about Harry." He laughed. "I killed him last night and dropped his body in your backyard right after you drove away on your bike." He glanced at his watch. "Right about now, the cops are realizing Harry wasn't the killer, and they don't have a clue who it is."

"You'll never get away with this." I pretended to be calm, but my heart raced.

He smirked. "I've had this planned for a long time. Last night, I stashed a car where I'll land my parachute. I hid a disguise in the trunk and put my new IDs in the glove compartment. No one will ever find me."

"Why are you using Hunter's Staggerwing?" I stalled, desperate to stop him.

"Good question. I was going to use the sky diving club's Beaver, but it's even better that you have the humiliation of crashing your uncle's airplane." He shrugged. "Hunter was always kind to me, so I'm glad he got called away. I didn't really want to kill him."

*He sounded almost human for a moment.*

"Time's up." He moved to the bench seat at the rear of the cabin, donned a parachute, and then moved forward. "Ready to die, Jett?"

I glanced up at him, my stomach in a knot. "Please, George, don't do this."

He squeezed my shoulder. "I remember reading about your parents' plane crash." A sinister laugh. "In a few minutes, you'll join them. But first, you'll feel the same terror they must've felt in those final seconds before their jet dived into the ocean."

My uncle's airplane didn't have an autopilot, so George set nose-down elevator trim, putting the airplane into a dive aimed at my home, a huge four-story target.

The air noise increased to a roar.

Just before he jumped out, he shouted, "Bye now. Enjoy the barbeque."

# THIRTY-NINE

George had left the throw-over control yoke on the left side. It
was connected to a vertical column that moved forward and aft
and controlled the elevator for nose up or down pitch and the ailerons
for banking the wings into turns. Belted into the right seat with my
hands bound behind me and my seat forward, my feet were free, and I
could reach the rudder pedals, but that wouldn't help me. Pulling out of
the dive would be a Herculean task.

Every second counted as the altimeter wound down much too
quickly.

I had to pull back the throttle and somehow get the plane's nose up.
Leaning forward to my left, I tried to grab the push-pull throttle with
my mouth, but just then the plane hit an air pocket. My face slammed
into the power quadrant, splitting my lip and smashing my nose.

Blood gushed onto the throttle, and my eyes watered as I spit blood
and tried again. Closing my mouth around the throttle knob, I pulled
back, but my bloody mouth slipped off. I clamped onto the knob with
my teeth and dragged it back to the idle position.

I had only a minute or two left to live as my ancestral home rose to
meet me.

Desperate to pull up the nose, I angled my left knee behind the vertical control column and pulled back with every ounce of strength I could muster, but with the elevator trim set to nose down the aerodynamic force was too strong.

Air rushing past the open doorway screamed at me.

The cabin biplane had quickly picked up speed in the dive. Pulling out would be like trying to stop a runaway freight train. I had to change the elevator trim setting. The trim wheel was attached to the right side of the vertical control column, which stood between the two pilot seats. A lucky break for me. I used my left knee to rotate the trim wheel to full nose-up trim, but with the airplane in a high-speed dive, pulling out would still be difficult.

I blinked away tears caused by my smashed nose, and the altimeter came into focus.

Five hundred feet and seconds before certain death.

Now that I'd reset the trim, I rammed my left knee against the forward side of the vertical control column, pulling back with all my strength.

Glancing out the left window, I spotted George gliding to a landing on Juno Beach.

*Must do something. Can't let that monster escape.*

The muscles in my left leg strained and vibrated with the effort of pulling out of the dive. If I eased off even a little, I'd die in a fiery crash with full fuel tanks. That had been a lucky break for George. My uncle, like most pilots, always kept the tanks full to avoid condensation.

Kelly's voice blared on the radio. "This is Bell Helicopter November Two Tango Sierra calling Jett Jorgensen in Staggerwing November One Hotel Victor. Do you copy?"

I could barely hear him above the rushing air noise. Unable to use the radio microphone with my hands tied behind my back, I couldn't answer him. Did he know where I was?

My eyes locked on Valhalla, its ramparts rising like gaping jaws full of fangs ready to devour the biplane. The stubborn aircraft's nose fought me for every inch it rose skyward.

It would be close.

Too close.

My heart pounded almost as hard as the aircraft vibrated, its speed above the red line on the airspeed indicator. Biplanes are strong, but if the speed continued to increase, the plane might break apart even if it didn't hit the castle first. Air noise from the slipstream and open doorway screamed like a banshee as my left leg shook from muscle strain, and blood steadily flowed out of my nose.

I prayed I'd miss my home and all my loved ones inside who were probably unaware of the impending disaster. I didn't dare use the rudder for an uncoordinated turn and risk entering a tight spiral. That would seal my fate.

As the airplane roared ever closer, I gritted my teeth, adrenaline humming through my veins as I coaxed the vertical control column back another inch with my aching left knee.

The altimeter wound down through a hundred feet.

A second or two left to live.

The nose passed through level on its way up as my stone castle filled my windshield. I don't know why, but George had left the landing gear down after takeoff. The airplane's belly just missed scraping the central ramparts on Valhalla, but the stone structure ripped away the main wheels. The high-speed impact dipped the plane's nose, and I barely pulled it up with my knee in time to miss a huge banyan tree.

In the blink of an eye, I blew past the turret towers on either side of the castle and out to sea. Relief flooded me as the excessive airspeed and nose-up trim helped me zoom up to a higher altitude. I had survived the dive, but I had to turn around and somehow land safely back at Aerodrome Estates.

I took a deep breath and tried to get my heart rate under control, then pushed the throttle forward using my sore mouth. After climbing a few hundred feet, I leveled off, moving the trim wheel with my trembling left knee, and setting the throttle to cruise power with my mouth. I gave my left leg a rest, and using the right rudder, I made small, skidding turns toward the coast. A banking turn required ailerons, but I couldn't reach the controls.

The airplane sounded normal again—no shrieking air noise, but my body hummed with adrenaline, tears ran down my cheeks, my nose and lip bled, and my left leg muscles spasmed. Dizzy from head trauma and pain, I tried to focus my eyes.

Using the rudder pedals, I managed to aim the airplane in the direction of the private airport at Aerodrome Estates. The light wind had shifted and favored me landing to the northwest on the grass runway.

When I had the field in sight, I leaned forward, eased the throttle back with my sore mouth, and began a gradual descent.

The engine coughed, spit oil on the windshield, and spewed smoke out the right side. Apparently, the dive above redline speed had damaged the engine. Would I make it to the airport?

*Oh, God, if the airplane catches fire, I'll never get out.*

The grass runway loomed in the distance. If I could hold my altitude a few minutes longer, I could shut down the engine and maybe prevent it from catching fire during my glide in. Black smoke swirled into the cockpit, choking me and making my eyes water.

Once I was sure I could glide to the runway, I pulled the throttle back to idle. Pain knifed my injured mouth as I pulled the fuel mixture control fully back, killing the engine. My left leg was ready to give out, but I needed it to keep me from crashing. I had to hold the nose up with my left knee long enough to skim over the runway and settle onto it.

I had managed to stop the propeller in a horizontal position, but I had no way of raising the damaged landing gear because the gear lever was out of reach on the left side of the control panel. I prayed the gear legs had sheared off flush with the belly.

My left leg cramped as I struggled to hold the elevator control back, hoping for a smooth touchdown with the plane's belly sliding on the grass. Instead, the gear legs dug into the ground, standing the plane on its nose. Momentum flipped the plane onto its back, and the sudden stop smashed my head into the instrument panel.

Everything went black.

I woke hanging upside-down from my seatbelt as thick black smoke poured inside, burning my lungs. Coughing, I leaned over and grabbed the window crank with my mouth. Pain contorted my face as I struggled with opening the side window. Acrid smoke swirled around me, and I gasped for breath.

Dizziness made my head spin while thundering rotor blades shook the airplane. The noise faded, someone shouted my name, and a fire extinguisher whooshed as it discharged into the engine.

Strong arms reached around me and unbuckled my lap belt. I fell in a heap against the roof, which was now under me. My rescuer wrestled me free and dragged me outside. My legs felt like rubber, and I collapsed onto him. He rolled me over, and my burning eyes gazed into the worried face of Kelly Mahone.

"Jett, are you okay? Your face is covered with blood."

I tried to speak, gasped, and erupted into a coughing fit.

He cut away the zip-tie binding my wrists, scooped me into his arms, and carried me to the helicopter. After depositing me on a front seat, he fastened my seatbelt. I tried to talk, but that triggered another coughing fit. He closed the door, ran around to the right side, and hopped aboard. We were quickly airborne and headed to a hospital helipad.

No matter how hard I tried, I couldn't speak. My raw throat and the metallic taste of blood made me feel like puking. I barely held it in.

Kelly landed on the hospital roof, and medics wheeled a gurney out. In seconds, I was strapped onto it and headed inside.

I had to tell Mike about George Stavros. The thought of him getting away made my stomach churn. Reaching out, I grasped Kelly's hand in a tight grip and made a writing motion with my other hand. The desperate look on my face must've convinced him it was important. He stopped the gurney and handed me his cell.

I texted Mike: *Killer is George Stavros posing as nurse Grace Simms. He parachuted onto Juno Beach. Don't let him escape!*

# FORTY

I was treated for smoke inhalation and contusions and released after a CT scan of my head. Gwen and Sophia picked me up at the hospital. They took turns hugging me.

Gwen's jaw dropped. "Jett, your face is a mess—black eyes, swollen nose, and a split, swollen lip."

"Does it hurt?" Sophia examined the injuries.

"Everything hurts, but I refused pain killers so I can think straight."

"We're so relieved you pulled out of that dive," Sophia said. "Tim's men saw the airplane coming and evacuated everyone to safety."

"We thought the killer was on board with you," Gwen said, helping me into the car. "Thank God you survived. How did he get you?"

I told them everything and ended with, "We have to move fast. We need dirty clothes from George's apartment so we can seal them in a plastic bag for Darcy's dogs. If the opportunity arises, the dogs can use the scent to identify him even with his new disguise."

"Good idea." Gwen made a U-turn. "It's just down the street near the hospital."

CSU had finished sweeping the apartment for clues to George's whereabouts. Crime-scene tape stretched across the door. Sophia picked the lock, and we ducked under the tape.

Sophia took a two-gallon Ziplock bag from the kitchen, and I found dirty clothes in the hamper. Meanwhile, Gwen searched the apartment for a hidden compartment.

She removed an air-conditioning vent cover. "I found a passport for Grace Simms and other IDs with Grace's name on them. Guess George won't be using that identity anymore."

"Wish we knew for sure if he plans to live as a man again." I stuffed some dirty underwear and a soiled shirt into the plastic bag.

Gwen held up a pill bottle. "He left behind the estrogen pills, and you said he left his wig inside the Staggerwing. He must intend to be a guy again."

Sophia nudged me. "What color was his hair under the wig?"

"Dark brown, but he can always dye it a different color or bleach it."

Sophia sealed the bag of dirty clothes and stuffed it into her giant handbag. "We'd better go before someone sees us here."

Just then, Mike walked in looking weary. "Gwen, Sophia, you shouldn't be here." He spotted me behind them, gasped, and pulled me into his arms for a long hug. "I'm so sorry, Jett. By the time I got your message and rushed over to Juno Beach, George was gone. I checked flights departing all the airports within a three-hour drive, plus trains and buses—nothing." He tilted my chin up. "Your face looks painful." He hugged me again.

"I'm okay." His hug flooded me with warmth. "Don't feel bad about this, Mike. George meticulously planned every aspect of the murders and his escape. Probably drove somewhere police wouldn't look, then donned a new disguise with new identity documents and boarded a flight."

Gwen patted his back. "Or maybe he's driving cross-country."

He sighed. "It's out of our hands now. The FBI took over the case. Serial killers are their area of expertise."

I took his hands in mine. "Mike, there's something you should know."

The serious look on my face commanded everyone's attention.

"What is it?" he asked.

"Your brother was George's first victim." I squeezed his hands. "He confessed everything to me before he parachuted out."

Mike sucked in his breath. "Did he say why?"

"Yeah, he said Matt shoved his head in a toilet."

Sophia put a hand on his shoulder. "Sick little creep probably deserved far worse than a swirly from your brother."

Mike pulled me in for another hug. "Thanks, Jett. I finally know who killed Matt and why." He sighed. "A normal person wouldn't have murdered him over that."

Gwen patted his back. "Sorry, Mike, but at least you have closure now."

Recovering, he glanced around. "I hope you ladies didn't take anything."

"We found something CSU missed." Gwen pointed at the bottle of estrogen pills and the IDs. "Looks like George is done pretending to be a woman."

"I'll pass this along. You should take Jett home now. She needs rest after her ordeal." He gave me a soft kiss on my forehead.

Since Sophia always carried an enormous handbag, it didn't occur to Mike to check it. We got away clean. I felt a little guilty not telling him about George's dirty laundry, but I knew he'd never let us keep it if he knew we had it.

Once we were in Gwen's car, I borrowed Sophia's cell and called Darcy. "Hey, I have a question about your dogs."

"How can we help?"

"I collected dirty underwear and a shirt from the killer's apartment and put the items in a Ziplock bag. If it takes a few months to locate him, will the dogs still be able to get enough scent to ID him?"

"Oh, yes, but keep the bag sealed until we're ready to send in the dogs. I heard about what happened in your uncle's airplane. It's all over the news. Are you alright?"

"A little banged up but determined to catch George Stavros. He'll change his name and appearance, so your dogs might be the only way to verify we have the right guy when we find him. No way I'm letting that monster get away."

"Mona can search the Internet, and you can tap your contacts at the three-letter intelligence agencies. Once you think you have a likely suspect, I'll bring Max and Dobie, and we'll nail the creep."

"Sounds good. I'll keep you informed." I handed back Sophia's phone as we pulled in front of Valhalla, still intact, no thanks to George.

Tim and Kelly met me at the car. I gave Kelly a warm hug and then Tim.

Kelly scrutinized my face. "How are you? Is your throat feeling better?"

"I'm good, thanks to you." I sighed. "I feel terrible about Hunter's Staggerwing."

"Hey, it's nothing that can't be fixed—minor engine damage, no fire, and the wings look pretty good, but he'll need a new prop and landing gear, and body and tail repairs."

Tears ran down my cheeks as I thought about my uncle's beautiful airplane lying in a heap on the grass.

Tim put an arm around me and guided me through the front door. "The way you flew the airplane with your hands tied behind your back and the controls on the opposite side was nothing short of miraculous."

I sniffled. "Trying not to die is a strong motivator."

"Kelly flew back and retrieved your shoulder bag from the airplane." He pointed at my bag on a table. "He also made arrangements for the plane to be dismantled and moved to your uncle's hangar after the feds release the accident scene." He paused. "Oh, and your Harley is still in the hangar. Would you like me to send someone to ride it back here?"

"No need. I'll get it later, or Hunter can ride it here when he returns from his flight, that is, if he's still speaking to me." I picked up my shoulder bag.

Gwen patted my back. "Don't be ridiculous. Hunter loves you more than anything. He'll be relieved you survived, and he knows how to fix airplanes."

Just then, my cell rang. I fished it out of my purse and answered, "Hello."

"Jett, it's Hunter. How badly are you hurt, sweetheart?"

"Just a little banged up is all. Uncle Hunter, I'm sorry I wrecked your beautiful airplane." I stifled a sob. "I feel terrible about it."

"Jett, baby, I almost lost you. Don't worry about my Staggerwing. Airplanes are replaceable—you're not. We'll make it a fun project and work on it together when you're feeling up to it." He paused. "I love you, sweetheart. Now get some rest and I'll see you when I get back from this airline trip."

"Love you too, Unc." I dropped the phone in my bag and glanced around the great hall to make sure the feds weren't waiting to interview me. "Can I talk with everybody in confidence?"

"Of course," Tim said.

Tim and Kelly sat on either side of me on a leather sofa.

Gwen and Sophia settled nearby and Mona joined us with Karin and my dogs.

After a flood of doggie kisses and worried looks from Mona and Karin, everyone settled in and waited for me to speak.

"Mike said the FBI is taking over the case, but I feel like we might have better luck than their people because Gwen and I know George Stavros. And I have some insight into his mindset. Unlike most serial killers, he's motivated solely by revenge. Now that he's killed everyone he wanted to kill, except me, he might go years before he kills again. That'll make him a lot harder to find, and it's a safe bet he won't take another job as a nurse."

"What do you want us to do?" Mona asked.

"George will have a new identity, so we'll focus mainly on his height and weight. I'm thinking we should search everywhere in the US and Canada for a man recently hired as a bush pilot, possibly to fly a radial-engine Beaver like the jump plane he used here."

Kelly said, "The Pacific Northwest, Alaska, and Canada are good places to start. He just left here today, so he'd be starting a new pilot job in a few days or maybe next week."

"Let's hope he applied for the job via the Internet. He'd have to include a forged pilot license that will have his height and weight. With any luck, we can narrow it down to a few suspects." Tim paused. "How do you intend to verify it's him if he changed his identity and appearance?"

Sophia glanced around and pulled the dirty clothes from her giant shoulder bag. "We have his scent. Darcy's dogs won't be fooled. They'll nail the dirtbag."

Tim and Kelly grinned.

I turned to Mona. "I'm counting on your hacking skills to locate him. I'll also reach out to my contacts at the three-letter agencies just to cover all the bases."

Mona nodded. "No worries, boss. You can count on me. I'll find the creep."

Karin said, "I just have one question. What will you do when you catch him?"

"How about I shoot him between the eyes—in self-defense, of course?" Sophia asked.

"It's impossible to predict what will happen when we find him. He might be unarmed." I arched a brow at Sophia.

"No problem. I'll bring one of them throw-down guns and put his prints on it."

I rolled my eyes. "We aren't criminals. We'll do this the right way and hand him over to the feds. With my testimony, they'll lock him up forever."

"And I'm coming with you," Gwen said. "I'll ask my captain for time off when we have some suspects to run down."

Tim cleared his throat. "Uh, Jett, there's a chance George will come after you when he hears on the news that you survived."

"Right," Kelly agreed. "You need to remain vigilant here at home."

"And I'll keep your security team on full alert," Tim said.

"Thanks, everyone." I stood. "Time for me to hit the sack." I turned to Sophia. "I'll leave my bedroom door open in case the dogs need to go out."

I took the elevator up to the fourth floor and headed down the south hallway where twelve-foot walls paneled in golden teak held paintings of Nordic landscapes and Viking battles.

My head pounded, and my body ached as I changed into a

nightgown and closed the heavy, rose-colored draperies. Preferring natural medicine, I swallowed a handful of systemic enzymes and slid beneath the covers on my king-size, four-poster bed.

Pratt and Whitney jumped up on the bed and snuggled against me. Their furry bodies comforted me, and I dropped into a deep, restorative sleep.

# FORTY-ONE

First thing Wednesday morning, I called in favors with my contacts at the DIA, NSA, and CIA. They agreed to employ their vast intelligence networks and search for a newly hired bush pilot working in a remote area, narrowing the search to pilots who fit George's height and approximate weight. These agencies tended not to share info with the FBI, giving me an edge.

When I gathered with everyone for breakfast, Sophia looked at me and said, "Whoa, Jett, you look like you were in a bar fight and lost. How bad is the pain?"

"I look worse than I feel." I gingerly touched my lip. "Everything is swollen, my black eyes are darker, and my face has turned a sick shade of bluish-green."

Karin handed me a plate of eggs scrambled with diced ham and shredded cheddar. She shook her head. "It looks bad, but your lip will heal fast. Your black eyes and swollen nose will take longer."

I shrugged. "Doesn't matter. The ball was last week."

"Don't you want to look pretty for your date with Mike on Saturday?" Mona asked.

"Oh, geez, I forgot about that, and Saturday is only a few days away." I licked my split lip. "I just can't catch a break with Mike."

"You can probably look okay with enough makeup," Sophia said, offering me some cinnamon toast.

"Ladies, I've seen my face. There's no way it'll look romance-ready by Saturday."

———

An hour after breakfast, I took a soothing swim in my heated pool, followed by a soak in the hot tub. The warm water relaxed my aching muscles and made me feel rejuvenated.

FBI agents visited me later that morning and questioned me about George Stavros and my abduction in the plane. They took notes and also recorded the interview.

Afterward, I walked them to the door. "Thank you for coming, and I hope you catch him soon."

They waved goodbye and drove away in a black SUV.

Sophia walked up as I closed the door. "Think the feds will catch him?"

"I doubt it. They think he'll continue his nursing career in a new location."

"Mona has been running Internet searches all morning," Sophia said. "I bet she'll find him."

I smiled and regretted it. My lip stung as I replied, "I have faith in her, but I'm counting on the NSA as a backup."

My doorbell boomed out Wagner's "Ride of the Valkyries." Representatives from the FAA and NTSB were at my door. I invited them in and spent the next hour answering their questions about my ordeal in Hunter's Staggerwing. I had already sent in my written accident report. Some of the questions the FAA guy asked gave me the impression he was fishing for a way to blame me for the accident. My tax dollars at work.

———

Thursday morning, I strode into my study, and sunlight filtering in through tall corner windows bathed my oak floor-to-ceiling bookcases in a warm light. Mona sat cross-legged with her computer on her lap, tapping furiously on the keys.

She thrust her fist in the air and yelled, "Score!"

"You found him?"

"Three strong possibilities." She showed me her screen.

"Good job, Mona." I fired up my late father's fully updated desktop computer. "Let's see if my spook friends agree with you." I checked my email and found info from a friend at the NSA on possible suspects located in Wyoming, Montana, and Alaska. The very same men Mona had already found.

Jackpot.

Sophia walked in, and I said, "Come and see what Mona found."

She read the report over my shoulder. "I'll pack my bag with several full magazines for our Glocks." Then she patted Mona's back. "Well done, my dear."

I hesitated. "All the suspects are in the far Northwest and are due to start new pilot jobs tomorrow. There's no way I'll get home in time for my date with Mike on Saturday."

"Reschedule it. Catching the guy who wants you dead is more important, and if you delay your date, you'll look better by then anyway."

"I guess you're right. It's just that Mike and I are finally on the same page, and I don't want to mess that up." I printed out the info.

She shrugged. "Hey, if he loves you, he'll understand, especially if you say you don't feel up to it physically."

"Maybe." I chewed my lip. "But he won't be happy we went after the killer."

"Don't tell him." Sophia nudged me. "Call Gwen and Darcy and pack a bag."

"First, I'll call the flight department at Jorgensen Industries and book the Gulfstream G650. That'll give us plenty of room for four passengers and Darcy's two big dogs."

"Better pack warm clothes. All those places are still cold in April, and Alaska might be freezing." She headed for the door.

I called after her, "And he won't recognize us if we're wearing hooded parkas."

She yelled back, "He wouldn't recognize *your* face anyway."

———

After hugging my doggies, I turned to Karin and Mona. "Thanks for looking after the fur babies while we're gone. We'll keep you posted on our progress."

Karin asked, "What did Tim say when you told him where you're going?"

I shot a glance at Sophia. "We didn't tell him. You can inform him we're gone after we're airborne."

Mona's eyes widened. "Why wouldn't you tell him?"

"Tim and his men have saved us so many times I've lost count. I don't want to drag him into a quasi-legal situation that might jeopardize him and his security company."

"Besides, four armed women with two big dogs should be more than enough to deal with one cowardly wienie who sneaks up on people," Sophia said.

Karin sighed. "What about Mike? Should I tell him what you're doing?"

"Don't tell Tim or Mike where we're going. They might come after us." I turned and tossed my bag into the SUV. "I'll text Mike during the flight and reschedule our date."

Karin and Mona waved as we drove next door to pick up Gwen.

She tossed her bag in the back and hopped in. "This is exciting. My boss gave me a few days off and permission to apprehend George if I hand him over to the feds." She lifted her shirt a little, exposing her aunt's antique brooch pinned to her waist. "I wore this for good luck."

"Whatever helps." I glanced back at her. "Darcy and her dogs will meet us at the jet."

I parked in the company hangar, and Captain Dan Duquesne helped us with our luggage.

He took my arm. "I heard about the plane crash. You sure you're up for this?"

"Don't worry. I look a lot worse than I feel. Let's go aboard so I can brief you and the copilot. I want you to know our mission plan."

Just then, Darcy arrived with her German shepherd, Max, and her big Doberman, Dobie. The dogs looked excited.

"Hi, Darcy. This is our pilot, Dan."

"A pleasure to meet you." He eyed the dogs. "Have they flown before?"

"Don't worry. My boys are good in any type of transportation as long as I'm with them." She introduced him to Max and Dobie. "They aren't pets. They're working dogs."

"I see," he said, petting them. "Let's get everyone on board and settled."

The copilot, Rob Owens, stowed our luggage and then joined us in the cabin.

I stood. "I'll brief the pilots on our mission, and then we can get going." I explained our plan to catch George Stavros, that we were armed, and ended with, "That's why we didn't want a flight attendant on this trip. Fewer people are at risk. I know how to work the galley, and we can fend for ourselves."

Dan smiled. "Flights with you are always interesting, Jett." He nodded at Gwen. "I remember your nurse outfits from last time."

It wasn't long before the pilots started the engines and taxied to the runway. Max and Dobie lay at Darcy's feet, already asleep before we took off.

I waited until we were over Texas before I sent a text to Mike: *Sorry, but we'll have to reschedule our date when I no longer look and feel like a crash victim. I'll call in a few days.*

Mike called immediately. I didn't dare answer and turned off my phone.

---

I looked out a passenger window as we approached Natrona County International Airport in Casper, Wyoming, and admired the majestic mountains. Was this where George had gone for a new start? Within minutes, we touched down like a feather and taxied to the terminal.

Our destination on the field was Wilderness Flying Service. They advertised flights to remote grass-strip airports with hunting and fishing lodges and campsites. One of their airplanes was a DeHavilland Beaver like the one George flew at Aerodrome Estates in Florida. Our target had applied for the pilot job using the name Gerald Stone.

We had flown into a time zone that was two hours earlier than Florida. The early afternoon weather was sunny and fifty degrees when we walked off the airplane and headed for Wilderness Flying Service. Darcy dressed the dogs in their orange work bandanas, and Gwen took the lead because she had a badge. We entered the lobby with the dogs and waited behind Gwen while she spoke to the woman at the reception desk.

She flashed her badge. "Hello, I'm Detective Gwen Pendragon, law enforcement from Florida in pursuit of a dangerous fugitive."

The young woman's jaw dropped. "Oh, my, I'm Jenny Jones ... how can I help?"

Gwen made a show of checking her electronic tablet. "You hired a new pilot named Gerald Stone. Where is he?"

Jenny stood. "Are you saying Gerry's a fugitive?"

"No, Jenny. Mr. Stone is a person-of-interest who may aid our investigation." Gwen glanced around. "Is he here?"

"He flew some tourists out to a wilderness camp and won't be back until tonight." She wrung her hands. "There's no cell reception there. Would you like to try reaching him on the radio?"

"No." Gwen paused. "I realize he just started work here, but does he have a locker?"

"Yes. It's in the pilot lounge."

"Do you know if he keeps anything in it?"

"All our pilots keep extra clothes and spare boots in their lockers."

"Good, show us his locker." Gwen glanced back at Darcy and her dogs.

Our group followed Jenny to the pilot lounge. She pointed at an unlocked locker that had Gerald Stone's name taped on the door.

Gwen, Sophia, and I moved aside while Darcy had Max and Dobie take scent from George's clothes in the Ziplock bag and then sniff Gerald's locker.

"The boots inside look worn. They'll offer a better scent than the clean clothes on hooks," Darcy said.

The dogs eagerly sniffed the boots and everything inside the locker. Afterward, they backed away and sat behind Darcy.

She looked at us and shook her head. "Sorry, he's not our guy."

Gwen turned to Jenny. "Thanks for your help. Bye, now."

I patted Darcy's back on the way out. "That's okay. I didn't expect to find him on our first try. Maybe he'll be at our next stop in Montana."

# FORTY-TWO

Our pilots had the jet fueled and ready to roll when we boarded. In minutes, we were airborne and headed for Missoula, Montana.

The captain announced, "Relax, ladies. We'll be on the ground in an hour and fifteen minutes. The weather is good, but it might be bumpy around the mountains, so keep your seatbelts fastened."

Sophia checked her Glock and asked, "Who're we looking for in Montana?"

I pulled out my list. "Brent Morgan started today as a pilot for Big Sky Adventures. They have a Beaver, a Cessna 180 on floats, and a Helio Courier."

Gwen had her seat reclined and seemed to be dozing. I glanced back at Darcy. She was reading a thriller novel, and her dogs were sound asleep at her feet. Not a stressful trip so far.

I dozed off for what felt like a few minutes. Dan's voice woke me when he announced we were landing. I looked out the window and admired the sundrenched valley. The air was so crisp and clear, I could see for a hundred miles. We parked in front of Big Sky Adventures, and I spotted their Beaver and the Cessna on amphibious floats.

The weather was still sunny, but it was late afternoon, and the temperature had dropped to forty degrees with a brisk wind. Darcy slipped on the dogs' bandanas, and I zipped up my parka as I left the airplane.

"Let's hope he's here," Gwen said, glancing back at us as we headed for the lobby. She turned around just in time to bump into a man in his late twenties. He had sky-blue eyes, black hair, and was the same height as George, but handsome.

He smiled at us. "I hope you're looking for me," he said, holding the door.

"Are you Brent Morgan?" Gwen asked.

I carefully listened to his voice, thinking he didn't sound like George.

He smiled again. "Yes, I am, and who might you all be?"

Gwen flashed her badge. "Detective Gwen Pendragon, and these are my associates." She introduced us.

Brent's eyes widened when he met me. "Jett, tell me who did this, and I'll make him wish he'd never been born."

I smiled a painful smile. "Thank you for offering, but he's destined for a permanent prison cell."

He cracked his knuckles. "I could tune him up before you take him into custody."

Sophia laughed. "I'd enjoy watching that."

Darcy cleared her throat after the dogs took scent from the bag. "And these are our specialty dogs, Max and Dobie."

She urged the dogs forward, and Brent petted them as they sniffed his hands and wagged their tails.

"Beautiful dogs," he said as they trotted behind Darcy and sat quietly.

I sighed. "Nice meeting you, Brent, but you aren't the guy we're looking for."

"I could be if you're willing to be flexible." He flashed another smile.

Sophia smirked. "We're on the trail of a serial killer, sugar buns. You don't want to be that guy."

His jaw dropped, but he recovered quickly. "No, but I'd like to take you lovely ladies out to dinner. Are you staying at a hotel in town?"

I glanced at my watch. "May as well spend the night here and continue on in the morning. Brent, do you know a nearby hotel that allows working dogs?"

"Yep, the Missoula Inn is only a few miles from here. I can take everyone in the company's ten-passenger van."

My friends nodded, so I said, "Thanks, Brent. Our plane is parked outside. We'll pick up the pilots and our luggage."

It had been a long day of flying, and Dan and Rob were happy to spend the night. The hotel had a restaurant that specialized in steaks, and the crisp mountain air had fueled our appetites.

I took Brent's arm as we walked into the restaurant. "You were kind to bring us here. We'd like you to be our guest for dinner tonight. It all goes on our expense account anyway." It didn't really, but I couldn't stick him with a huge dinner bill.

He smiled. "Well, as long as you don't have to pay for it, that's great."

We enjoyed a delicious meal, and before he left, Brent handed me his card. "Call me in the morning, and I'll give your group a ride back to the airport."

———

We took turns hugging Brent before we boarded our jet at 9:00 a.m. for the flight to Alaska. His body felt a lot warmer than the brisk thirty-five degrees swirling around us.

Darcy and Gwen waved at him as they ushered the dogs aboard the plane.

I shivered. "My Florida blood isn't used to this cold air."

Brent laughed. "If you think this is cold, wait until you get to Alaska."

"I might have to buy some long underwear."

"I wish I could come with you and keep you warm." He gave me another hug. "Look me up when you're finished in Alaska."

I kissed his cheek. "Thanks for everything."

Sophia squeezed his left butt cheek. "Take care, sugar buns."

Brent grinned and waved goodbye.

———

Five hours later, I looked out a passenger window as we made our approach to Nome, Alaska. It was located on the southwestern side of the Seward Peninsula along Norton Sound, which flowed into the Bering Sea. The local time was two hours earlier than Montana, which put us on the ground at noon. The weather was cloudy and twenty-seven degrees.

*Maybe I should've stayed in Florida.*

I unbuckled my seatbelt, stood, and stretched. "Well, ladies, let's hope the third time's the charm. We're looking for Tom Denton at Barlow Freight Service. The company uses a Beaver like the one in Florida." I glanced out. "There's one parked over there."

Gwen headed for the door. "Let's check out their office. Maybe he has a locker."

I stopped at the cockpit. "Dan, we'll spend the night here, but first please have the jet fueled up and ready to go."

Gwen, Darcy, Sophia, and I zipped up our hooded parkas, slipped handguns into our pockets, and trudged across the ramp with Max and Dobie wearing their work bandanas. The cold, humid air cut into me like a knife, but it energized the dogs. Happy to stretch their legs, they ran circles around us during the walk from the airplane.

I followed everyone inside. Scents of fresh-brewed coffee and hints of Old Spice aftershave wafted through the freight company's warm office.

I stamped my feet on the doormat and lowered my hood. "Wow, it's cold out there!"

A man who appeared to be in his late fifties glanced up from behind a desk. "Cold? It's almost above freezing—much warmer than last month." He regarded our shivering little group. "You're not from around here." He chuckled. "At least the dogs look happy."

Gwen stepped forward and flashed her badge. "I need to talk to your new pilot. Is Tom Denton working today?"

"Hold on, Miss." He stood. "What's this about?"

"We're hunting a serial killer. If Tom's our man, he'll have changed his appearance, and he'll be using phony IDs." She gestured at Darcy and her pooches. "The dogs are here to sniff him out."

His eyes widened. "How many people has he murdered?"

"Eight that we know of. And he tried to kill me." I offered my hand. "Jett Jorgensen."

His jaw dropped when he noticed my injured face. "The killer did that?"

"It could've been worse," I said. "And you are?"

"Sorry, I'm Fred Barlow. I own this company, so if my new pilot is a criminal, I need to know everything."

Darcy moved forward with her dogs. "Tom might be innocent. We checked pilots in Wyoming and Montana before we flew here. We're looking into newly hired bush pilots who match the height and weight of the serial killer. Does he have a locker?"

"No locker, sorry."

Sophia asked, "Where is he now?"

"He's on a freight run with several stops. Won't be back until tonight."

I checked a route map hanging on a wall. "What's his last stop?"

He walked around his desk and tapped a spot on the map. "White Mountain Airport. It's sixty-three flight miles from here."

I turned to my friends. "Should we wait for him to return?"

Gwen glanced out the window. "This looks like a busy airport. Lots of people might be put at risk if we wait."

"Then let's rent a four-wheel-drive SUV, drive over to White Mountain Airport, and nail the dirtbag," Sophia suggested.

Fred shook his head. "Forget it. That airport is on a narrow plateau, and the only way up there is by air, snowmobile, or dog sled."

"Sounds like the perfect place to trap him." I gazed out the front window at the Beaver on the ramp. "Do you know who owns that airplane?"

"It's my backup plane, but the engine needs a new cylinder." He pointed at a package. "The part arrived last evening, and I plan on installing it after lunch."

"I'll help you. It has the same engine as my uncle's Staggerwing. We've worked on it together many times." I felt a wave of sadness thinking about Hunter's wrecked plane.

"It'll be dark soon." He rubbed his beard. "My buddy said I can use his heated hangar."

Sophia looked outside. "Dark soon? It's just a few minutes after noon."

"We only have about five hours of daylight in April. Gets dark around two-thirty p.m." He checked his watch. "We'll grab a quick lunch across the street and then get started on that engine. You can leave the dogs here while we're eating."

"Do we have time for that?" I glanced at my watch. "It's important we intercept him before he gets back."

"We'll finish in plenty of time, but first you ladies need fuel in your bodies to weather the cold temperatures."

A half hour passed while we finished our hot lunches.

Fred sighed. "I hate to say it, but Tom might be your guy. I needed a pilot, and he was well qualified, but when he walked in … there was something about his eyes—gave me the creeps."

"Our guy definitely has creepy eyes with a touch of crazy." I shook my head. "I'll never forget the last time I saw him."

Fred nudged Gwen. "I hope you're carrying. Alaskan bush pilots are always armed, you know, for safety reasons in case of an off-field landing."

"What weapon does Tom carry?" Gwen asked.

"He's strapped with a Glock 19 handgun and keeps a .30-06 Springfield rifle in the cargo hold."

Sophia pulled out her pistol and racked the slide. "Sounds like we might end up in a shootout."

"We're not taking any chances," Gwen said. "If he draws on us, shoot him."

Sophia grinned. "No problem. I never miss."

Fred stared at her, his mouth agape.

I grinned. "It's true."

He checked the time. "We'd better get cracking on that engine."

# FORTY-THREE

Our pilots checked into an airport hotel with my friends and the dogs. My team would wait in comfort for my call.

It was pitch dark when we finished working on the engine. I stepped inside the bathroom and took a few minutes to wash the grease off my hands. Finished, I came out just as Fred zipped up his parka and started the tug.

After bundling up and donning warm gloves, I followed him outside. A light snow had fallen, and the temperature had dropped to sixteen degrees when he pulled the airplane out of the heated hangar.

My breath formed a white cloud when I asked, "Fred, is there a warm place for us to wait at White Mountain Airport?"

"Yeah, they have a heated building where supplies from the flights are stored."

I showed him my pilot license. "I've flown many radial engine aircraft, including Beavers. I'd like to rent this one for a few hours."

He looked me up and down, then pulled a double-barrel shotgun from the cargo hold, checked it was loaded, and cocked it. "I'll let you fly it, but I'm riding shotgun."

Apparently, he meant that literally.

I glanced at my watch. "We have to get there before your pilot arrives."

"It's only a thirty-minute flight. We'll land before he does, but it'll be close."

Before we did the preflight inspection, I called Gwen on my cell. "Round up everyone. We're ready to roll."

———

Fred dialed in the radio frequency for the automated runway lights and keyed the mic to turn them on. I lowered the flaps after lining up for a landing to the northwest on runway 33 at White Mountain. A full moon broke free of the clouds long enough to illuminate the steep sides of the narrow plateau and the sheer drop off at both ends of the short, three-thousand-foot runway. A tiny native village ran along one side well behind the storage building.

"Wow, even dogsleds and snowmobiles wouldn't have an easy time getting up there, and I'd hate to slide off the end of that runway." I adjusted the throttle.

"If you run off the northwest end, you'll save your family the burial costs." He chuckled. "There's a cemetery at the bottom of the cliff."

Turbulence jostled the plane as I scanned the instrument panel. "If you're trying to help me relax, it's not working." I grabbed the mic and announced to the cabin, "Keep your seatbelts fastened tight and hang on to the dogs. We're landing now."

Fred reached over and patted my knee. "Be ready for some nasty gusts, Jett, and put her down nice and gentle."

The Beaver's big balloon tires helped cushion my touchdown on the snow-covered runway. Then a gust caught us, and I did some fancy footwork on the rudder pedals to keep us straight. The end of the runway was fast approaching when the brakes finally gained some traction.

"Good job, Jett." He pointed. "Take that turnoff and park in front of the building."

"Should we hide the airplane?" I asked. "He might be suspicious if he sees it."

"Nah, he knew about the bad cylinder. He'll probably think I flew it up here for a short test flight after fixing it."

"I hope you're right." I parked and shut down the engine. "I have an idea. Before your pilot lands, my friends and I will hide behind the building. Help him unload and then keep him inside a few minutes while we sneak around the outside and let the dogs sniff his cockpit. If they react to his scent, we'll know he's our guy and nail him."

"Good. And if he's not your serial killer, we'll all get together for drinks back in Nome."

"Fingers crossed." I smiled and went aft into the cabin to share the plan.

———

"There he is, ladies." Fred's breath made a cloud as he pointed southeast. "He just switched on his landing lights, so you've got about five minutes before he gets here."

A brisk wind blew ground snow into swirls around us. The temperature on the plateau was only eight degrees. Being a Florida girl, I couldn't imagine why anyone would want to live in this climate. Maybe that was why the killer thought no one would look for him in Alaska.

I glanced down at Max and Dobie, alert and wearing their work bandanas. "Oh boy, Fred, I didn't think—how will you explain paw prints in the snow?"

He rubbed his beard and gave it some thought. "Easy, I'll say I delivered two sled dogs. The villagers use them for most of their transportation needs."

"That sounds good." Darcy snapped on their leashes and led the dogs inside as we followed. She wiped their feet so they wouldn't leave wet prints on the floor, and we wiped our boots. Then we went out the back door, leaving Fred inside.

Sophia, Gwen, and I followed Darcy as she and the dogs eased around the side of the building. We hid behind an equipment shed and waited. The deep, throaty sound of the Beaver's R-985 radial engine grew louder as the airplane approached the building.

I pulled out my pistol, checked the magazine, and racked the slide. "Are we ready for this?" My feet were already freezing inside the thick boots.

Sophia checked her weapon's laser sight. "I was born ready."

"Simmer down, Annie Oakley," Gwen said. "We're taking him alive if possible."

Darcy had the bag containing George's dirty clothes zipped inside her parka. "I'll keep the dogs back until you signal us."

"Okay, we'll wait a few minutes and then take a peek." I tightened my hood.

Gwen eased around the shed and whispered, "Sophia, stay with Darcy until we wave you forward. Come on, Jett."

I followed her to the corner of the building and peeked around the side. Fred helped his pilot unload a few packages. They were too far away for us to see their faces.

Sound carried downwind on the snow-covered plateau. I heard Fred say, "Let's have a cup of hot coffee inside before we head back."

We waited a minute to make sure they were done unloading, then waved Darcy and Sophia forward with Max and Dobie.

"Darcy, take the dogs and check his airplane. We'll stand guard," Gwen said. "Sophia, cover the plane's door, I'll watch the side, and Jett can take the front."

We spread out while Darcy unleashed the dogs. They entered through the cargo door near the back and sniffed their way to the cockpit.

A loud gunshot echoed from inside the storage building.

I looked back at Gwen and Sophia. "Sounded like a pistol, but who fired it?"

Fred's pilot burst through the building's door holding the shotgun. He stopped and stared at us—three people bundled in parkas standing around his airplane in the dark about sixty feet away.

"Who the hell are you?" he shouted, raising the shotgun.

I was closest and thought he sounded like George Stavros. I fired, grazing his right shoulder. The shotgun slipped from his hand, and he bolted into the darkness.

Two sharp barks from inside the airplane distracted me, indicating the dogs had found George's scent in the cockpit. Fred's new pilot was indeed the serial killer, but he ran away before any of us could fire another shot.

I spotted him sprinting down the runway, disappearing into the darkness. This had been his first flight into White Mountain, and I suspected he hadn't seen the sheer cliff at the far end during his approach in the dark. He didn't know he was trapped.

Fred's shotgun lay discarded in the snow, and I checked it. Two shells were still loaded.

Sophia and Gwen joined me, and Darcy ran up to us with her dogs.

"He's definitely the killer," Darcy said. "Where is he?"

I pointed at the runway. "He ran that way. Can you send the dogs after him?"

"Max and Dobie, find and hold!" Darcy gave them one more sniff of the clothes and pointed.

The dogs were downwind of George and must've picked up his scent, because they bolted down the runway and vanished into the darkness with Darcy and Sophia following.

Gwen glanced at the building. "We'd better check on Fred first."

We hurried inside and found Fred on the floor, moaning. I didn't see any blood. Gwen unzipped his parka, revealing a bullet-proof vest and one nine-millimeter bullet embedded in the lower chest area.

"You're wearing a Kevlar vest." I smiled. "I don't know when you put that on, but I'm glad you did." I laid his shotgun on a table close to him.

Fred moaned and sat up. "I slipped it on while you were in the bathroom back in Nome." He rubbed his chest. "Thought I was being clever when I tried to trick him by asking if he had a hard time adjusting to the drastic temperature difference between Florida and Alaska. Bastard shot me with his Glock and took my shotgun. Did you get him?"

"The dogs are chasing him on the runway." I helped him into a chair.

"Better get after him. I'll be fine—probably just a cracked rib and the wind knocked out of me."

Darcy limped in. "Hurry. I fell hard on some ice, but Sophia ran after him."

"Take those battery-operated floodlights." Fred pointed at a shelf near the door.

We grabbed the lights and ran outside. Darcy limped after us. The powerful lights illuminated our path, but it also made us potential targets as we ran toward distant barking.

I struggled for breath in the freezing air as I ran as fast as I could on the slick snow. About two hundred yards from the end of the runway, the dark clouds parted, and a bright full moon lit up the landscape. My lungs burned as I hurried toward distant shapes of people and dogs.

Gwen and I neared the end of the runway and spotted Sophia about sixty feet ahead. She was half that distance behind the dogs and George.

Our fugitive halted at the end of the runway, the dogs trapping him at the edge of the cliff. Panicked, he drew his handgun and aimed it at Dobie. Max leaped up and locked his jaws around his gun arm, making him miss when he squeezed the trigger. Dobie chomped down on his other arm, and George kept firing, trying to hit them.

The dogs tugged viciously at his arms, shaking their heads side-to-side and snarling. Terrified, George kept firing, his bullets flying everywhere. Gwen and I dived onto the ground, but Sophia stood firm to take aim, and a stray bullet hit her.

She fell onto her back, and I panicked, thinking I'd lost her.

Gwen yelled, "Stay down."

I crawled to Sophia the way soldiers crawl under barbed wire on an obstacle course and prayed I'd find her alive. Bullets buzzed past me, a few hitting nearby. Sixty feet seemed like sixty miles. I feared time might be running out for my dear friend lying on the snow-covered runway.

I was ten feet from Sophia when the firing stopped. George had run out of bullets, and he couldn't reload with the dogs holding his arms. He dropped his weapon, probably thinking that would make the dogs let go of him. They didn't.

I rushed to Sophia and shined my light on her. Blood darkened the snow around her left upper pant leg.

She struggled into a sitting position. "Dirtbag got me in the thigh. Shoot him!"

I was so relieved she was alive, I hugged her. "I thought I lost you. Never scare me like that again."

"Scumbag got lucky. No way a wienie like him could take out a Calabrese."

Gwen rushed up. "Is she okay?"

I ripped her pants a little for a better look at the wound. "Looks like a deep graze on the side of her thigh."

Thirty feet away, George's screams echoed across the plateau.

Gwen aimed her weapon at him. "The dogs are jerking him around too much. I can't get a clean shot in the dark without risking hitting them."

Darcy had limped close enough to take in the scene. She shouted, "Max, Dobie, release!"

The dogs released their prey, and he lurched backward from their snapping jaws.

A fatal move.

Loose snow at the edge of the cliff gave way, and in an instant, George dropped from view, his terrified screams echoing off the rock wall.

The dogs nuzzled each other and sniffed where his blood had dripped onto the snow. They peeked over the cliff and then ran back to us.

"Let me help you." Darcy pulled off a knit cap she wore under her hood and pressed it against Sophia's wound, then used a leash to tie it against her thigh.

I hugged Sophia again. "How bad is it?"

"It burns, but it's just a flesh wound." She clutched my arm. "Help me up."

"You should stay here while we get something to use as a stretcher," Gwen said.

"No, I wanna see what happened to him." She grabbed Gwen's arm too.

We pulled her to her feet and helped her walk to the cliff. Gwen kept a tight grip on her while I shined my floodlight downward.

I spotted George's silver parka in the moonlight. His body was impaled on a large gravestone, the pointed centerpiece protruding from his darkening chest. "Looks like his killing days are over."

"Hah, I love it—dropped dead like so many of his victims." Sophia leaned against Gwen. "I vote we leave him there."

I shrugged. "He's already in a graveyard."

Darcy picked up George's handgun and handed it to Gwen.

"I'll contact the FBI when we get back to Nome," Gwen said. "They can deal with his body. Let's get Sophia and Fred to a hospital."

I felt a brief wave of unease. "We never got a close look. What if it wasn't George?"

"It's him." Darcy patted my back. "As my motto says, 'The nose knows.' My dogs never make a scent mistake."

Max and Dobie gave quick barks as if agreeing with her. Gwen and I trudged back to the airport building, holding Sophia between us. Fred sat inside, sipping hot coffee.

His chest obviously hurt him, but he insisted, "You fly home in the plane we came in, Jett, and I'll fly the other one back."

Sophia sat beside him. "Look, Fred, we know you're a tough guy, but are you sure you're up to flying a plane right now?"

"Pretty lady, I'm always up for flying." He lowered his voice and leaned close. "And up for other things too, if you know what I mean." He winked.

Sophia grinned. "I may be tiny, sweet cheeks, but even wounded, I'm still way too much woman for you in your present condition."

"I can wait." He helped her up and walked stiffly with us out to the airplane. He turned to Sophia. "You're welcome to visit me anytime. Alaska is pleasant in the summer."

Gwen took his arm. "I'll ride back with you, Fred. You can finish flirting with Sophia after we land safely in Nome and get you two patched up."

# FORTY-FOUR

The FBI collected George's remains and closed the case after interviewing Fred, my friends, and me. Technically, we hadn't broken any laws, except maybe carrying handguns that weren't registered in Alaska. The Special Agent handling the case, angry that we'd tracked down the serial killer without him, threatened us with weapons charges.

Sophia called her eldest son in New York. Thirty minutes later, the Special Agent received a phone call and apologized to us. He wished us a safe trip home.

Sophia explained, "Nobody messes with our family. Dominic has dirt on all the major players."

Turned out she had a deep graze on the side of her thigh. After a little morphine, some stitches, and prescription pain pills for the flight home, Sophia was good to go. Fred had a nasty bruise on his chest and a cracked rib. Thank God for Kevlar vests.

We said our goodbyes to Fred and boarded the jet for the long flight home. The dogs curled up together and fell asleep at Darcy's feet. Several hours later, I woke when Dan announced we were about to land at PBI.

Home at last.

———

It had been a week since our manhunt in Alaska, and I was grateful to be back in the warm Florida sunshine.

Home on Banyan Isle, Mike called and was angry I'd gone after the killer, especially since I'd said I wouldn't. But then he rescheduled our date for this evening. Tim wasn't upset with me. He understood me not wanting to put his security company at risk.

I wore a sexy cocktail dress, and Mike picked me up for the date I'd purchased at the charity ball. Thank God my split lip and injured nose had healed, my face was no longer swollen, and makeup hid fading bruises under my eyes.

We drove to The Breakers Hotel, and I sat across from him in the Seafood Bar. Our window table overlooked the Atlantic Ocean, glistening under an almost-full moon.

Mike looked handsome in a navy suit, but his demeanor was still frosty. "Have you recovered from your crash injuries and your trip to the freezing Northwest?" he asked.

"Yes, but I still remember the cold Alaskan air cutting into me like a sharp blade. I wonder why people choose to live there." I took a sip of red wine.

He shrugged. "It all depends on what you're used to, and Alaska is a beautiful place."

Time to stop skating around the real issue. "Look, Mike, I'm really sorry, but I couldn't live with the constant threat of George Stavros wanting to kill me. I needed closure, and I couldn't involve you because you're a police detective."

"Gwen's a police detective. You told *her*." He frowned. "And you took her with you."

"True, but she knew all the prep-school victims and the killer, and her boss gave her a few days off." I sighed. "Admit it. You would have stopped me, and I'd still be looking over my shoulder."

Mike clenched his jaw and took a breath. "I don't know how you found him so fast, but I'm confident the FBI would've tracked him down if you'd given them the chance."

I took a gulp of wine and tried to think of a way to appease him.

His warm hand grasped mine. "Jett, I would've stopped you because I care about you, and I didn't want you to get hurt. I heard you barely escaped being gunned down by a shotgun, and then had to duck bullets from George's pistol."

"Yeah, and Sophia got hit in the thigh. Just a deep graze, thank God."

He squeezed my hand. "You've had too many close calls since you came home from the Navy."

I looked into his eyes and saw what he'd been hiding for so long.

*Mike still loves me.*

I smiled. "Well, Mike, maybe, if you spent more time with me, I'd be safer."

Leaning forward, I pulled him close and gave him a deep, sensual kiss.

He reciprocated, his lips burning into mine.

# AFTERWORD

Banyan Isle is a fictitious residential barrier island on the east coast of South Florida, north of Singer Island, and south of Juno Beach. References to fictitious Garnet, Florida, Diamond Lake, and the surrounding area are from *Sniffers Agency—The Nose Knows*, a cozy mystery novel written by S.L. Menear and her mother, D.M. Littlefield. Private Investigator Darcy McKay and her specialty dogs from the Sniffers Agency will also appear in future Jettine Jorgensen Mysteries. All the other locations mentioned in *Dropped Dead* are real places, except the author added a clubhouse at Naked Lady Ranch and rearranged hangars at North County Airport.

The airplanes described in the book are real, and the author has flown many of them. The author chose not to include standard Vernier controls for the throttle, propeller control, and mixture control in the Beechcraft D17S Staggerwing to avoid complicating the action scene for non-pilot readers.

Chief Pilot Kelly Mahon of the Mid America Flight Museum was kind to help the author with the Staggerwing emergency scene. He made a video inside the cockpit to verify that Jett could indeed fly the airplane from the right seat with her hands tied behind her back and the control yoke on the left side. Thank you, Kelly.

White Mountain Airport in Alaska is a real airport as described, and a cemetery is at the bottom of the cliff. The author's dear friend, world-record-holding pilot Ruth Jacobs, was a long-time resident of Alaska and helped her choose the ideal airport for the book's climax. Thank you, Ruth.

Jett's Timber-shepherd puppies, Pratt and Whitney, are based on the author's real dogs who enriched her world for fourteen wonderful years.

Sharon appreciates Niko Bujaj and his fabulous Islander Grill and Tiki Bar on Singer Island for their delicious food, live music, and creative atmosphere for her writing.

# ACKNOWLEDGMENTS

First and foremost, I thank my Lord and Savior, Jesus Christ, for my many blessings and for keeping me and my loved ones safe during the pandemic.

Although I know how to do all the things Jett does in the story, I always get a second and third opinion on the action scenes so I don't forget to include something important.

Many thanks to Chief Pilot Kelly Mahon for his advice and expertise, and thanks to his employer, the unique Mid America Flight Museum for their excellent work preserving warbirds and vintage airplanes in flying condition so the public can truly appreciate how these magnificent aircraft look, sound, and feel as they come alive in flight. They are always grateful for donations which can be sent to: Mid America Flight Museum, 602 Mike Hall Parkway, Mount Pleasant, TX 75455.

Thank you to my friend, retired airline captain, aircraft mechanic, and vintage airplane restorer Jeff Rowland, who is always willing to share his expertise.

I resisted damaging the rare and beautiful cabin biplane, a 1944 Beechcraft D17S Staggerwing, even though the one in the book is imaginary, so I must thank vintage airplane pilots Marc and Lynn Rossi for convincing me to make the climactic landing scene more realistic by crashing the airplane. It will be restored in the next book.

Special thanks to PADI Tec Deep Instructor Justin Newton and all the dive professionals at Pura Vida Divers on Singer Island, Florida, for their expert advice.

I'd also like to thank author and professional diver Jeffrey Philips and marine biologist and professional diver Kip Peterson for their time and talent, helping me make the dive scenes as vivid and accurate as possible.

As always, a heartfelt thanks to my treasured critique buddies, Fred Lichtenberg, George A. Bernstein, D.M. Littlefield, Suzanne Berglind, and Vicky Edwards.

# DEAD ENDS

## A JETTINE JORGENSEN MYSTERY, BOOK 3

Waves crashed on shore as I stood under a sprawling banyan tree in my Banyan Isle backyard near the beach gate leading to the Atlantic Ocean. "Okay, this is far enough. I swear those so-called senior citizens can hear a pin drop from a hundred yards."

Tim Goldy, owner of Trident Security, the firm responsible for protecting my home, stood beside Sophia DeLuca, my dog nanny, house manager, and trusted friend.

Tim shook his head. "Jett, I thought you said all the people attending this International Mystery Fest range in age from sixty-five to eighty-five."

I nodded. "But they're a lively bunch, and they can afford the best hearing aids."

"Lively is an understatement." Sophia chuckled. "The ones on my floor are playing musical bedrooms, and they're all heavy drinkers."

Tim grinned. "At least they don't have to worry about unwanted pregnancies."

"It's not all fun and games. There were some heated arguments at dinner last night about who should be the next president when Edith Pickering steps down tomorrow." I shrugged. "I don't know why they're making such a fuss. The International Mystery Lovers is just a club."

"A very exclusive club, according to Count Medici." Sophia leaned down and accepted the frisbee my honey-colored male Timber-shepherd brought her. She tossed it and said, "That Italian count is a hottie. I wouldn't mind getting to know him better."

"I thought you were smitten with John Caldarelli." I threw the other frisbee for my black and tan female Timber-shepherd.

"Sure, I like him, but we just started dating two months ago. It's not like I'm tied to John, and Paolo is royalty."

"So are several other guests, and Mystery Fest is being held here in South Florida for the first time. Past years were in Monaco, London, Paris, Venice, and Edinburgh. Edith Pickering is expecting us to make a good impression on twenty international A-listers and four bestselling authors."

Tim nudged me. "Uh, Jett, why are we meeting?"

"I think we need to beef up security inside the castle and have guards patrol the first floor and all the hallways on the upper floors, especially at night."

"There's no way anyone can break in without my men catching them, so I assume you're concerned about what the Mystery Fest guests might do," Tim said. "Are you worried about theft?"

"No, they're all wealthy, it's just that this is the first time I've had guests I don't know at Valhalla, and I'm responsible for their safety." I glanced out at the sun rising over the sparkling ocean as a warm sea breeze caressed me. "They're such party animals, I'm worried they'll drink too much and fall off a balcony or get lost looking for their rooms ..."

"Relax, my men handle situations like this all the time. We'll keep everyone safe."

"Okay, then plan on starting the indoor patrols tonight at nine." I turned and called back Pratt and Whitney, my six-month-old puppies named after my favorite aircraft engine manufacturer.

We headed across to my oceanfront terrace and found my best friend and next-door neighbor Gwen Pendragon waiting for us.

Twenty-eight, Gwen was a homicide detective with the Palm Beach Police.

"Hey, Gwen, what brings you over so early?" I asked.

"Do you remember Kitty Kensington, a young Palm Beach socialite who attended your charity ball two months ago with Muffy Murdoch and Bunty Berenson?"

"She and Muffy bought dates with Snake at the bachelor auction." I chuckled. "They kept him up until dawn night-clubbing in West Palm Beach."

"Well, she vanished from a trendy local club last night, and Muffy and Bunty want to hire you and Darcy's Sniffers Agency to find her. They asked for Sophia and me to help. They want the same women who caught the Body-Drop Killer."

Sophia, a slender four-foot-ten and sixty years old, was the daughter of a late New York Mafia kingpin. She pulled a Glock 26 from her waistband holster and checked the magazine. "I'm ready for action."

I shook my head. "I'll call Darcy and set up a meeting. Where should we meet with them?"

Gwen checked her watch. "Bunty and Muffy will be here at eleven a.m."

Tim cleared his throat. "If there's nothing else, I'll head to the office and schedule those extra guards for your home tonight."

I nodded and waved goodbye.

Loud giggles erupted near the infinity pool as three female guests burst through the French doors. Baron von Helsig from Germany, clad in a red bikini marble-bagger, chased the women into the pool.

It was impossible not to notice his manhood bouncing around on his way past. "I really didn't want to see that," I said, covering my eyes.

Sophia shielded her eyes from the sun so she could get a closer look. "Huh, not bad for a guy in his seventies, and he's royalty too. Hubba, hubba."

I rolled my eyes. "Do I need to worry about you now?"

We entered the great hall through oceanfront glass French doors.

Valhalla Castle had been built by my great-great-grandfather as a tribute to his Viking heritage. Although it was a world apart from my late Cherokee shaman mother's native American upbringing, she had loved it here.

I scanned the wall opposite the tall glass windows. Ancient Viking weapons and paintings depicting elaborate battle scenes adorned the twenty-foot-high oak-paneled wall.

Then I noticed it.

Halfway down the wall at eye level, a battle hatchet was missing.

Pratt and Whitney tilted their heads, sniffing the air. Before I had a chance to comment on the missing weapon, the dogs ran out of the room and disappeared down a long hallway.

I elbowed Gwen. "Look, a hatchet is missing from its mount."

Loud doggie howls echoed down the hall from the south wing.

Sophia grabbed my arm. "It's never anything good when they do that."

We hurried down the hallway, following their wails, and found the dogs in my study.

Lord Edmund Helmsley from London lay sprawled face-down on the oak floor with the missing Viking hatchet buried in his skull. A pool of congealed blood had formed a halo around his head.

———

**Available in Paperback and eBook from Your Favorite Bookstore or Online Retailer**

# ABOUT THE AUTHOR

S.L. Menear is a retired airline pilot. US Airways hired Sharon in 1980 as their first woman pilot, bypassing the flight engineer position. The men in her new-hire class gave her the nickname, Bombshell. She flew Boeing 727s and 737s, DC-9s, and BAC 1-11 airliners and was promoted to captain in her seventh year.

Before her pilot career, Sharon worked as a water-sports model and then traveled the world as a flight attendant with Pan American World Airways.

Sharon also enjoyed flying antique airplanes, experimental aircraft, and Third-World fighter airplanes. She has flown many of the airplanes in her Samantha Starr Series featuring a woman pilot: *Flight to Redemption, Flight to Destiny, Triple Threat, Stranded,* and *Vanished,* Books 1 - 5. Samantha Starr will return soon in Book 6.

Jettine Jorgensen Mysteries will continue with Book 3 – *Dead Ends.*

Sharon also co-wrote *Life, Love, & Laughter: 50 Short Stories,* with her mother, D.M. (Dorothy) Littlefield. They also co-wrote a standalone cozy mystery, *Sniffers Agency-The Nose Knows* and two children's novels, *Journey into the Land of the Wingless Giants* and *Enchanted.*

Sharon's leisure activities included scuba diving, powered paragliding, snow skiing, surfing, horseback riding, aerobatic flying, sailing, and driving sports cars and motorcycles.

Her beloved Timber-shepherds, Pratt and Whitney, were her faithful companions for fourteen years, and they produced eight darling puppies. When she lived in Texas, Sharon enjoyed riding her beautiful black and white paint stallion, Chief, who kept her mother's mares happy, fathering several adorable foals.

Retired now, Sharon lives and writes on an island in South Florida. She is an active member of Mystery Writers of America, International Thriller Writers, Sisters in Crime, and Florida Writers Association.

Sharon can be contacted at...

**www.slmenear.com**

 facebook.com/slmenear

www.ingramcontent.com/pod-product-compliance
Lightning Source LLC
Chambersburg PA
CBHW030651020726
47493CB00006B/1969